The Organization
Sequel to Asset Management

Annette Mori & Erin O'Reilly

The Organization
Sequel to Asset Management

Annette Mori & Erin O'Reilly

Affinity
Rainbow Publications

2017

Editor: JoSelle Vanderhooft
Proof Editor: Alexis Smith
Cover Design: Irish Dragon Designs

Acknowledgments

Annette Mori

The biggest acknowledgment goes to my cowriter, Erin O'Reilly, who teased me along to finally complete the continuation of the story. It was such an honor and a privilege to work with Erin on this project. I'm sure that like with my first love, if I ever cowrite a book again, I will undoubtedly compare that experience with this first one and it will be hard to surpass. I am honored to call her a friend and have her support me in my journey. I would also like to express my gratitude to Affinity Rainbow Publications and the wonderful trio (JM Dragon, Erin O'Reilly, and Nancy Kaufman) who continue to provide feedback to tighten up manuscripts that need assistance and publish my sometimes unconventional work. I am eternally grateful for the opportunities they give me to let my stories see the light of day. My other family members who are also very supportive include my nephew, Aaron, his wife, Chelsea, my two sisters, Val and Kim, and my father who struggles to read my books with one eye.

Thanks to JoSelle Vanderhooft for her magic as the final editor to tighten the story even further. Inevitably, there are those pesky final errors that slip through, so many thanks to Amy Herman-Pall for a final proof of the manuscript. Nancy Kaufman is a rock star with her covers and a promoter extraordinaire. A huge thanks to all the other readers and fellow writers who kept pushing for a continuation of the story via e-mails, sneaky messages embedded into the reviews of *Asset Management*, and posts on Facebook (you know who you are). The Affinity authors are an especially supportive group and often share posts or send words of encouragement. Finally, my wife, Jody, continues her support in so many ways. I need a keeper, and she always jumps in to make sure I have everything I need.

Erin O'Reilly

I do not have enough words to praise Annette, who invited me to write the sequel to *Asset Management* with her. We have two very different approaches to writing, and through this whole process she was patient with me and my need to think things to death before putting my ideas on paper.

Thank you goes out to everyone on the Affinity team who helped make this story possible. Without them and their support, I would be a lesser author.

Finally, thank you to the readers who take the time to read my stories and comment for it is with feedback—both positive and negative—that I can continue to grow as an author.

Dedication

To Mel for reasons I know she understands.

To my wife who I love dearly for her patience and her ability to take care of me when I fail to do that myself.

For Lisa

Table of Contents

Chapter One   1
Chapter Two   12
Chapter Three   23
Chapter Four   30
Chapter Five   42
Chapter Six   57
Chapter Seven   64
Chapter Eight   74
Chapter Nine   91
Chapter Ten   101
Chapter Eleven   108
Chapter Twelve   118
Chapter Thirteen   137
Chapter Fourteen   145
Chapter Fifteen   151
Chapter Sixteen   166
Chapter Seventeen   174
Chapter Eighteen   183
Chapter Nineteen   195
Chapter Twenty   208
Chapter Twenty-one   217
Chapter Twenty-two   230
Chapter Twenty-three   240
Chapter Twenty-four   249
About the Author   263
Other Books from Affinity eBook Press   265

Also by Annette Mori

Captivated
The Termination
The Review
The Ultimate Betrayal
Locked Inside
Out of This World
Asset Management
The Incredibly True Adventure of Two Elves in Love
(Affinity 2014 Christmas Collection)
Love Forever, Live Forever
The True Story of Valentine's Day
Vampire Pussy…Cat
Nicky's Christmas Miracle X3
(*It's in Her Kiss*, Affinity's Charity Anthology)

Also by Erin O'Reilly

Specter of Fear
Next Time
Ready for Love
Return to Me
If I Were a Boy
Through the Darkness
Deception
Fearless
'55 Ford
Fractured
Specter of Fear
That Kiss
Revelations

Wolf at the Door
Sandcastles

Writing with JM Dragon

Take Me as I Am
Against All Odds
Earthbound
Quest for Love
New Beginnings
Atonement

When Hell Meets Heaven Series

Echoes of the Past
Paradox of Love
The End Game
Requiem

Chapter One

Val opened the door to reveal her compact quarters and sighed, "Hovel sweet hovel," before sniffing her clothes and saying, "Ick." Surveillance work was boring and dirty and she hated doing it. The warehouse she had just been staking out was repulsive, and she wouldn't be surprised if she caught some disgusting disease.

Going straight to her sink and then washing her hands thoroughly, she began singing "Happy Birthday" to herself like she'd been taught as a little girl by her mother, who was a nurse. She turned around and faced her deluxe, stainless-steel refrigerator and opened the door to the freezer.

Peering inside, she found one lonely pint of Ben and Jerry's Chocolate Chip Cookie Dough. Otherwise, the freezer was like a barren desert. She popped the top of the carton and looked inside. One measly spoonful of her treat was left at the bottom. "God damn it, Char."

Val was furious. She was tired, dirty, and hungry— not necessarily in that order. She marched out of her quarters and down the hall, and started banging on the first door to the left. She absolutely did not care one bit if she interrupted Char and Toni in whatever stage of lovemaking they might

1

be in. It was late at night, so she knew that would undoubtedly be occurring.

New love, ugh, they're like rabbits for shit's sake. They had raided her fridge for the last time. *Isn't anything sacred anymore?*

Bang, bang, bang

"Open the fucking door, Char! You better have at least one full pint of ice cream left, or so help me, I'll forget we're on the same side and put a god damn bullet in your hand for stealing my main food source!"

Val instantly regretted her words. Char was like a sister to her—Val was just cranky tonight. Maggie—head of The Organization, a covert group of women working toward eliminating the sleazier side of society—had relegated her to watch what those animals were doing to the young girls, and it made her skin crawl. If it were up to her, she would have killed them all, but she had her orders and the last thing The Organization needed was for her to compromise the sting they were setting up.

Images of the past returned, and a cold fury washed over her. At least she'd been the one to put the bullet in Viktor Borsky's head. It almost scared her to think that the one event had given her more joy than anything in her life—past or present.

Val was an impatient person, and the fact it took them eighteen months to take down Viktor was unacceptable to her. She wanted to move faster with Leonid, the newly appointed head of the Russian mob. He'd been able to reestablish Viktor's slave trade business in mere months. Unfortunately, he was twice as cunning and ten times as ruthless as Viktor. Leonid was also a paranoid bastard who vetted his employees carefully, so they hadn't found a way in to his inner circle yet.

Val didn't generally agree with her fellow agent Ronda's perspective on how to address the Russian mob, but in this instance, she thought her colleague had the right idea. Ronda's answer to the problem was to execute every last one of them. Val thought that was the perfect solution and right up her alley. She excelled at executions.

As far as Val could tell, his only Achilles heel was his beautiful new wife. He had numerous enemies and didn't want his wife to get caught in the crossfire. She, however, refused to feel like a prisoner in her own home and insisted on living life as a normal person without a string of bodyguards to protect her. His jealousy was legendary, and he'd already terminated three bodyguards for what he perceived as their inappropriate attention toward his wife.

Val was about to break the door down when a disheveled redhead opened it and blinked at her. Behind her, a dark-haired woman peered around her lover with an unrepentant smirk.

"Jesus, Val, it's midnight. I didn't realize you would be back so soon. What happened? Anything we need to know about?" Char asked.

"No, I'm just in a foul mood. Maggie took pity on me tonight and sent Ronda to finish the shift. She probably thinks I'll go off the deep end and shoot all the fuckers before we have a chance to infiltrate the organization. You know how she is—always wants to wait for an opportunity to cut off the head of the snake. I'd be more worried about Ronda. Now that is one crazy-ass bitch," Val answered.

"Ronda's calmed down quite a bit now that Cindy is calling the shots. That's what you need, Val, the love of a good woman. It ought to calm you right down," Toni, Char's lover, piped up from behind her.

"No thanks. My job here isn't exactly conducive to a healthy, loving relationship." Val held up her hand. "Nope,

3

don't want to get involved with another agent who might be just as bat-shit crazy as I am. I prefer living my life just the way it is right now. I get an itch and I find a beautiful woman to scratch it for one night only. That's the rule and I'm sticking to it."

Char looked at Toni and smiled before placing a gentle kiss on her lips. "That's the way I felt before I met Toni. Your day may come. Never say never."

"Can we get to the more important subject of where I can get my fucking ice cream? I want my own untouched pint of perfection, not something you two got cooties all over. I know you incorporate it into your little love games, and I'm not interested in any additional flavor." Val shuddered.

"Try Dani. I think she may have a Chocolate Chip Cookie Dough left. She might still be in the lab, though. She was working on some new prototype. She won't even disclose anything about it to me. I'll pay you in ice cream if you can manage to get her to spill the beans." Toni chuckled.

"Thanks for the tip, but I'm staying clear of any discussion of your egghead inventions. I'm the muscle part of the operation. I don't understand what the two of you are talking about most of the time, but I'm happy to try out any new weapon. Ronda and Sophie got to have all the fun with those poison darts, so I'm next in line to try out any new prototype." Val shook her head. "Next time you decide to raid my fridge, I expect a replacement before the night is over."

"But the whole reason to raid your fridge is because we're too lazy to go out and get our own," Char reasoned.

"Not my problem. Next time I won't be so nice," Val growled.

"Who said you were nice this time?" Toni grinned. "Never mind, I'm on to you. Face it, Val, your bark is much bigger than your bite."

Val pulled her Glock from her shoulder holster and pointed it at Toni. "I've killed for far less. Don't push it, Toni. Consider yourself warned."

She secured her gun back in the holster. After she turned and began walking toward the lab, Toni whispered, "She wouldn't really shoot one of us, would she?"

Val chuckled. She enjoyed keeping people guessing. She was a coldhearted killer and that would never change, but of course that wouldn't extend to one of her sisters in The Organization. However, she didn't want them to know that deep down inside she'd die before she let any of them come to harm.

†

Val stalked down the hallway and entered the lab, vowing not to admit to Maggie that lately she was on the verge of losing it. Flashbacks from her past kept playing in her head late at night when she had nothing better to occupy her active mind. She lamented that they were returning. She thought she'd conquered her fears, but that part of her life just wouldn't let go of her.

Tonight when she watched a man drag a struggling, chained young girl into the cement basement of the industrial complex, it all came flooding back. She felt the cold steel against her wrists and smelled the coppery scent of her own blood. Twelve years was a long time and she should have been able to forget, but tonight she couldn't. When she'd reached for her phone, her hand was shaking uncontrollably. She called Maggie and asked for a replacement, and Maggie had sent Ronda without asking why. That was how Maggie was. She never pried, so she never knew the horrors that had befallen Val before Maggie caught her in the midst of picking that rich fart's pocket.

Val blinked against the bright lights of the lab as she pushed open the door and saw a familiar head bent over one of the special computers. Val had a soft spot in her heart for Dani, who had her own skeletons and nightmares to overcome. Dani was a sweet kid, but Val wouldn't think of revealing any of her terrifying nightmares to her. Dani's physical barriers after being shot still plagued her, and the nightly reminders had not lessened. She simply could not accept that she wasn't able to move about as well as she could before the undercover mission went terribly wrong.

"Hey, kiddo," she said, her voice softer than usual, "your big sis told me you might have a few extra pints of Ben and Jerry's hidden away in your freezer. If you can see your way to liberating them for me, it might save her life." Val smiled.

Dani looked up and chuckled. "Stole your ice cream again, did she?"

"I keep threatening to shoot her, but she never listens. Next time I'm making good on my threats. You tell her that," Val growled. "I don't understand why she doesn't steal from you."

Dani shrugged. "I think she likes to rile you up. It's been quiet for her since they got back from vacation, and I'm fairly certain she's getting antsy and bored. You *are* her favorite entertainment at the moment."

"Now I'm definitely going to put a bullet in her."

"Please don't do that. She's the only sister I have, and she does have redeeming qualities," Dani pleaded half-jokingly.

"I'm just kidding, but she does piss me off sometimes."

"Yeah, me too, but you know she'd risk her life for either one of us." Dani struggled to stand and wobbled before Val rushed over and steadied her. "Come on, I'll get you my secret stash right now."

"Where's your crutches? You look like you might need a little extra help tonight. You've been pushing it lately, haven't you?" Val frowned.

"Geez, suddenly I have six mothers and Maggie to contend with. I don't need you playing that role as well. I'm just a little stiff from sitting for so long. I'll let you offer your arm to steady me until I work out my stiffness, but I don't need the silver sticks tonight." Dani latched on to Val's arm and took a few tentative steps as Val walked alongside.

"So what were you working on? You had that intense look you get when it's something really innovative," Val remarked.

The glint in Dani's eyes told Val everything she needed to know. This was a special project that she imagined Dani was particularly proud of.

"I think I've developed an algorithm that will predict where Leonid's wife will go with 85 percent accuracy. This means we can track her movements and eventually track Leonid's. He accompanies her 38 percent of the time. Sixteen percent of that is at social functions that will provide us with the opportunity to get close enough to use Toni's biological bug." Dani's smile disappeared. "I know that still leaves us without an in to their organization, but it's a start. He isn't as easy to infiltrate as Viktor was. So far we haven't been able to plant tracking devices on his guards in the same manner that we used with Viktor's cell phones."

"That's brilliant, Dani. I know you and Toni will figure out a way to get in. I have faith in both of you, but don't tell Toni that; she'll just get a bigger head. Fucking

7

brainiac is already such a smartass. We can't have her becoming too confident, now can we?"

Dani laughed. "How come you're not afraid I'll get too cocky?"

"You? Never. You're the sweetest person in this cynical organization. Everyone else is arrogant, badass, or a sociopath like me."

Dani smacked Val's arm. "You're not a sociopath. I see beneath that badass exterior you try to present to others."

"Shhh, you're ruining my street cred by saying those words out loud." Val grinned.

†

The echo of Leonid's confident footsteps reverberated in the dingy warehouse. His shiny Italian loafers contrasted sharply with the dark and foreboding room. A low-wattage bulb hung from the ceiling, barely illuminating the large man sitting in a plain wooden chair. Zip ties securely fastened his feet and hands to the legs and arms of the chair. A dark stain stretched out below the man and formed an even pattern of liquid slowly spreading across the cement. Two men bookended Leonid as he walked farther into the cavernous room.

Leonid narrowed his gaze at the man and noted the droplet of sweat that traveled down the side of his face. His wide-eyed stare didn't mask what Leonid presumed was terror. He counted on his reputation to keep his men in line, and when they stepped out of line, his response was quick and deadly. Leonid took joy in personally carrying out each execution for actual and perceived indiscretions.

Sometimes he took his time, torturing the intended victim, and at other times, he was quick and merciful. His mercy, however, was never the result of his desire to end the agony quickly, but rather his limited time to deal with the problem. Tonight he planned to resolve the situation quickly because he had plans with his wife for the evening.

Before sending his intended target to the depths of hell, he always patiently explained his reasoning. Men deserved to know why Leonid decided to execute them. "You did not perform your duties with honor. I warned you not to look at my wife as if she were a piece of meat to devour. Your eyes should have traveled everywhere else but upon my wife to ensure her safety at all times. I thought you Italians knew the importance of family and respect for another man's property," Leonid pronounced before turning to one of his bodyguards, who handed him a gun.

Without further delay, he lifted the gun, placed it against the condemned man's forehead, and pulled the trigger. Blood and brain material exploded from the back of his head. Leonid looked at his hand in disgust when he realized a small amount of blood splatter had landed there.

Leonid handed the gun to the man who had provided it and in an even tone said, "Please take this trash out for me. Consider him fired. I need you to find a replacement for him, and don't bring another Italian into my inner circle. From now on, we only hire Russians. I made an exception for Gina's brother, but those wops think with their dicks, not their heads. Even a woman would be a better choice." Leonid paused. "Yes, that is a much better idea. I do not trust my Russian comrades. Bring me a woman qualified to keep Gina safe. I don't care where you get her, fly to Russia if you have to, but I want the best. Put her through a comprehensive screening before bringing her to me for final approval."

Leonid snapped his fingers and the other bodyguard pulled a clean handkerchief and a small container of Purell from his pocket. After Leonid coated his hands with the liquid sanitizer, he wiped them dry and handed the soiled cotton cloth to his employee. "Get me a new shirt and be sure to send his family flowers. I wouldn't want those uncivilized wops to think we lack respect."

Leonid laughed as he walked away from his poor selection of a bodyguard to protect his most prized possession—his wife.

✝

Until she'd received the call from Val, Maggie was content to sit and listen to her favorite CD, *The Four Seasons*. Pinching the bridge of her nose, she reflected on Val's strained request. Val was slowly unraveling, and Maggie wasn't sure she would be able to use her much longer unless Val got the help she needed to chase away her demons.

So far, they hadn't managed to figure out a way into Leonid's inner circle. She sighed, realizing that as much as she didn't want to call Antonio, his offer of assistance might be their only option. Her most trusted team had listened intently to her explanation of their connection, but Sophie's training as a former FBI agent made her remain guarded.

Connecting with Antonio again was dangerous on so many levels. Their philosophies not only differed, but she was afraid her feelings for him might resurface after she'd learned about his wife's recent fight with cancer. Sevilla hadn't survived, and Antonio had been alone now for over two years. The presence of another woman was no longer the barrier in rekindling the old flame.

Her private cell rang and she scrunched her face as she looked at the number flashing on the screen. She didn't recognize it. Only those she trusted most in The Organization had this number, but something was instinctively telling her to answer the phone.

10

"Hello," she hesitantly spoke into the tiny device.

As Antonio's rich baritone oozed through the speaker, she envisioned his broad smile.

"How did you get this number?" She immediately regretted her sharp tone. She listened to his explanation and learned about the recent developments in Leonid's organization. "Yes, I think I may have someone who would be nearly perfect for the job. My major concern is that lately she's displaying abnormal amounts of stress and instability, and that is not like her. Unfortunately, she's the only one who can speak fluent Russian and possesses all the other needed attributes." Maggie sighed.

She continued to listen to Antonio's information. "I suppose we don't have much choice at this point, because this opportunity isn't likely going to present itself again. I understand and appreciate that you have assets that are also at risk, but I don't like to send someone into the lion's den without thoroughly evaluating our choices.... I'll call you tomorrow.... Yes, I know what to do to set the stage.... Dani has been looking for a challenge—I believe this will provide her with a big one if we decide to use my person for this job."

Chapter Two

Val wasn't sure what to think about the summons to the small conference room on the other side of the lab. She knew Maggie trusted her, but normally Maggie activated her when she needed Val to perform very specific duties that tended to hover on the periphery of the action. Her eyebrow rose when she noticed the high-powered agents of The Organization lounging in the conference room. She hadn't expected that.

She was happy to see that Ronda was one of them. They had similar worldviews and tended to want to act more quickly than the others, who gravitated toward a more strategic approach. She smiled when Sophie nodded to her. Sophie was a hard one to figure out. She wasn't exactly in line with Ronda and Val, but she wasn't inclined to agree with the heavy thinkers either. Over the past month, Val had detected some tension between Maggie and Sophie and wondered what that was all about. Maybe this meeting would enlighten her.

Kim, Sophie's lover, was absently stroking Sophie's hand. Val suspected her caresses were an attempt to reduce the visible tension in Sophie's rigid posture.

Dani sat next to Char and Toni. Toni and Dani were whispering to one another—two eggheads relishing each other's brilliance. Val wasn't stupid, but next to those two, she felt inferior.

Maggie cleared her throat, and seven sets of eyes turned in her direction. "There's been a new development that will require immediate action. I've decided it's in our best interest to work collaboratively with Antonio to take down Leonid Petrov. Since Antonio has already managed to infiltrate his organization and place two individuals very close to Leonid, he's offered us an opportunity to combine forces. It seems Leonid is looking for a new bodyguard for his wife and is adamant that this person be Russian and a woman."

The team began looking around the room, clearly trying to decipher which agent Maggie would choose for this dangerous assignment.

"I must be missing something, because while we're all women, none of us speak Russian well enough to fool Leonid. Not even Char could pull that off." Sophie removed her hand from Kim's and folded her arms across her chest.

A foreboding sense of unease slowly crept into her body as Val realized why Maggie had invited her to the party. She hadn't ever wanted anyone to stick their nose in her business, and now she had to reveal a little of her history.

"I speak fluent Russian," Val offered.

"Thank you, Val, I was just getting to that," Maggie explained.

"What the fuck, Val. I never knew that," Char interjected.

13

Val glared at Char. "You haven't exactly told your life story to any of us, have you? I prefer to keep my past exactly where it belongs—ancient history. I think the term *don't ask, don't tell* applies here. Suffice it to say, Leonid will not question my Russian roots."

"Everyone is entitled to their privacy, so no questions. I've made my decision and now I need the rest of you to support the plan. Dani, Toni, and Sophie, you need to perform your magic to create a solid background for Val. There can be no holes in her identity for them to drive through. Kim, we may need your special brand of expertise later if we require a disguise that will enable another person to have access to Leonid's residence or his central operations hub. Ronda, you're on retainer in case we need firepower quickly. Char, I need to meet with you later as my co-strategist. I want to pick your brain for ideas." Maggie looked at each agent as she laid out her instructions.

"As much as I hate to admit this, I'd like to work with Ronda as backup firepower. We understand one another," Sophie offered.

Maggie nodded. "Toni, can you work on your special biologic tracking device? We now have a way to begin tracking Leonid more accurately than before. I appreciate all the progress you've made, Dani, but now that we have an in, the tracking must be 100 percent accurate. We'll also need a way to stay in constant communication with Val without blowing her cover. I believe that you and Dani have been refining your prototype. Will it be ready in less than twelve hours?"

Toni grinned at Dani. "It's ready now."

"We'll need more than one item of clothing, because we can't very well have her wear the same jacket or shirt every day. Will you be putting it in her bras or panties?" Maggie inquired.

"It was actually Dani's idea to place the device in lingerie. She's a clever little minx." Toni fist-bumped Dani.

"One for every day of the week, but I didn't stitch the name of each day into the thongs. That was way too tacky and there wasn't enough material for us to do that. I sure hope you like wearing thongs." Dani grinned.

"Can I wash the thongs and still have the communication device work?"

Toni nodded.

"How is that even possible?" Val asked.

"Trade secret, my friend, but think waterproof watches or cameras. It's not that complicated. Now you can't shoot me when I take your ice cream because my invention will be saving your ass." Toni chuckled. "You need me."

"You promise the device is completely undetectable? I wouldn't put it past Leonid or one of his henchmen to insist on frisking every inch of my body, and these guys think nothing of stripping you down—and taking particular pleasure in touching the more intimate areas." Val's eyes searched Toni's for assurance.

"Aww, I have no idea how you can endure that. I guess that's why I was never in the position of trying to seduce any of those sick fucks. I wouldn't even want them touching my arm!" Toni exclaimed.

"It's a good thing I have no problem stripping down to my birthday suit, because I'll break their fucking arms if they try to feel me up," Val declared.

Sophie raised her eyebrow. "Not that this conversation isn't fascinating, but can we get back on track now? Oh, and you might want to try to control your gas. I for one don't want to hear you farting over the commlink." Sophie smirked at Val.

"Just couldn't resist that jab, could you? And here I thought Toni was the juvenile one of the bunch," Val retorted.

"Okay, enough. We have work to do." Maggie stood. "Sophie, can I have a word with you in private? Kim, you don't mind, do you?"

Toni, Dani, Ronda, and Val exchanged looks but didn't question Maggie's request.

Kim smiled at Maggie. "Of course not."

"I need to brief Sophie on something while the rest of you get started. Toni and Dani, before you finalize your work on the commlink, can you please get to work on that background for Val? Sophie will join you in a bit. Don't underestimate Leonid's expertise in ferreting out a fake." Maggie frowned. "He has the best technological support money can buy. It's a little-known fact that the Russians are leaders in cybersecurity. He has a key player at Kaspersky Lab, which is the first Russian company counted as one of the world's leading software organizations. There are rumors that the CEO was tied to Russian intelligence."

"No wonder we've been having such a fit trying to break into his computer system," Toni whispered in Dani's ear.

Val was curious about the private meeting with Sophie, but she would never think to question Maggie. She didn't know what to do with herself after Maggie and Sophie left, so she just watched the others. Kim walked over to the section of the lab that housed her latex masterpieces, while Toni and Dani made a beeline for the main computer. Ronda shrugged and walked out after Sophie and Maggie. Val thought she might be heading to Cindy's unit. They had an affair going on that wasn't as secret as they thought it was. Chancing a rejection, Val decided to learn more about what Dani and Toni intended to do when creating her persona.

Val had always been a loner and carefully kept everyone at a distance. She and Char had shared their perspectives about keeping people at arm's length, but that was all. Val's gaze turned to Toni, who was cautious around her, but always eager to share her research.

"Mind if I hang out and see what you're doing and get a head start on memorizing my background?" Val asked as she strolled over to Toni.

Dani waved her over. "Not at all, we'd love to show you what we're doing."

"Yeah, and maybe get your perspective on what to build into it," Toni added.

Val smiled. For maybe the first time, she felt included. No one had ever bothered to ask her opinion before. She was now an integral part of the team, not just the firepower relegated to the periphery of a mission. "Thanks." Val's face flushed and was embarrassed they may have noticed.

†

Maggie motioned for Sophie to sit in her comfortable brown leather chair. Maggie noted Sophie's introspective expression and applauded her patience.

"Would you care for some tea or coffee?" Maggie asked.

"No, I think I'd rather you get right to it."

"Very well. I am not going to reveal a lot of Val's very personal history, but I do want to set things up a bit."

Sophie raised her eyebrow.

"I brought Val into The Organization when she was almost thirteen. Suffice it to say that she's suffered things beyond what you or I can even begin to imagine. I won't go into detail other than to say that under that tough exterior is a

17

very vulnerable woman. I want to make sure nothing bad happens to Val. If I had another choice, I wouldn't put her in this position, but I don't. I need you to prepare her for what to expect as an undercover agent. I trust you to make sure you adequately groom her for this mission. I know you still have your misgivings about working with Antonio and I understand, but if you can't support this 100 percent, you need to tell me now. Val is as dear to me as Char, and I need to know you will do everything in your power to protect her."

Sophie's chilly gaze penetrated Maggie, and Maggie felt like several hours passed before she responded. "Why aren't you asking Char?"

"Char is a brilliant strategist and a very good undercover agent, but she doesn't have the right skills to mentor someone. Besides, Char and Val fight like sisters. I know they love and respect each other, but they also tend to push one another's buttons."

Sophie nodded. "You have my commitment. Now that I've made that decision, I won't waver. I'll not raise another objection to Antonio again. I've come to trust your judgment. Val saved our asses on the last mission, and I intend to make sure she comes out of this alive and well."

"Thank you, Sophie. Don't let her hard exterior keep you from imparting all of your wisdom and expertise," Maggie warned.

"Oh don't worry about that. Remember, I've been dealing with Toni for the last several years. She's damn near impossible to get through to sometimes. Val will be a piece of cake compared to her."

"Don't be so sure about that," Maggie quipped.

†

Holding a pint of Chocolate Chip Cookie Dough, Sophie was about to knock on the solid wood door when it opened. She hoped Val wouldn't be too pissed when she learned that Toni had snuck in a tiny device into the ice cream that once ingested would allow them to provide audio instructions.

Val narrowed her eyes and focused on the treat. "A bribe?"

"No, a peace offering because I'm not any good at subterfuge. I apologize in advance if I am abrupt in my approach. Kim has tact. I do not," Sophie stated.

"Perfect. I don't respond well to bullshit anyway." Val waved her hand toward her couch and walked into her small quarters.

Sophie followed her inside. All the living spaces in the primary hub of operations were cramped units that took some time to get used to. Anyone with a tendency toward claustrophobia complained bitterly. Dani's inventions designed to fool the casual observer that these units had windows to the outside world only went so far if carefully inspected. Dani never explained exactly how they worked, other than describing a high-tech, ever-changing image connected to a timer designed to emulate whatever was happening on the outside. Dani tried to show her how she'd intersected data from an anemometer and barometer with thousands of images and sounds to reproduce what would be seen and heard in any location in the world. When Sophie asked why she didn't just install a camera on the outside and project images from it on the window, Dani had acted like she was offended. She'd huffed and said that was child's play, and people liked variety. Sophie preferred the Fiji Islands and set the dial accordingly, but she was still getting used to all the new technology. For most, they did the trick, complete with the requisite bird sounds in the morning.

When Val pointed to the Ultrasuede couch, Sophie sat and placed the ice cream on the small oak coffee table. An empty ice cream container on it had a dirty spoon sticking up like a periscope watching every move Sophie made. She wondered if Val would go to the tiny kitchen to retrieve a new spoon or use this one.

She didn't have to wait long to find out as Val shrugged, sat in the matching recliner, retrieved the dirty spoon, flipped off the lid of the new ice cream, and dug in with gusto.

"Okay. Spill," Val said through a mouthful of ice cream. "Mmmm, so good. Points for buttering me up before you tell me what the fuck is going on."

"We have no more than two days to get you ready for your assignment. I will instruct and you will shut the fuck up and listen. You saved my ass when you shot Viktor, and now I'm about to save yours."

Val set the spoon on the table, leaned back in her chair, folded her arms across her chest, and glared.

"Good start. It's easier with the stoic badasses versus the incorrigible smartasses. First thing you need to do is prove your worth to Leonid. I like your creative approach of taking off your clothes before they maul you—with the excuse of checking for wires and guns. That will work fine, but then you need to break someone's bones. My guess is that at least one of the bodyguards will reach for you and you'll need to take him down. I assume you have advanced martial arts training?"

Val nodded.

"Good. You get extra brownie points if you manage to get his gun and turn it back on him. The key is to control the situation without directly threatening Leonid."

"You know, Sophie, you're as much a psycho as Ronda. I like that about you, which is the only reason I'm

20

listening to your instruction without rearranging your face. If there is one thing I'm good at, it's taking care of myself and getting out of impossible situations," Val stated.

"Don't get too cocky, because that, my friend, will get you killed."

Val smiled and Sophie wasn't sure what that was about. Was she mocking her or agreeing? It wasn't a smirk, though, so she took that as a good sign.

"Okay, here's the hardest part. I could never do it, but sometimes when you're in deep cover, you have to do things that might turn your stomach. I know you've killed before, but can you kill someone Leonid directs you to kill? If you can't, you better figure out how to prove your loyalty some other way. Think about that tonight, because you'll want to work that out before you're presented with a test that has consequences you can't take back."

Val frowned. "I never considered that. Depending on who I might be asked to kill, I suppose I would rather die than terminate someone who didn't deserve that sentence."

"Shit. I guess I expected that—a moral assassin. You'll just have to keep that commlink open at all times so we can barrel in and save your righteous ass." Sophie chuckled.

"No offense, Sophie, but how in the hell did you get mixed up with the brainiac and the thespian? You're more like me," Val observed.

"We developed a college friendship and sometimes opposites attract, you know."

"Is Kim your one true love?"

"Yeah, she is. She's the only one who can calm the savage beast. She's the kindest, gentlest, sweetest person I know. She's good for me, just like Cindy is good for Ronda. You could use someone like that in your life."

Val reached for the spoon again and dug out another chunk of ice cream. "I prefer living alone. Lovey-dovey coupledom isn't my cup of tea. They'd only disappoint me. Sex I like; love I don't."

"Hey, is there any chance I can get some coffee? We might be at this a little while. I'd like to tell you what I know about the inner workings of the Russian mob. It might help you."

Val jumped up. "Oh shit, yeah, sorry. See, I'm a terrible host and even worse at relationships. I have no manners and that usually doesn't go over too well with women."

Val was somewhat of an enigma to Sophie. She'd watched as Val interacted with Kimiko, the young girl she had rescued from the previous mob boss, Viktor. Val was patient, tender, and loving with Kimiko, and all Val's roughness dissipated whenever they were in the same room. Sophie suspected if Val ever did fall in love, she would make an excellent partner. All the love she tried to hide would spill out of the tough exterior if only someone could crack that hard shell.

Chapter Three

Val squinted at the enormous mansion laid out in all its glory. *Same Bat time, same Bat channel.* Val chuckled to herself as she thought about the many hours she'd spent in front of the TV trying to master the English language and being hooked on *Batman.* It was ridiculous and campy, but she loved that show. She remembered how Maggie would just smile when she walked by and found her glued to the TV.

Leonid's mansion was nearly a carbon copy of Viktor's—gaudy and overwhelming. She thought they both tried too hard to prove their immense wealth and standing in the community as a whole.

Val strode confidently to the front door and pushed the doorbell. Big surprise when two burly men ushered her inside and attempted to frisk her. In less than fifteen seconds, she broke one bodyguard's nose, wrenched the gun from the other, and pointed the muzzle in his face. She hadn't done anything particularly fancy—one head butt and a wrenched wrist had done the trick. Val was quick—she was very, very quick.

23

The bodyguard with the broken nose hadn't learned his lesson and lunged for her. Without breaking a sweat, Val roundhouse-kicked him and sent him flailing to the ground.

"Oomf."

Obviously thinking she might be distracted, the other bodyguard attempted to retrieve his gun, and Val rewarded him with an elbow to the face and the second broken nose of the day. She then shot his leg for having the audacity to try to get his gun back.

Rich baritone laughter filled the foyer, and Val got her first look at Leonid. She was surprised to see the handsome, chiseled face surrounding cold, gray eyes, and her body had an immediate reaction to his laughter. Something about his laugh was familiar, and for a split second the dungeon from her past flashed before her eyes. Stuffing the fear deep inside, she met his steely gaze with her own penetrating stare.

Val set the gun on the marble pedestal. She removed her backpack, set it on the floor, and proceeded to strip. She noted the bodyguards warily watching as they looked back and forth between their boss and her.

Standing completely naked before Leonid, she stated, "I do not like to be touched. The next time I will kill them. As you can see, I am not wearing a wire, nor do I currently have a weapon." Val glanced at the pedestal with the stolen gun and smirked.

"Duly noted," Leonid remarked. "You may put your clothes back on. Normally I would conduct an interview, but I believe you just passed the first test. You are Russian, yet you speak perfect English? I don't detect an accent."

Val shrugged. "One of my many talents. Do you need proof of my Russian background?"

Leonid narrowed his eyes. "Not necessary. My background checks are thorough. My wife is not Russian and does not speak the language. I suppose it is a plus that you speak perfect English."

The bodyguard she'd shot groaned as he held on to his leg.

Leonid glanced to his left and gave an almost imperceptible nod to another large man standing on the other side of the room. "Take care of this mess. If the blood leaves a stain, terminate him. That will be the test of his worthiness to continue to serve me. I do hope he manages to protect the floor from his blood better than he protected me."

The injured man stared wide-eyed at Leonid and tried to stem the flow of blood.

Leonid turned his icy-gray eyes in Val's direction and commanded, "Come. I will show you to your room. I trust the accommodations will meet your requirements. You won't object to one of my men checking your bag?"

Val shrugged. "Fine by me."

She followed Leonid and another large man who had miraculously appeared by his side as soon as the other guard moved toward the temporarily incapacitated guards.

"How did the small female overpower my best guards?" Leonid asked him in Russian.

Val smiled to herself as she contemplated his calculated use of the language. She would answer him back in flawless Russian.

"Never underestimate me. It will be a fatal mistake," Val growled, her voice was low, but loud enough for Leonid to hear every syllable.

He turned and caught Val's eyes in a laser stare. "For one who lacks the equipment, Verushka, you have very big brass ones. I will be sure not to underestimate you, and I am counting on that to protect my precious property."

Val cringed internally when Leonid referred to his wife that way, but left her face blank. She knew not to let the misogynist bastard trip her up by revealing a reaction of disgust. "Vera. I prefer to be called Vera."

Leonid nodded. "Very well. Vera. Your Russian is flawless."

Val thought the name they had chosen for her alternate identity was perfect. She'd always admired the 1960s model, Countess Vera von Lehndorff-Steinort, and Vera was close to her real name. She'd also read somewhere it meant "truth." The irony was that she was a stranger to everyone, and no one person knew who she was or her full backstory. She was suddenly reminded of her father and the realization he and Leonid were cut from the same cloth dawned on her. She hated them both.

The fake name also meant "faith." The Organization was putting their faith in her to find a way to work with Antonio's undercover agents, whoever they were, to once again unravel the newly formed slave trade that seemed stronger and less vulnerable than Viktor's previous organization.

No one knew who Antonio's plants were and Val had no idea if they were in close contact or even communicated. Maggie had assured her that she had faith in her skills at discerning who was working on their side and who wasn't. Her survival and fighting skills were excellent but she wasn't as sure with her insight into others. *How the hell am I supposed to work with someone without knowing their identity?*

Leonid snapped his fingers and the big blond man picked up Val's bag and then handed him a pager. Leonid opened the door and motioned Val into a spacious bedroom complete with a large flat-screen television and a love seat. The room was larger than her whole quarters back at the compound.

Leonid tossed Val the pager and she caught it. "You

will carry this at all times. You are on call 24/7. Whenever my wife wishes to go outside this compound, you are responsible for her safety. If one hair on her head is harmed, consider your employment terminated," Leonid threatened.

"I will give you six months and if I still desire your generous compensation package, I may reconsider giving you more time. Don't ever threaten me again, because you won't like my response. I'm the best you'll ever find, so don't give me a reason to quit before I start."

Leonid laughed. "Brass something. You remind me of myself when I was younger."

Val watched impassively as the man rifled through her bag, tossing out her pen and electric toothbrush along with all the clothes, including the underwear.

"Asshole," she muttered as they left.

†

Val took a look around the room. She opened the door to her right and found an enormous walk-in closet filled with a variety of clothing, from expensive evening gowns to casual shirts and pants. Neatly pressed jeans lined one corner. Silk and cotton shirts butted up against casual and business pants.

Val pulled one of the shirts from the hanger and looked at the tag. Size eight—her size. She didn't want to know how Leonid knew that. She suspected the fake persona Dani had created had every possible piece of information to make her existence believable—down to the size of her underwear and bras. She wouldn't need to wear the underwear he provided for her, so she needed to make a big show of tossing aside whatever was available in the dresser and replacing it with the pairs Dani had placed in her bag.

Val walked to the rich mahogany dresser containing

what she assumed would be underwear, socks, and other clothing exactly her size, like t-shirts and shorts. She opened the first drawer and yanked out the several pairs of neatly folded underwear and threw them on the floor. She didn't bother to fold the ones on the bed that the ape had pulled from her bag before she shoved them in the drawer and closed it.

Val jumped when inside her head she heard, *"Good job, grasshopper. Although I might not have challenged him quite as much as you did."*

"What the fuck?" she cried out.

"Careful, don't say another word. Act like you just stubbed your toe or something. Leonid will definitely have your room bugged. He's a paranoid bastard. Now, you didn't think we would leave you completely incommunicado with us, did you? Toni found a way to put a biological commlink inside your ear so we can communicate with you. Sorry we didn't tell you before you left today. It was a last-minute enhancement because the undies only let us hear what's going on and we needed a way to talk to you."

Val listened to Sophie laugh inside her head and vowed to kick her ass when this mission was over. Though she had to admit, she might find this humorous if the shoe were on the other foot.

"Well, I guess I should be impressed that Leonid has good taste in women's clothing," Val said to the empty room. She figured that should explain her earlier expletive.

"Nice recovery."

Val wanted to tell Sophie to shut the fuck up, but she knew she couldn't react. That pissed her off even more, and she knew Sophie would have a big laugh at her expense. She would probably have plenty of time over the next couple of months to think of ways to get her back.

She put the rest of her belongings back in her pack

and looked around the room for a place to store her bag and finally found a corner in the closet. She had hoped they wouldn't examine too closely some of the other ordinary contents like her pen with the tranquilizer darts, and the electric toothbrush with a disruptor hidden inside. The man hadn't given either item a second look as he pulled them from the side pocket and tossed them next to her meager supply of clothes. She plopped on the bed and decided she would take advantage of her free time and get in a quick nap before meeting the pain-in-the-ass wife.

Chapter Four

Paulie Maggio grabbed his sister's wrist and twisted. "Don't you fuck this up for me." He gave her tall and willowy frame, her long white-blonde hair, and her eyes the color of a clear summer's sky a once-over before sneering.

"You leave a bruise and I'll make sure Leonid knows it was you." Gina smirked. "And you know what he does to anyone who harms what is his."

"I'm warning you." Paulie let go but moved so he was toe-to-toe with her. "If you leave him, he will hunt you down, and then you will be on the wrong side of his gun."

"I said he was a pig, not that I was going anywhere." She motioned at the palatial house in front of her. "This is what I've dreamed of all my life."

Paulie noted her sarcastic tone as he pulled her into a hug. "If you fuck this up, we are both dead," he whispered. "I have big plans for the future, so you should keep that in mind before you do something you'll regret."

"Let go of me," Gina whispered back. "His spies will tell him we're planning something."

Paulie took a step back. He knew listening devices were everywhere and that he'd be dead with one wrong word. His sister was his ticket to the big time, and he'd make sure she played nice with Leonid until his plans were in place. He grabbed her arm again, making sure he didn't squeeze too hard but enough to get his point across. "Are you with me?"

Gina nodded while looking at the Hummer limousine that came to a stop near the mansion's front door.

Leonid Petrov emerged from the vehicle and beckoned her to join him.

"Make sure you don't get me killed in your grandiose scheme," she said before walking away.

✝

"Darling, what took you so long? I've been waiting for over an hour." Gina wrapped her arms around her husband's neck and kissed him passionately. The act made her stomach turn, but she'd made her choice, and because of who the man was, she had to live with her decision. She knew all the right words and actions to keep Leonid happy.

She and her brother grew up on the wrong side of the tracks, dirt-poor and with alcoholic and drug addicted parents who were absent for most of their lives. They were survivors and knew how to play the game, doing whatever was necessary to win. Paulie was also tall, but where her features were on the fairer-side, he was dark with obsidian hair and skin that revealed his Southern Italian roots. The only thing that distinguished them as siblings was the distinctive color of their eyes. Of the two of them, he was the more brutal in taking what he wanted. He'd never known how to finesse a situation to his advantage, but his intellect and cunning made him a formidable ally and enemy. Whatever he was planning,

31

she hoped her relationship with Leonid would stay intact. She would never jeopardize the sweet deal she had going for her with the man in her arms.

"Come on, let's go inside and find somewhere private," she cooed. "I want to be alone with you." Her stomach lurched and she choked back the bile that threatened to rise.

I've made my bed and have to sleep in it.

†

Gina grinned inwardly at how easily Leonid would succumb to her overtures. He was a ruthless mobster, and she suspected he'd killed all the bodyguards she'd had over the eight months they'd been married. She was under no illusion that he was anything other than cold and calculating in all his dealings except with her. It had taken her a while to figure out, but she now knew how to walk the narrow line so he didn't realize she was manipulating him into revealing many of his secrets—secrets that, if the time came, she would use against him. No one was better at twisting situations to their benefit than she was, and that always gave her the upper hand.

He was rough when he took her, and to her dismay, that was becoming a daily occurrence—sometimes even more. Fortunately, it never took long and all he ever wanted was for her to spread her legs and let him enter her. For that, she was grateful. The thought of doing anything else with him was even more repulsive and sickening than what she did with him now. Her involvement with the man was a means to an end and the reward outweighed her sacrifice, but she now questioned the wisdom of the path she'd chosen.

Paulie was another problem for her. She needed to keep him in check before he went on a tear and ruined this for them both.

A knock at the door had her pulling on her light yellow silk robe. "Come in."

A short, round woman opened the door. "Ma'am, I have a tray for you. The mister said to bring it," she said in a heavy accent.

"Thank you, Irina." Gina sat up in bed and allowed the maid to place the tray over her legs. "This looks great. Please tell Cook thank you for me."

"*Da*," Irina said as she backed out of the room.

Gina shook her head. She was no threat to any of them, but over time, she'd noticed that no one in the household ever turned their back on her. Fear was pervasive in everyone who associated with Leonid. He was a vile, evil man, and she was glad he hadn't turned that evil on her. For a fleeting second, she wondered how long that would last. How long could she keep up the pretense of being a dutiful, loving wife before it became too much for her?

†

Leonid stretched and rolled his head from side to side, attempting to lessen the tension in his neck. He leaned back in his brick-red leather chair specially formulated to mold to his body. His den was where he often pondered his next business strategy.

Something felt off to him, and he wondered about the new bodyguard he'd just hired. She seemed familiar, yet at the moment he couldn't place where or how he knew her.

Vera came highly recommended, and if what he'd read in the dossier was correct, she was not exaggerating— she really was the best. She'd certainly proven that by effectively taking out two of his best men. Her arrogance unnerved him, and when he'd complimented her audacity by comparing her to his younger self, the lie left a bad taste in his mouth. No woman could ever compare to his greatness, but he needed her to feel comfortable in her new role. She was like a tightly coiled snake—ready to strike at any moment—and he, Leonid, would be her snake charmer.

Leonid pressed a button on his desk to summon his personal assistant. It was time to introduce Vera to his wife, who was another source of tension. Lately, she wasn't complying with his wishes like a dutiful wife should. Her insistence on frequent excursions and her challenge to his decision to hire another guard for her irritated him. Lately she'd also been asking more questions about his business, and that was unacceptable. Wives did not belong tinkering in matters solely reserved for men.

His personal assistant entered the room and stood before him in silence. Leonid had trained him well. Ivan would wait for instructions until Leonid spoke.

"Bring my wife to me. I need to discuss my latest hire."

Ivan nodded and quickly left the den.

The security camera showed Ivan leading his beautiful wife down the hallway. She looked stunning in her casual outfit. He was unnerved by how exquisite she always looked regardless of what she wore. Although he preferred that she dress with more flare and elegance, even during the day, he had to admit she would look good in a paper sack. If he didn't know any better, he might attribute her casual attire to a subtle form of rebellion. He'd often asked her to wear something a bit classier than a pair of jeans, but it wasn't a hill he was willing to die on. Still, he did worry that if he let the small things go, perhaps he would have trouble when needing to control her on the larger issues like when to begin having children and how to raise them.

Gina entered the den, and Ivan quietly closed the door behind her. She walked to Leonid and placed her hands on his neck, where she massaged his tense muscles. This was something he applauded. A good wife should take care of her husband's aches and pains, and Gina had a sixth sense for knowing when he needed the extra attention.

"Leonid, my love, you work too hard. Your neck is like a steel rod. Why won't you let me help you with the business?"

Leonid clenched his jaw and took his time to answer so he wouldn't explode and do something he might regret later. "Do not worry your pretty head. Business is for the men to attend to. What plans do you have for today?"

Gina stopped massaging and instead stroked his neck before gliding her hand over his chest as she moved to sit on the corner of his desk. The touch was a tease to Leonid and he wished he had more time as his erection grew, but a small problem needed his personal attention today.

"Well, since I can't help you, I thought I'd do a little shopping."

"*Da.* That is acceptable. I hired a new bodyguard for you."

"What happened to, what's his name? Donnie?" Gina asked.

"I decided he was not a good fit. I will introduce you. She will accompany you today."

Gina raised her eyebrow.

Leonid held up his hand. "You will have two guards and that is final. I do not wish to hear another word on the subject."

Gina smiled. "Of course, my love. At least you hired a woman. The men are boorish and not at all good at helping me pick out clothes."

"Ah, now that is better. I like this more compliant side. You are far too beautiful to argue with."

Leonid pushed the button on the desk and the door opened to reveal Ivan, who quietly entered the den.

"Bring Vera here. She is to accompany Gina to the fancy boutiques today."

Ivan nodded and left.

☦

Gina looked at the tall woman with interest when she entered her husband's den. Her body was lean and muscular. She had long, blonde hair pulled back in a ponytail, and her eyes were the color of steel. She exuded an air of danger. The fact she was beautiful in a rugged sort of way only added to her mysterious allure. The woman was a step up from the goons Leonid hired to protect her in the past, and if Gina played her cards right, she wouldn't have to put up with Paulie anymore either. She only needed one bodyguard, and the woman was a far better choice.

"This is my wife, Gina. I expect you to guard her with your life," Leonid said.

"I know my duties," Vera grumbled.

The low timbre of the woman's voice made Gina shiver. She looked at Leonid. "What's her name?"

"Vera, but that shouldn't concern you. Her only duty is to protect you." Leonid looked at the bodyguard. "That is her only purpose."

Gina slipped off the desk and moved toward the woman, resisting the urge to hold out her hand in greeting. Leonid would see that as a sign that she regarded the woman

36

as her equal. "I hope you like shopping, Vera," she quipped. "We will be leaving in fifteen minutes. Be outside by my car waiting for me, and don't be late." Gina left the room, hoping neither Leonid nor Vera heard the tremor in her voice—she sensed that both were equally dangerous.

☩

Gina emerged from the mansion and saw her new bodyguard standing by her sleek, black Porsche Boxster Spyder.

"I hope you weren't expecting to drive." She gave Vera her most insincere smile. "No one drives my baby but me. Get in." She watched as Vera opened her door. "Thank you." She slid behind the wheel and fired up the engine.

Just as Vera closed her door, Gina smashed on the gas pedal and took off with the wheels screeching. She laughed as she sped out into the street with the tires kicking up gravel.

Gina laughed as the wind blew through her hair, then glanced over at her passenger. Vera's arms were crossed and she was looking bored.

The tires squealed as Gina guided the car to the curb. "So what's your story, badass?"

"No story, princess. Just drive."

"Listen, you work for me and you'll show the respect due to me. I am not a princess and never have been. You're going shopping with me and you'll like it. Do you understand?"

"I work for Leonid, not you, and that doesn't include conversation," Vera growled.

"You do know that one word from me and my dear husband will have no problem ending your life with a bullet." She fixed the woman with a glare. "Got it?"

"I don't respond well to threats. I have an understanding with Leonid, and as long as I do my job, he'll leave me alone. You should never underestimate me."

Gina reached across the middle console and grabbed the woman's arm. "I'm the one you shouldn't underestimate, because I have the power here." She put the car in gear and sped off down the street. Her jaw tightened as anger tensed her body.

How dare she speak to me like that?

Gina kept her eyes on the road until they approached Chez Bennet, seething at the woman's impudence. Vera had sat there stoically for the entire drive. If it was the last thing Gina did, she'd get a rise out of her new bodyguard.

†

Val wouldn't give the spoiled-rotten wife the satisfaction of responding to her last threat as they screeched up to the boutique. She hated the fact that the woman unnerved her. Val hadn't ever met a more beautiful woman and she'd known her fair share. Yet Gina's beauty wasn't the only thing setting off alarm bells. Something about her was familiar, and Val just couldn't put her finger on it, but she would. Eventually. She always figured things out.

She cringed when Gina got out of the car and slammed her door before Val could release her seat belt and follow. "God damn pain in the ass."

"Having trouble with the missus, are you?" Sophie chirped in her ear.

"Shut the fuck up, Sophie, or I swear I will come after you as soon as this mission is complete," she hissed.

"Temper, temper." Sophie laughed.

Val wanted to abort the mission and tell Maggie she wasn't cut out for field work if it meant babysitting some

38

prima donna. She could cut her losses before she ended up killing Gina out of frustration.

Val rushed to the boutique's door several steps behind her charge and grabbed her wrist. "If have to handcuff you to me to keep track of you, I will."

"Let go of me." Gina looked around her. "Don't you know he has people everywhere watching me? If they see you manhandling me, it will get back to him. Now let go and act nice."

Val was surprised at her response and considered whether Gina might have more to her than she wanted the world to see. Perhaps she'd been a little harsh in her initial assessment. "I'm sorry. I just need to make sure you're protected. That is my job. Did I hurt you?"

"No," she said softly. "Just watch yourself. You have no idea who you're dealing with." Gina shook her head. "You're the fifth bodyguard I've had since I've been here." She sighed. "I don't want to be responsible for anyone else having a bullet in their head."

Val stared into Gina's eyes and saw the frightened look in them. She hated the fact she was beginning to view Gina as an innocent victim because surely she would know all about her husband's business. She needed to stay on track and not get distracted by the woman's apparent vulnerability.

"You needn't worry about me. I've been taking care of myself since the age of twelve and have managed to survive against odds far worse than you can imagine. I'm the best in the business and no one gets a leg up on me, but I do appreciate your concern."

Gina closed her eyes. "I'm sure you are more than capable, Vera, but it would be foolish to underestimate someone as powerful as my husband." She nodded. "I'm sure this is not to your liking, but I need a new little black dress for this evening's dinner with the mayor." She looked up and down Val's body. "I think you would look nice in a tux for the event."

"Leonid stocked my closet, but I don't believe he included a tux in the mix. You buying?" Val smirked.

"Of course I'm not. Whose card do you think I'll be using?" Gina grinned. "I think you will look rather handsome in a tux and all the women there will be swooning over you." She laughed. "And to think you'll be all mine."

"If I didn't know any better, I'd think you're flirting with me, and honestly I'm not interested in being number five in the body count. Although, I have to admit you're almost worth the risk." Val gave her a once-over. "*Almost* being the operative word."

Gina let out a hearty laugh. "I think I'm going to like you being my bodyguard." She winked. "I flirt with everyone, but never one of my bodyguards…until now."

"Careful. You're playing with fire, little girl, and little girls who play with fire get burned," Val bantered back.

"Ouch. You certainly are a hot one. Come on, let's shop, and then we can have a late lunch. My treat."

"Now how can I resist such a generous offer? Do I get to give you my opinion on your selection for this evening? I can definitely appreciate a woman who fills out a sexy black dress nicely, as I suspect you will."

"All comments will be welcomed." Gina ran a finger down Val's arm. "Let me know if the dress meets your satisfaction."

"Oh, I will, I definitely will. I'll need to, of course, remain with you at all times, including inside the dressing room. You aren't shy, are you?"

"Just a word of warning. I suspect the woman who always waits on me is on Leonid's payroll."

"Spoilsport. I suppose a quick check of the dressing room would suffice. Don't want to get the boss irritated on my first day."

"What the hell game are you playing, Val? You better stop flirting with Gina. She is not your mission," Sophie warned.

Val shook her head as if doing that would let her lose her own personal Jiminy Cricket.

"I do think you should check out the dressing area and perhaps stand guard while I change. You never know how many of Leonid's enemies might be lurking in one of the rooms." Gina grinned and waved her arm. "Shall we?"

Chapter Five

Sophie walked into the main lab and looked around at her colleagues, who all seemed to be engrossed in their work. Toni was chewing on the end of her pen, and Sophie was about to warn her about getting ink all over her lips when she stopped herself and grinned.

I think I'll just let it happen, and maybe she'll absently kiss Char and pass on the love.

Kimiko sat plastered next to Toni, watching the screen quietly and taking in every keystroke. Sophie marveled at how far she'd come from the shy, frightened young girl she'd first met. Char had been working with her every day on her English, and Kimiko seemed to have mastered the complicated language well enough to communicate with most everyone.

Kimiko pointed at the screen and whispered something to Toni.

"Damn, thanks, Kimiko, I missed that," Toni muttered.

Empty ice cream and potato chip containers littered the lab, and Sophie shook her head at what a horde of pigs her friends were. She started picking up the trash and tossing it into the can she'd brought down several months ago after lamenting what a disgrace the lab had turned into now that a bunch of science geeks had taken it over at all hours of the day and night.

"Maggie asked me to gather the troops in an hour or so. It seems Antonio would like to meet with us now that Val is in place," Sophie called out.

Toni glanced up and gave her a bleary-eyed look. She stopped chewing on her pen, but not before the blue ink dotted her lip.

Kimiko pointed at her mouth. "Blue, Miss Toni."

"Huh?" Toni asked.

Sophie laughed. "You got ink all over your mouth, again."

Dani swiveled her chair around. "God, Toni, you never learn. Char won't be kissing those lips until you rub them raw again removing that beautiful blue lipstick."

"Shit." Toni grabbed a moist towelette from the dispenser on the desk and began vigorously scrubbing her mouth.

Kimiko giggled.

Char and Kim entered the lab, followed by Maggie.

Kim immediately crossed the room and placed a gentle kiss on Sophie's lips.

"Good afternoon, love." Sophie knew she probably had a goofy look on her face, but she didn't mind the whole world knowing how much she loved Kim.

Char shook her head as she glanced over at Toni furiously wiping her mouth. She strolled over and kissed the top of her head, then turned her head in Sophie's direction. "You let her get ink all over that beautiful mouth, didn't you, Sophie?"

"I'm not her keeper anymore. That job went to you the minute you stuck your tongue down her throat," Sophie answered.

"Asshole," Char muttered. "So how is our little field agent doing?"

"The dumbass is flirting with the wife," Sophie responded.

"Val is many things, but a dumbass is not one of them," Maggie interjected.

Sophie turned around and caught the steely gaze from their usually gracious leader. "Sorry. I didn't mean to disparage her. She took out two guards in the first five minutes and is on a shopping spree with the wife right now. Nothing much to report yet. I don't get the feeling it will be particularly easy to gather information from Leonid. He doesn't seem to respect women too much, and I doubt he'll take Val under his wing and reveal any of his secrets."

"So did Val shit a brick when you let her know we could communicate with her?" Toni asked.

Sophie laughed. "Yeah, I don't think she's very happy with my little inspirational messages."

"I appreciate the camaraderie all of you have, but I do caution you not to get carried away. This is a very serious and dangerous undertaking and I am quite fond of Val. We are here to ensure her safety, not to poke the bear," Maggie quietly chastised.

Ronda bounded into the lab. "What did I miss? How's Val reacting to you chirping in her ear?" She smirked.

"Asked and answered. When you get here on time, you get the gossip, and when you come late, you miss out," Sophie said.

"Antonio should be here shortly. Thank you all for coming, and I appreciate you treating him respectfully. I know we haven't always thought he was on the same side as us, but in this situation, we most definitely are. I am not suggesting we will combine forces in the future, but I believe at this point we both have the same goal and could use one another's resources."

†

Gina closed the door to her bedroom suite, looked at the packages on her bed, and lifted one eyebrow. The day of shopping had been remarkable to say the least. Her new bodyguard proved to be much more interesting than the others had been. Gina did not doubt that Vera would kill in less than a blink of the eye, and for some reason that gave her comfort. For the first time since she'd known Leonid, she didn't fear that one of his associates would harm her. Did she regard Vera as an associate of her husband? No. If she read her right, Vera was her own person and loyal to no one.

"Yet she makes me feel safe," she whispered.

She knew that her rooms just like all the others in the mansion had both sound and video monitoring. She had no privacy and had long since accepted that as a part of her life now. The only time she could let her hair down was when she went shopping, and even then, Leonid's men were with her or lurking in the shadows, giving her little freedom to be herself. Today was different. She remembered Vera standing stoically outside the dressing room. The look on her bodyguard's face when Gina opened the door and asked her to zip her dress was a mixture of amusement and something else. Desire.

I think I saw desire in her eyes.

A knock on her door made Gina straighten her back and shoulders. She knew who it was and what would be coming next. The door opened and Leonid strolled in.

45

"I hope you bought the perfect dress for this evening," he said, moving toward her.

"Yes, it's a black Vera Wang cocktail dress." Gina smiled. "I know how you like me in black."

"And your new bodyguard. Was she satisfactory?"

Gina knew he was testing her and didn't hesitate in her response. "I had to set her straight on the ground rules of shopping before we entered the store," she said. "I don't think she's had much experience in that area."

"Would you like me to replace her?"

She could see the suspicion in her husband's eyes, and Gina moved closer and ran a finger down his chest. "No. With her I won't have to worry about her eyes undressing me all the time like the others."

"Why did you buy her a tux?"

Gina smiled. "Because it is befitting that my bodyguard look the part, and a tux allows her to fade into the background at these events." She moved her hand lower. "Don't you agree?" She wrapped her fingers around the bulge in his pants and resisted the urge to throw up. Now that she was the aggressor, she knew Leonid would reject her, and that made touching him palatable.

Leonid took her hand and removed it. "I haven't time to satisfy your needs now. Perhaps later." He roughly kissed her before leaving the room.

Gina watched him go, resisting the urge to wipe her lips and opted instead to take a bath in hope of scrubbing away the disgust she felt each time Leonid touched her.

†

Maggie glanced at the security monitor—Antonio. His arrival made her suck in a breath. He was still a very handsome man, and she had to admit she was still attracted

46

to him. Even though she hadn't seen him for nearly ten years, the nervous flurries in her stomach reappeared just like the first time she'd met him over twenty years ago.

"Ronda, will you please go up and greet our guest and then bring him down to this meeting room? Oh, and I'd prefer that you not put a gun to his head. After all, I did invite him to our complex," Maggie added wryly.

Ronda nodded and a hint of a smile appeared.

Sophie was eyeing her warily, and Maggie wondered if she really had let go of her misgivings about joining forces with Antonio. Kim nudged Sophie and her expression softened. Maggie was thankful that Kim was able to ease some of Sophie's hesitation because Sophie had proven she was a valuable member of The Organization.

"Toni, I know you and Dani have been working on an exciting new prototype. Would you be willing to share this with Antonio? I believe it has great value in our combined mission."

"Sure. I think we have everything worked out except for the minor eye irritation, but frankly I don't give a shit if Leonid's eyes get a little itchy," Toni responded.

When the door to the hub opened, all eyes turned to watch as Ronda and Antonio entered the room.

Antonio's smoldering, brown eyes swept the meeting space, and Maggie was sure he noted where every person was situated and their reaction to his arrival. The slight graying at the temples of his almost-black hair added to his distinguished appearance.

Antonio quickly crossed over to Maggie and swept her into his arms. The hug was a surprise, and he hung on to her a tad bit longer than an old friend should. When he finally let go, he surprised her again with a quick peck on her lips. It certainly wouldn't be considered a passionate kiss, but it also was one step above a friendly one. "*Amore mio*, you are as lovely as I remember. Ah, perhaps a bit lovelier."

"You haven't changed a bit, have you? Still quite the charmer and consummate liar." Maggie chuckled. "Why don't we discuss how we can help one another. I suggest we all take a seat at the conference table and you can bring us up-to-date on the resources you have in place."

Antonio gestured for Maggie to take a seat as he pulled out her chair. Toni, Dani, Sophie, Kim, Char, and Ronda filled in the empty spaces and waited for Maggie to lead the discussion.

Antonio pulled a thumb drive from his pocket and directed his gaze at Dani. "Dani, I presume you have a laptop connected to a projector that I can use?"

"Kind of old school, but yeah, I can make it work," Dani responded.

Antonio chuckled. "I almost forgot I was in the company of two well-renowned technological geniuses. It may be old school, but I do believe it will provide you with the necessary information."

Dani wobbled as she awkwardly stood and plucked the thumb drive from Antonio's hand as Toni retrieved a laptop and booted it up. She pressed a button on the side of the device and a crystal-clear three-dimensional image of an eagle soaring over a mountaintop hovered in the air in front of them. She held out her hand and Dani handed her the portable drive. After plugging in the thumb drive, she moved her hand in the air and pointed at the laptop to activate the drive. "Just tell me which file to open."

"Repulsive Bastard," Antonio drolly replied.

"Hmm. No hidden messages there. I like it," Toni stated.

The image of the eagle dissolved and the two dimensional picture hovered in the air as the team waited patiently for Antonio to explain.

Maggie noted the extraordinarily beautiful woman on the right with long blonde hair and striking light blue eyes. The man on the left had dark Mediterranean features but bore a slight resemblance to the woman. The facial structure, shape of their eyes, and full generous lips were nearly identical. She was sure the others on her team had noted the similarity of features.

"Siblings?" she inquired.

"You always were quite perceptive, Maggie. Yes, they are brother and sister. The woman is far more cunning than her brother, but unfortunately they are a package deal. Gina managed to find a way into Leonid's inner circle and brought her brother along for the ride. Honestly, I don't completely trust either one of them. They grew up on the streets and have a survivor's instinct, but no real loyalty to anyone or anything besides money."

Sophie crossed her arms over her chest. "Fuck. Gina is the wife."

Antonio turned toward Sophie. "Sophie, did you have something to add to the conversation?"

"Yes, as a matter of fact, I do. Your inside person, Gina, is playing a dangerous game, and I don't believe she is prepared for the consequences. I knew it was a bad idea to join forces with you. Why exactly did you come to us if you already have your people inside? Our organizations don't exactly have the same set of rules governing our behavior," Sophie groused.

Maggie shot Sophie a look of warning, but she supposed it was better to let her air her feelings and get everything out in the open so they could move on and successfully work together.

49

"I find it quite fascinating how you've conveniently drawn your heavy lines of morality, yet you and I are not as different as you might like to fool yourself into thinking."

"We are nothing alike," Sophie barked.

Antonio raised an eyebrow. "I seem to recall that your funds come from illegal operations. How is that different from where I obtain the capital to fund my missions?"

"What missions? You're a mobster who makes money from gambling and drugs. You kill without remorse, and I haven't seen any evidence of you using your funds for the greater good."

"I'll excuse your lack of respect and complete ignorance because youth sometimes skews one's view of the world. However, I will take this opportunity to set you straight on a few pieces of misinformation."

Antonio folded his hands in front of him on the desk and took a deep breath. "I regret ever having dabbled in the drug business. The lucrative nature of that particular enterprise was very enticing at the time, and the primary reason for the discord between Maggie and myself. I've since seen the error of my ways. Surely there are mistakes in your past that you regret. While you were still in diapers, I was fighting and winning against the same lowlifes you and the rest of Maggie's organization fight against today."

Antonio glanced at Maggie. "Now that you've brought Toni, Sophie, and Kim into your organization, the means by which you fund your missions are just as illegal and morally questionable as my gambling establishments. I make no apologies for any person I've eliminated over the years. Every single one of those bastards deserved it, unless you believe I should have allowed rapists, child molesters, and human traffickers to continue to live."

Maggie could hear the quiet fury in his voice and rushed to settle Sophie. "He's right, Sophie, and if you take a few moments to consider his arguments, I believe you will agree they're valid."

Kim touched Sophie's arm. "Honey, I trust him, and I believe we all have the same end goal."

Sophie relaxed her arms. "I suppose I owe you an apology, Antonio. I guess we aren't as different as I initially thought. It's hard to shed my FBI training and the information they pounded into my head about organized crime."

"Apology accepted. Now, if I might return to the dilemma in front of us. I'd like to hold off on having your person reveal herself to Gina and her brother, Paulie. Besides, they've been inside for quite some time now and haven't managed to penetrate Leonid's organization in any way that we can take advantage of. I was hoping you had a plan to expedite the mission."

"I know I'm not smart about strategy, but explain to me why Val can't just take him out and then we can access his accounts like we did with Viktor?" Ronda asked.

Maggie smiled. "Leonid has a brother in Russia, as well as links to a high-level American. Once Leonid is eliminated, that person will fall too. Leonid has protected his assets in a different manner than Viktor did, and we haven't been able to break through the security measures he has in place that will enable us to access his accounts. Unless we decimate his financial resources his brother will simply take over."

"I think I have a way to break the passcodes or get useful information about the security measures, but we may need Gina or Val to make it work," Toni interjected.

"That sounds promising, let's hear your plan," Antonio responded.

✝

Dressed and ready for another boring night schmoozing and playing the part of Leonid's dumb blonde wife, Gina descended the long, winding staircase. Paulie was in the foyer glaring at her with his arms folded over his chest, and she drew in a deep breath. His body language was angry, and that always spelled trouble.

"What's the matter?" Gina asked.

"As if you have to ask," Paulie sneered and moved closer to her.

"If I knew I wouldn't be asking. Obviously something has set you off. What is it this time?"

"Your new bodyguard." Paulie's voice was full of venom, and Gina could see he was ready to explode.

"What about her? She hasn't even been here a day and already you have a problem? Lighten up, Paulie. She's not a threat to you." Gina touched his arm. "You're still my number-one bodyguard. I thought I'd spare you the shopping experience." A grin crossed her lips. "Besides, I needed to break this one in, and what better way than a day out shopping?"

"I don't like her," Paulie said belligerently.

"Have you even met her?"

"Don't need to. I can spot a badass when I see one, and she's as dangerous as they come."

Gina smiled. "That should make you happy since you'll know she'll keep me safe."

Paulie shrugged. "I don't trust her and will be watching her."

"I would expect nothing less." Gina hooked her arm in Paulie's. "I'm ready for a glass of wine. Will you join me?"

Just as they were about to enter the living room, Gina turned and saw Vera standing at the bottom of the staircase. She had to catch her breath. Nothing had prepared her for the vision of her latest bodyguard decked out in a tuxedo. The woman exuded power and danger, and Gina found that oddly exciting.

Gina tugged at her brother's arm. "Come and meet my other bodyguard." She smiled. "Vera, this is my brother, Paulie Maggio. He fills in as my bodyguard when you're not available."

Vera nodded. "Shall I wait here for you?"

"No. Come with us, and you can practice guarding me this evening. That will consist of you standing out of the way but close enough to save me if I need it." Gina laughed inwardly. She knew Leonid was watching this exchange and knew she'd nailed it. "Come along, a glass of Pinot is calling my name. My husband should be joining us shortly."

Next to her, she heard Paulie grumble and knew the question of Vera was not over. Gina figured Paulie's plans included taking over a part if not all of Leonid's business, and she feared for him. If Vera lived up to what her brother thought of her, she might prove to be an ally and not an enemy. If she decided she could trust Vera, she'd have to find a place where they could talk and not be overheard. Paulie was the only family she had, and she would not let harm come to him. He was in over his head but didn't have the sense to know it.

†

Val was glad Sophie had stopped chirping in her ear. It was starting to unravel her already hypersensitive emotions. She'd had to call upon every ounce of willpower not to grab Gina and kiss her senseless when she first saw her in that sexy black dress. She didn't miss Gina's reaction to her either. She knew that under very different circumstances, she would have had Gina naked and squirming underneath her, begging for release. Lust, pure and simple, stared back at her through those alluring sky-blue eyes.

She wanted to snap Paulie's neck, and if he hadn't been Gina's brother, she might have acted on her need to wipe that scowl off his face. In her mind, he was just another slimy bastard deserving of her personal brand of justice. Val had many years of practice not letting her thoughts show on her face, but somehow that little shit had taken an instant dislike to her.

Val waited patiently for Leonid to arrive and was careful to remain a respectable distance from Gina. She would make sure Gina's safety was her only concern tonight. She felt oddly protective of the mobster's wife. The woman was starting to get under Val's skin, and she didn't like that feeling one bit.

✝

Ronda strolled into the lab and warily eyed the shimmering coral cocktail dress hanging from the rolling wardrobe stand. The blonde wig on the table looked like a hairy mop.

Kim looked up from whatever she was focusing on at her adapted workstation. She was the only agent whose workspace didn't have computers or other high-tech gadgets. Instead, it included a top-of-the-line sewing machine and special equipment designed to produce nearly flawless latex masks or other facial prosthetics.

"Oh no. I'm not wearing that." Ronda pointed to the skimpy dress. "I heard Val is wearing a tux. Why can't I wear one?"

"Because we can't afford to have you stick out like a sore thumb. You would be far too dashing in a tux and might attract unwanted attention," Kim patiently explained.

"Pfft. Like I won't attract attention in a slinky dress and heels. I don't do dresses, and I definitely can't walk in those fucking things." Ronda pointed to the four-inch Jimmy Choo heels on the floor next to the rolling wardrobe.

Someone snickered, and Ronda turned around to catch Toni covering her mouth. "I'm about to rearrange your fucking face, you little egghead. Go ahead, laugh one more time and see what happens."

Toni smirked. "I wore a dress when Kim suggested it was the only option and I looked hot, so buck up, little dyke, and do what she says. She's always right about what to wear." Toni's smirk turned into a glare. "You got your area of expertise and so does she. I don't hear Kim challenging your specific selection of explosives."

"Why can't Char or you do this?" Ronda looked back at Kim. "Or how about you, Kim? I seem to recall your special talent for blending into high society. You're the one with the theater degree," she whined.

"Maggie didn't want to take the chance that any of us would be recognized. Kim didn't have time to make a mask for one of us. From what I've learned, it sounds like Leonid is a lot smarter than Viktor was. He may have gotten ahold of some old security film from the Republican fundraiser the rest of us attended, and he often uses fancy face-recognition software to identify potential threats. At least that's the rumor," Toni explained.

"I hate every last one of you," Ronda declared.

"No, you don't," Kim responded.

"Yes, I do. I really, really do." Ronda held out her hands. "Give me the fucking dress."

Kim gently placed it across her arms.

"I don't have to stay long, do I? I can just get the fancy communication bot to Val and she'll take it from there, right?" Ronda pleaded.

Ronda felt a presence and turned around to see Maggie smiling behind her. Ronda didn't know how Maggie managed to do it, but she was the stealthiest person Ronda knew.

"You'll have to stay long enough to ensure your exit doesn't get noticed as an oddity. Don't leave before dinner is finished. Kim, can you teach Ronda how to walk in heels?" Maggie directed.

"Would love to," Kim answered.

"Fuck," Ronda mumbled.

Chapter Six

The black, armored limousine pulled around the circular driveway and stopped at the front door of the mayor's home. One of Leonid's men got out and scanned the area before opening the back door. Leonid held up his hand and waved the man away.

"Tonight is very important, and I know for certain that some of my enemies will be here. It is your job to stay close to my wife, and if the situation arises, don't hesitate to use your gun. If any harm comes to her it will mean your life." He curled his lip and glared at Vera. "Do I make myself clear?"

"Yes," Vera answered.

Leonid turned his attention to Gina, his expression softening for a second. "You are so lovely this evening. Everyone will be jealous of me for having such a ravishing wife." He opened the door and waited for his three bodyguards to surround him and Gina. "Do not let any man other than myself approach her."

"I will make certain they do not," Vera said.

†

Ronda kept tugging at the peach dress that clung to her body like a second skin. The quick lesson on heels was barely sufficient to hide her discomfort. She knew that when she reached the mayor's mansion, she would have to stop fidgeting or risk unnecessary exposure. Oddly she was less bothered by her arm casually looped through Antonio's, who provided a perfect escort for the event. The cesspool of crooked politicians afforded both Antonio and Leonid the same level of access to powerful men, all the way up to the president. However, it wasn't usual for both men to receive invites to the same events. Sophie seemed to have a huge issue with Antonio, but Ronda agreed with Char and Maggie—Antonio was probably the least abhorrent mobster in DC and not much different from most of the politicians.

She walked carefully to the front door after just as cautiously emerging from Antonio's limousine.

"Ronda, you look lovely. Do not fidget; you will fit in just fine, and I am proud to be an escort to such a beautiful woman," Antonio said.

"Save your charm for Maggie. You know it doesn't have the same effect on me. If I so much as see a smirk on Val's face, I'll take my revenge out on every last one of you, including you, Mr. Smooth."

Antonio's chuckle filled the air as they reached the door.

†

Gina looked out over the room and saw the same old, tired faces she always saw at such functions. The mayor was busy glad-handing everyone while his wife stood by with a false smile plastered on her face. The mayor was in a tight race for reelection and Leonid would support him as long as he continued to ignore his illegal dealings. The place was loaded with men like her husband who would secure the mayor's next term. In return the mayor would turn a blind eye to their dealings.

Her attention turned to the woman standing next to her. Vera certainly looked handsome in her tuxedo, and Gina had noticed all the eyes that turned in their direction when they entered the room.

"It's too bad we had to buy that off the rack," she said. "Tomorrow we will go and have you fitted for one."

Vera only nodded.

Vexed, Gina said, "Your life is in my hands. I suggest you never forget that." She took a flute of champagne from the tray one of the many servers offered her. When the woman holding the tray glanced appreciatively at her bodyguard, Gina growled. The server quickly left. She narrowed her eyes and took a sip of her drink before placing the glass on a nearby table.

When Gina saw Vera's arrogant smirk, she scowled at her. "Arrogance isn't your best suit, so I'd knock it off if you know what's good for you." She looked over and saw Leonid looking at them. "He's watching, so play nice."

"Denial doesn't look any better on you, and I always play nice. Name the time and the place and we can have a play date." Val turned away from Leonid and faced Gina with a broad grin.

"You are a cocky shit, aren't you?" Gina smirked. "I play for keeps."

"I believe you're already kept. Leonid has you on a short leash, and I don't think you have the guts to play on my team. Your mouth is making declarations your ass can't pay for."

"Is that a dare? You might be surprised."

"Gina, who is this gorgeous woman?" Janet, the mayor's wife, an attractive platinum blonde with enormous breasts interrupted as she strolled up to them.

Gina watched as Janet, ran her gaze over Vera's body and smiled. "She's mine."

Janet quirked her eyebrow. "Does Leonid know this? He doesn't seem like the sharing type."

"I'm here to ensure Gina's safety. I work for Leonid, but I don't belong to anyone. What about you, Ms....? Do you belong to someone like Gina does?" Vera asked.

Gina glared at both women. "Janet, if you want to ensure that your husband has our support, I'd suggest you run along. You're way out of your league here."

"Hmmph. I was only trying to be hospitable, but I can see I've ruffled some feathers here, and I don't really need to get involved in whatever game you two are playing." Janet stalked off and grabbed a glass of champagne on her way toward a small group talking quietly in the corner.

"I don't know what your endgame is, but know this, Vera—I always play to win, and trust me when I tell you it's a dangerous game you're playing," Gina growled. "Now go fetch one of those waiters and bring me some more champagne."

"I'm paid to protect you, not to be your fucking lapdog. Go get it yourself, you spoiled little shit. Oh, and as long as you're going to get yourself a drink, I'll take a Perrier, please." Vera chuckled.

"Is there a problem here?" Leonid asked.

Where the hell did he come from? I always know where he is at these functions. "No, darling." Gina ran a finger down his studded shirt. "The mayor's wife thought Vera could be persuaded to be her bodyguard."

Leonid looked at Vera. "Is that true?"

"She made an offer. I turned her down," Vera responded.

Leonid narrowed his eyes. "Janet did not seem pleased. Her husband is a puppet, but a puppet we need, so perhaps you can play nice with her. Stop lingering in this corner and mingle with the guests. Vera is not going anywhere, so don't worry about Janet hiring her away from her duty to you."

Vera nodded.

Gina gulped down her rejoinder and watched as Leonid's attention turned to an exquisite-looking couple who had just entered the main room.

"Son of a bitch," Leonid snarled.

✝

Val followed the direction of Leonid's eyes and nearly choked at the sight of Ronda decked out in a slinky dress. It took all her willpower not to burst into laughter. Fortunately, Leonid's eyes didn't leave Antonio and Ronda long enough to notice the brief reaction. When Val glanced back at Gina, she sensed Gina hadn't missed the split-second response.

Sophie had warned her that Ronda would be accompanying Antonio to the event so Ronda could transfer Toni's new gadget, but she hadn't mentioned what Kim had picked out for her to wear. Val wasn't sure how the device worked or what she would need to do with it when she received it. But she suspected Sophie or someone else would instruct her how to ensure it absorbed into Leonid's skin just as soon as she had it.

She watched as Antonio and Ronda boldly strode toward them as Leonid looked as though he might explode right before her eyes.

"Leonid. I see you have a new bodyguard for your wife. It is so difficult to get good help these days, isn't it?"

"How dare you speak to me in such a manner! My wife and who I choose to protect her is none of your damn business." His nostrils flared and his jaw tightened.

Antonio waved his hand. "Merely an observation. Your temper will be your downfall, Leonid. I would advise you to tread lightly. You never know whom you're going to piss off that won't bow down to your form of coercion." He drew closer and whispered, "Tick tock, Leonid, your time is drawing near."

Leonid balled his hand. "You should watch that mouth of yours."

Gina took her husband's hand. "Darling, the mayor is looking at you. Didn't you need to speak with him?"

Val wasn't sure what Antonio was trying to do, but she needed to get control of the situation and fast. Leonid was volatile and completely devoid of emotion. She wouldn't put it past him to light up the place and damn the consequences.

In a move too quick for any of them to register, Val had a Glock against Antonio's back. "Apologize to Mr. Borsky." She made sure Leonid saw the gun but that it was out of anyone else's view.

"I meant no disrespect. By all means, please don't let me keep you from the mayor," Antonio relented.

"I can have her kill you or not," Leonid said before baring his teeth. "You wouldn't have a problem with that, would you, Vera?"

Val smirked. "Well, I would hate to get blood all over this nice tux and it might prematurely end the party, but I suppose those are minor wrinkles to work out."

Leonid grinned. "You have a point." He glared at Antonio. "I'd watch my back if I were you." He took Gina's arm. "Come with me. I believe the mayor is motioning for us."

As soon as Leonid turned around, Ronda bumped into Val, and Val felt a small package slip into her jacket pocket. Ronda was so fast, only an expert spy would have realized what had just occurred.

Val followed a few steps behind Gina and Leonid and smiled inside, knowing part one of the plan was done. She hoped Sophie wouldn't start filling her head with instructions yet. She needed to pay attention to what was happening at the mayor's house lest Gina begin to notice her subtle reaction to Sophie's intermittent communications.

Chapter Seven

Leonid unzipped the small leather case. He pulled out the compact blood-glucose monitoring system and pricked his finger. After he booted up his top-of-the-line computer using both the retinal and hand-scan security access, he quickly pressed a droplet of blood onto the small indent on the special keyboard to open the secure communication program. It would allow him to speak with his younger brother, Alexei, who operated the Russian portion of their vast slave trade empire. The program operated much like Skype, but with failsafe security to keep out any prying eyes.

A handsome younger version of Leonid filled the large monitor. His charming smile was a disarming attribute that he used to his advantage. "Good evening, brother. I hope you are well. I am hearing disturbing things that I am confident you are already aware of."

"Yes, I know there is a varmint among us. For the moment, this person is useful to me and believes their ill-advised plans are still unknown. When the moment is right, I will follow this parasite back to their little hidey-hole and exterminate the whole nest of them."

"You have a plan to smoke them out?" Alexei asked.

"We will be vermin-free by the time you come to visit, and then our business will flourish without interference from any pests. There is never a lack of demand for our product," Leonid answered.

"How is your lovely wife?"

Leonid's eyes narrowed. "She is well for the time being. I will expect her to produce a son for me soon, and then we shall see. Her beauty is somewhat distracting, but no one is irreplaceable—even someone as lovely as Gina."

"Hmmm. I thought you may have fallen in love with this one, brother, but I see love has still yet to bite you. Perhaps a Russian beauty will capture your heart one day."

Leonid chuckled. "I will leave love to you, little brother, but I suspect it will be many years before you manage to run through all your many liaisons."

"Will you contact me after you've resolved your pest problem? I have a few nervous customers who are wary after what happened to Viktor. Fucking *sookas* managed to delay our business-expansion plans. I do hope your pest problem is tied to them."

"*Da*, do not worry, little brother. My plan has been in the works for many months. Nothing I have done so far is without reason," Leonid assured him.

"Be well, big brother. I will talk to you soon. Trust no one," Alexei warned.

"I trust no other but you."

†

When Val returned to her room, she pulled the small bag from her pocket and managed to unobtrusively inspect it after carefully laying her jacket on the chair. Her sleight-of-hand tricks often came in handy when hiding from the cameras. She wasn't sure what she was supposed to do with the tiny vial. She hoped it would be easy to transmit without detection. Toni's biologic tracking device was a whole helluva lot simpler, because all one had to do was hand someone a business card and voila, the device burrowed into the person's skin and stayed there for several weeks. That was how Toni had tracked Char's every move, but Char was smart enough to realize Toni had given her the *special card*. That was all before Toni, Sophie, and Kim had joined The Organization and the two groups had combined forces to take Viktor down.

"What a little social butterfly you are," Sophie said in Val's head.

She was getting tired of Sophie's running commentary that was unnecessary to the operation. All she wanted were the facts, not a bunch of bullshit teasing.

"Okay, listen, Leonid needs to ingest the nanobot," Sophie said, almost as if she had heard Val's thoughts. *"I know that's more difficult to achieve, but Toni couldn't get the advanced tracking device into paper so you could transfer it easily to his skin. She said we couldn't take the chance that the larger version would be detected through the slight rise in the paper. I guess she learned her lesson with Char. Besides, I don't suspect he will ignore you brushing against him, even if you make it seem like an accident. This guy is shrewd, so be careful."*

Val seriously wanted to spit something back, but she couldn't, and it irritated her to no end knowing that Sophie was taking great pleasure in the one-sided communication.

"By the way, stop playing with fire. Your continued flirtation with the boss's wife is very ill-advised. I swear, you and Toni might have been cut from the same cloth."

Val wanted to purge the little communication device from her body as she gave a low growl to indicate her opinion on the last piece of advice Sophie chirped in her ear. Besides the irritation of the limited one-way communication, she needed to get the message to Sophie that Toni and Dani should start working on a scrambling device so she could talk with ease in Leonid's fortress of intrusion. At the top of her list of aggravations was the fact someone was watching her every move and listening to her 24/7.

"Nighty-night and sweet dreams, Val. Keep them clean, will you? You'll only frustrate yourself further with something you can never have. Oh, and by the way, don't thank me yet, but we're working on a scrambling device because I know this one-sided communication is filling that volcano of yours with lava, and we can't afford to have you blow and demolish all our carefully laid plans."

Val ripped off her tuxedo shirt, unzipped and stepped out of her pants, then pulled the down comforter on her bed aside. She tossed her bra on top of the pile of clothes littering the only chair in the room but left her special thong on.

The antique chair wasn't really her cup of tea. She preferred more modern furniture, but Leonid, like Viktor, flaunted his wealth with over-the-top antiques and art. *It must be a Russian mobster thing.* But she had to admit she did enjoy sleeping in the 1800 thread-count Egyptian cotton sheets. As she slipped into the cool sheets, she sighed. Her mind went to the conversation she'd had with Gina in the gardens earlier that evening while Leonid was talking business with the mayor. Sophie was right, she was entering dangerous territory, but somehow, she couldn't help herself.

†

Sophie sauntered into the central hub where Toni and Dani had their heads bent over a piece of paper. She glanced at the complicated document and shook her head. More than likely, this was their latest brainstorm. She couldn't even imagine what this new invention entailed.

Dani's head popped up and she smiled. "Hey, Soph. What's up?"

"Do you know where Maggie is?"

"She went to her quarters with Antonio after he came back from the mayor's house a few minutes ago." Dani started laughing.

Toni looked up and grinned. "Ronda was bitching from the moment they arrived back at the compound until Antonio and Maggie left. I had to text Cindy to get her to come rescue us from it. Cindy told her she looked hot, and that shut her right up. They hightailed it out of here after that. I'm pretty sure they're doing the horizontal mambo right now."

Dani smiled. "You better hurry to Maggie's quarters if you want to catch her before she and Antonio reconnect, if you know what I mean. They were all googly-eyed with each other. I've never seen Maggie react that way around anyone else."

Sophie frowned. She still wasn't sure about Antonio, but apparently, the decision had already been made to work with him. "Thanks. I guess I'll head to her quarters now to give them an update." She looked at the others in the room. "I'm not sure about Val's ability to get the nanobot into Leonid without compromising her cover. As much as I hate to admit it, I think it's time to involve Gina." Sophie shook her head. "I wish we had a way to get Val's input. This one-way communication is nearly impossible to effectively design the perfect strategy. Maybe I should consult with Char. I just have a feeling Gina as his wife will have more opportunity than Val."

"I should have waited until I was able to design something that would absorb into his skin through an innocuous card or something." Toni balled her hand on the desk.

"That would have put us back several months or more. Have faith in Val's ability to work with Gina," Dani added.

"That's what I'm worried about. Val and Gina have engaged in a dangerous game of shameless flirting, and I know Leonid has every room in the house bugged. All it takes is one minor slipup and they're both toast," Sophie cautioned with a grim look on her face. "I don't think we have much longer to come up with a way to scramble his listening devices. Although it's a risk to let the two of them have unfettered conversations with one another, we have to take the chance."

"Well, shit, I wish we had waited to place her in a risky position. I was starting to like Val. Her curmudgeonly ways are vaguely reminiscent of how you act, Sophie. Underneath that badass exterior is a loyal, caring woman, and I would hate for us to lose such a great agent." Toni let out a long sigh.

"You got that right. Val is really a big pussycat. I love her like a big sister, and I swear if Gina causes her cover to be blown, I'll have to find an ingenious way to get revenge." Dani narrowed her eyes as she spoke.

"Toni, can you call Char and send her to Maggie's quarters? I think it's time for a powwow," Sophie directed.

"Sure thing. Hey, when you get it all figured out, would you mind bringing us up to speed?" Toni asked.

"Of course. Why don't you two stop your mad scientist routine and head to bed and we can connect in the morning. I'll bet Char gets irritated when she has to track you down at midnight." Sophie waved as she exited the main hub.

†

Sophie was in a quandary because she wasn't too thrilled about interrupting Maggie and Antonio, but she wasn't at all confident about Val's ability to arrange for Leonid to ingest the nanobot. On the other hand, she also wasn't excited about involving Gina in the mission. It didn't matter that she was one of Antonio's agents, Sophie's gut told her Gina was a self-centered amateur who was only out for number one. She sensed that if she was threatened, she would sacrifice every single person in The Organization to save her hide and get what she wanted. Sophie had a bad feeling about all of this and no one seemed to be heeding her warnings.

Sophie knocked lightly on Maggie's door and waited for her to answer.

"Sophie, come in. You're frowning," Maggie said as Sophie stepped into the room. "Has something gone wrong?"

Sophie stepped into Maggie's small quarters. She felt relieved she hadn't caught them in a compromising position, half-dressed and on the verge of having sex. "Not yet, but I am concerned this nanobot device will be difficult to activate. Val doesn't get close enough to Leonid to ensure he will ingest it, and I don't think Antonio's inside person is our answer. I asked Dani to call Char and maybe the three of us—"

Antonio cleared his throat.

"Oh, sorry, the four of us, can put our heads together and figure out how we're going to overcome the obstacles and give Val some more precise instructions." Sophie looked directly at Antonio.

"Sophie, you may be surprised to hear that I agree with you. Gina and Paulie are unfortunately in this for the money and don't have the same sense of loyalty to our brothers and sisters as we do. I hope it does not astound you, but there is honor among thieves and mobsters."

"Make yourself comfortable, Sophie. Can I get you a drink?" Maggie asked.

"Sure, why not." She pointed to an open bottle of wine. "I'll have a glass of whatever you're having."

Maggie answered the light knock on the door as Antonio poured Sophie a glass of wine.

"My, my, my, this is an unlikely pairing. Hello, Antonio, and Sophie. Did you two kiss and make up?" Char asked.

"Shut up, smartass. We have a problem, and it's going to take more than my brainpower to solve it. Val doesn't get close enough to Leonid to spike his drink, and I don't trust either of Antonio's inside agents. So that leaves us with very few options. Any idea, oh great strategist?" Sophie asked.

"Hmmm, that is a pickle. I suppose finesse and subtlety are our friends. Unfortunately, Val isn't too good at either. I suggest we exercise a bit of patience and see how things play out. Val is wired, so whenever she's close to Gina, Paulie, or Leonid, we'll be able to hear everything that goes on. Why don't you instruct Val to find ways to give us clues whenever they're somewhere else than his fortress. We probably should have arranged for a bartender at the mayor's house, and then we could have dropped the nanobot in his drink. Problem solved."

"Coulda, shoulda, woulda...too bad that ship has sailed. Why the hell didn't you suggest that earlier?" Sophie narrowed her eyes. "This is turning into one big clusterfuck. We have one of our own on the inside and no way of protecting her. The only thing that is working is the listening device in her ass." She was shaking. "We've just given her a device she can only use if she involves Antonio's plant, who is unreliable at best."

Char stood next to Sophie. "You all were too anxious and failed to consult me before you jumped into this."

"You were doing your lawyer thing and we didn't have time to go over all the finer points. We had a window of opportunity and took it." Sophie folded her arms over her chest.

"Well, it looks like we might want to wait for another window of opportunity, then. Patience does not seem to be your strong point, Sophie." Char raised an eyebrow.

"We barely had time to arrange for Ronda and Antonio to attend the private party. I don't think it would have been possible to get a bartender in there at that late stage. Toni just perfected the nanobot, and frankly, she has some questions about whether it will work or not," Maggie interjected. "We can't let Leonid slip through our fingers…we cannot allow that to happen. We have to work with what we have."

"Sophie, I think you better tell Val to hold tight until the odds shift more in our favor, but if she sees an opportunity, she should take it," Antonio suggested.

"I'm more worried about how difficult it will be to keep Val's cover intact with her being watched and monitored every second she's in that fortress, and I do mean fortress. So far, it's been nearly impenetrable." Sophie blew out a breath and rubbed a hand across her face. "They don't let a single maintenance person inside unless they've fully vetted them. We need to get to Val some way to scramble the signals so she can communicate with us and talk freely with Gina." Her eyes scanned the room, then landed on Maggie. "We have to keep her safe."

"She knew going in what the odds were. Trust her to know what to do." Maggie lifted a shoulder. "I worry about her too."

"We need a plan," Sophie said softly.

"We'll devise one. I'll meet with Dani and Toni tomorrow and see where we're at with their new prototype, but that isn't going to solve the problem of how we can get it to her. Gina does like her little shopping trips, so that's going to be our best bet. If we send Ronda again, I'm sure she'll blow a gasket." Maggie glanced at Char. "Perhaps we can send you in one of Kim's disguises. At least you enjoy shopping."

"That sounds fun. I'll work on a plan. Not that your company isn't riveting, but my mad scientist knocked off early—well, early for her—so I plan on taking advantage of the rare moment we'll have to spend together. Ta-ta. See you all in the morning." Char waved and let herself out.

"Yeah, I think I will be going as well. Kim gets a little cranky when I don't get back at a reasonable hour. Good night." Sophie waved at Antonio and Maggie, who looked rather cozy sitting together on the couch.

Chapter Eight

Toni was antsy when she opened her eyes and looked at the clock. After Char had slipped into bed last night, she'd brought Toni up to speed on the latest developments, and Toni was worried. She'd only known Val for a little while, but she surmised that patience wasn't her strong suit. If they didn't find a way to enable Gina and Val to talk freely or a means of secure two-way communication, Val would blow her cover and quite possibly get herself killed.

Char would be devastated if something happened to Val. Toni gingerly pushed the covers aside and slipped out of bed. She'd bet her left breast Dani was already working on the scrambler. They'd talked about a few ideas that would allow Val to utilize the device without anyone watching or listening in. The main problem was how to create an audio feed that would replace their conversation and sync nicely with whatever video feed Leonid was sure to review every day. The other problem was figuring out where Val would keep the device. They had to ensure it would fit into something Val wore every day, like her underwear, but that already had her commlink.

Toni smacked her head. "God, I'm so dense. That's perfect. She wears that smartwatch Dani got her every day."

"What?" Char flopped over and grumbled, "It's six and we didn't get to sleep until one. At this point, not even coffee will help."

"Sorry, hon, I need to head to the lab. I'll make it up to you later, I promise." Toni grabbed her shorts and a T-shirt that she'd thrown on the floor and quickly put them on.

Char waved her hand in the air. "Fine, at least you did earn yourself some brownie points last night. I'll forgive you if you do that thing with your tongue again tonight."

Toni grinned. "It would be my pleasure."

†

"Wakey, wakey, Little Miss Sunshine."

Val squinted at the watch sitting on the nightstand, noting the time. It was only seven. She was going to kill Sophie after this job was complete. She just knew Sophie was enjoying every single minute of chirping in her ear. Val began planning her revenge for the next time they sparred in the gym.

"We're working on a way to scramble the audio and video feed Leonid has on you and replace it with something innocuous, but we need just a little more time and we're hoping another shopping trip is on the horizon. Char will be the one to make the drop this time. She'll be in one of Kim's disguises. We're gonna swap out your smartwatch. You'll need to make it easy for her by loosening the band. I know this is a little difficult for your little pea brain to absorb so early in the morning, but can you give me a sign you understand?"

Val sat up. "Fucking birds chirping at the ass crack of dawn. Next time I get a chance I'm gonna shoot the little fuckers."

"Such a grumpy goose you are in the morning. No wonder you don't have a steady girlfriend. We'll be in touch later. Give us a few days and then find a way to suggest a shopping trip and don't forget to tell us where you'll be."

Val yawned and stretched before strutting into the bathroom to brush her teeth. She wasn't a morning person, but now that Sophie had awakened her, she knew she wouldn't be able to go back to sleep. She needed to pound something before she exploded. Thank God she wasn't expected to babysit Gina until later in the day. Val smiled. Gina wasn't a morning person either; she never woke up before ten.

We'd be compatible in that respect.

Val grabbed her workout clothes and quickly dressed. She then strapped her gun to her thigh and exited her room. Her Glock and her watch were her idea of the perfect accessories to any outfit, and she never went anywhere without them.

✝

Sweat poured down Val's neck and tickled the center of her back as she battered the large punching bag. She imagined Leonid's face as she beat on it. He didn't deserve Gina. She hated imaging Leonid pounding Gina during sex. She'd be able to take Gina to new heights of arousal and pleasure her in a way Leonid could never imagine, but he was the one she slept with every night. She was just a throwaway possession to him, not a precious human being.

Fucking animal.

Over the sounds of her fist connecting with the bag, Val heard the subtle click of the door to the gym and detected the scent that was uniquely Gina. Val had been surprised by the sweet citrus odor when she first met Gina. She'd assumed Gina would be the type of woman to wear an expensive perfume that would undoubtedly make Val gag when she came too close. Women always thought overpowering perfumes drove men and women crazy, but Val preferred the fresh, clean scent usually attached to those who were more down-to-earth. She sucked in a breath while waiting patiently for Gina to approach.

Gina walked over to Val and ran a finger down her arm. "Quite the muscles you have."

"Careful." Val turned away from where she suspected the camera and microphone were hidden and whispered barely loud enough for Gina to hear, "The walls have eyes and ears."

"Hmm, not in here."

Val wasn't so sure about that. She knew men like Leonid, and they weren't the kind to leave a crack in their security. She shook her head subtly to let Gina know her doubts. "Is there something you need? Because I've still got an hour left in my workout and you're interrupting my mojo."

"Today we're going shopping and I want you along. I'll even let you drive." Once again Gina ran her finger down Val's arm. "You're all sweaty." She grinned. "I like."

"Oh joy. Just how I want to spend my day. Why can't Paulie take you? I've been doing double duty while he sits on his fat ass."

"Paulie is such a bore." Gina took a step closer. "He doesn't have, shall we say, your appeal. I want you to see what I buy and tell me what you think."

Val sighed. "Fine, but do we have to leave right now, or can I finish my workout, take a shower, and meet you out front?"

Val hoped her acting was convincing and that she appeared irritated at having to accompany Gina on her shopping trip. She still believed the room was wired, and Gina was dancing dangerously on an edge Val wasn't willing to step out on. Inside, though, she was grateful for the chance to let her team provide them with the necessary device to communicate more freely.

"I can wait right here for you and watch you work out and shower." Her gaze moved over Val's body. "I will especially like watching you shower," she said in a low growl.

Val gritted her teeth and muttered, "You are bound and determined to get both of us killed." In a normal voice, she added, "I don't need a spotter, so just move along and get ready. I'll cut my workout short if that'll make you happy."

Val punched the bag, stepped back, and when it swung back and connected with Gina, sending her to the floor of the gym, she smiled. "Oh sorry, I didn't realize how close you were."

With a grin, Gina got off the floor. "Some punch you have there. You must be very strong."

The door opened and Leonid walked in wearing workout clothes. "What are you doing here?" he asked Gina.

"Arranging for a shopping trip, my darling." She walked over to him and kissed him. "You look good in those clothes. Maybe we should leave Vera to it and have some alone time."

"No. This is my gym time. I want you both to leave now."

"I was under the impression I had access to all of the facilities. It's important that I remain in top form if I'm going

78

to adequately protect Gina. You'll need to let me know if there is an alternate workout facility or specific times I need to avoid using this room." Val widened her stance and looked directly at Leonid.

"*Da*. You can use the servants' workout room when I am using this one." He scowled at Val. "If my wife wants to go shopping, then why are you still here? Get ready to go with her." This wasn't the first time Val had noticed the small cracks in his cool exterior with the resulting flash of anger directed at her. It was something she would need to pay close attention to.

Val nodded, spun on her heel, and moved to the door. Inside she was seething. *I'm going to enjoy putting a bullet in that asshole's head as soon as Maggie gives me the go-ahead, and she better not let someone else have that honor.*

"I might as well go with you," Gina said, trailing behind her.

✝

Dani's tongue poked out of the corner of her mouth as she bent her head to look at a tiny metal square. She moved her eyes from the computer screen to the small device for a little while, then frowned and muttered, "God damn it."

Noticing her bloodshot eyes, Toni suspected Dani had been working on the scrambler all night. She felt guilty for turning in early last night when she knew that Dani wouldn't leave it be. She was close to fixing the flaw, and that meant pushing through until she'd worked out the bugs. By the sound of it, Toni surmised the device was still causing her grief.

"What's it doing now?" Toni asked.

"I can't get the program to adjust to lip movements to simulate the fake replacement audio program we'll be supplying. We might have to switch both audio and video feeds somehow, and we don't have enough video of Gina to manipulate more than a couple of scenes. It'll be obvious if we keep looping the same scene over and over. It would be far better to have the audio sync with what is actually seen through Leonid's cameras."

"Can I take a look at the programming?" Toni asked.

Dani pushed her chair back. "Sure."

Toni rolled over another chair, and her fingers flew over the keyboard as she typed in new code. She could sense Dani leaning over her shoulder.

"That's brilliant, Toni. Damn, why didn't I think of that?" Dani touched the screen with a finger. "Here, just change that to—"

"Oh, yeah, that'll work," Toni exclaimed.

"Finishing each other's sentences again like an old married couple," Char said. "I should be jealous, but you two are simply poetry in motion. It's such a beautiful thing to witness. I can almost see the sparks of genius flow between your brains. Am I hearing that you've almost perfected the scrambler?"

Toni nodded and looked up at Dani to see her grinning and nodding. "Hey, I thought you'd sleep in. How come you're up already?" Toni asked.

"How quickly they forget." Char shook her head. "I couldn't get back to sleep after you tried sneaking out of bed. I kept thinking about that tongue thing."

"Do you have to flaunt your sex life in front of me? I've been frozen out again because I broke another date." Dani sighed.

"All work and no play," Char singsonged. "Seriously, you need to work less and enjoy life more. I worry about you sometimes. Candy's a nice girl and she's had it rough with her ex, so I don't think she wants anything remotely similar to her last relationship."

Dani had started to open her mouth when Char put up her hand. "I'm not suggesting you would ever be abusive, but there are more ways to kill a budding relationship, and taking someone for granted is one of them."

"I'll take a vacation when we shut down that bastard Leonid, and Val comes back to us safe and sound. Val's special—"

Char raised her eyebrow. "Don't tell me you're in love with her."

"No, it's not like that. I just understand damage. I get her, that's all." Dani let out a small sigh and returned her attention to the screen.

†

Sophie leaned back in the recliner and took a sip of coffee. She couldn't help the Cheshire grin on her face. Taunting Val was becoming an addiction. She had to admit that being Val's connection to The Organization and her mentor on deep cover was fun. Sophie heard stirring in the master bedroom and looked up to see Kim ambling into the living room.

"How long have you been up?" Kim lifted her arms above her head and stretched.

"Since about seven. I needed to update Val on our progress with the scrambler."

Kim raised her eyebrow. "You woke her up at seven in the morning? That's not very nice. You know you did it to push her buttons. Why?"

"Okay, I admit it, I get a perverse pleasure out of poking the bear. I like Val; it's just that she's so much fun to tease. If I didn't genuinely care about her, I wouldn't even bother to mess with her. It's a cop thing. We always razzed the ones we liked the most."

"You spies and cops are a different breed. Theater people don't do that to each other. So where are we at with the scrambler? Wanna bet Dani spent all night working on it?"

"Nope, I'm not taking that bet. Toni probably slipped out of bed early to join her. I'm guessing the two eggheads are deep into fixing the problems, and I wouldn't be surprised if we have something we can get to Val today if we're able to rendezvous through another shopping trip. Do you have Char's disguise ready?"

Kim grinned before nodding.

"I know that smile, and I think you enjoy tweaking Char as much as I enjoy needling Val. Are you sure you theater types don't have your own set of rules that include a few pranks here and there?"

"You think Char will mind turning into a large, garish woman who sort of resembles Tammy Faye—you know, the wife of that disgraced preacher?" Kim giggled.

Sophie laughed. "We should head to the lab and find out."

†

"Okay, stop distracting me. I need to concentrate on the final adjustments to the code," Toni told Char before looking in Dani's direction. "Do you think we'll be done with this today?"

Dani nodded. "You just opened the floodgates with your modification. That was the key. I'm confident we can finish today. We'll need to do some final testing, of course, but this will be so sweet. All Val will have to do is activate it and the new audio stream will match their gestures and sync

82

enough to fool Leonid. They should be able to talk freely whenever she uses the device."

"I don't understand how you're able to sync the audio and video." Char leaned over the computer screen.

"Just think of this like a really advanced foreign movie. Hollywood hasn't come nearly as far with dubbing technology as we have. Granted, they've come a long way, but our technology is almost seamless. Leonid won't be able to detect any anomalies. We're almost done, but no offense, hon, you're getting in the way of our making history here," Toni answered

Char slapped her hand to her chest. "I am so wounded. I guess the honeymoon's over. I'm just a distraction now." She chuckled.

The door to the lab clanged open and Sophie charged in with Kim trailing her.

"Well, look what the cat dragged in. What's up, Soph?" Dani asked.

"Just checking on how far you are with the device. Kim has the disguise ready, so as soon as you brainiacs have the bugs worked out, we can listen in and coordinate with Val on the next shopping excursion."

"Sounds like a good plan. So, what did you work up for me? I hope it's something fun," Char said.

Kim grinned. "Oh it's fun all right."

"I'm not sure I like the sound of that." Char rested her hand on Toni's chair.

"Hey, what's not to like about Tammy Faye Bakker?" Kim chuckled.

"You're kidding, right?" Char asked.

"No, she's not. She's really not," Sophie answered.

Dani and Toni started snickering.

"Hey, stop laughing or I'll make you go in my place, and I know how much you love to shop."

"No can do. You want this device ready today, don't you?" Toni asked.

Dani craned her neck and signaled to Toni that she wanted to take over.

"You have a solution?" Toni asked as she turned the monitor toward Dani and pushed the keyboard in front of her.

Dani nodded and began to enter code into the program. "I got it. Take a look, Toni."

Toni glanced at the screen. "Yeah, that looks about right. Let's do a little test right now. Char, will you please sit in my lap and tell me that you want to rip off my clothes and fuck me 'til I scream?"

"You're kidding, right?" Char asked.

Toni grinned. "Nope, we need to test how the code works and what it will do to sync the video and audio of the live demonstration."

"I swear you two have the oddest ways to test your inventions."

"We might be geeks, but we know how to make our work interesting," Toni remarked.

"Fine." Char sat on Toni's lap and deadpanned, "I want to rip your clothes off and fuck you until you scream."

"Waiter, check please," Toni quipped.

"Listen, it's working." Dani began typing on the keyboard again. "Let me play it back for you to hear while I increase the volume on the computer. I think it's ready for prime time. We can do a few more tests, but I feel confident that if a shopping trip is on the horizon, Char should be able to do her magic and replace Val's smartwatch with the new and improved model."

Toni shifted her eyes to Sophie when she heard her groan. "Jesus, Soph, you look constipated or something."

"Why do we have to work with fucking amateurs? It's bad enough Val has to be the one to do this deep-cover assignment. I just know that Gina is going to get her killed. Antonio should have never deployed that twit in the first place."

Kim frowned. "What's going on?"

"Gina is blatantly flirting with Val in Leonid's workout facility. I can barely hear Val trying to warn her, but the stupid little shit won't listen. On the plus side, it sounds like a shopping trip is planned for today. Do you think it's possible to get this device you're working on to her soon enough to take advantage of this opportunity?" Sophie asked.

Char climbed out of Toni's lap. "I don't think we should wait. It sounds like Gina is operating fast and loose. We can't afford to place Val in any more danger than she already is. Kim, I'm ready for you to do your magic. Sophie, can you let Val know we'll make the switch today and that we need her to give us an advance hint about their location? Good job, honey." Char leaned down and gave Toni a chaste kiss on her lips.

"I'll have you ready within the hour, and then Sophie can tell us where to send you," Kim remarked.

†

Val tore off her workout clothes and stalked into the shower. "I hate working with amateurs," she hissed under her breath, having been told that Gina was the inside agent she was supposed to be working with. She wasn't sure if the bathroom was bugged, but at this point she was frustrated enough not to care.

When Gina ran her hand along Val's arm, it had taken every ounce of willpower not to throw the little tease on the mats and rip her clothes off. Gina was playing a dangerous game, and Val wasn't making any headway in her efforts to keep Gina from blowing her cover. In fact, she wasn't convinced Leonid hadn't already clued into their attraction to one another. He wasn't a stupid man, and the rare flash of emotion she'd seen this morning, let Val know her days were probably numbered. They needed to speed up this mission or both of them would leave in pine boxes.

Val stepped out of the shower, dried off, and quickly donned her bra and thong. She hadn't fully pulled up her underwear when Sophie's voice boomed in her ear.

"Where the fuck have you been? The device is ready and we need to know a location for today's swap. Don't forget to put on your watch, and be sure to wear it whenever you need to speak freely after the exchange."

Val hated that she couldn't bark back at Sophie. Letting Sophie know where they were headed today and when they were leaving wouldn't be a problem, but exercising restraint was another story. Val wanted to give her a piece of her mind, but she was already dancing along the edge, and talking too much to herself would be a surefire way to tip off Leonid and his goons.

Val grabbed her watch and fastened it to her wrist. She buckled it loosely enough for whoever they sent to slip it off and put another in its place. She picked up the worn jeans she'd tossed on the chair in her room and stepped into them. The T-shirt she intended to wear lay semi-crinkled on the bed, and she pivoted to grab it.

As she pulled it over her head, Sophie spoke again.

"Char will make the exchange. She's dressed as Tammy Faye Bakker's ugly twin. Don't laugh when you see her."

Val couldn't help it; she started chuckling, and when she yanked the bedroom door open, she came face-to-face with Gina, who raised her eyebrow.

"Is something funny?" Gina scowled. "I don't appreciate being laughed at."

Val didn't want to reveal the upcoming exchange to Gina or Leonid, who was certainly listening in, so she ignored the question. "Are you ready? I don't have all day to just piss away."

"You have all day if I say so." Gina took a step closer. "And I say you have all day to do my bidding. Let's go. I've decided to let you drive me today."

"Oh, I'm just bursting with joy. What a magnanimous woman you are. Shall I bend over and kiss your feet in appreciation?" Val's sarcasm dripped from her lips as the corner of her mouth turned up in amusement at Gina's sour expression.

"Let's go." Gina turned and walked away.

"See if you can delay for five minutes so we can get into position to follow you. We will make the exchange at the first shop you go to," Sophie said.

†

Paulie watched as Gina and her body guard exited the house before grabbing his sister's arm.

"Where do you think you're going?" He moved so he was standing over Gina and puffed out his chest. He grinned when she flinched.

"I told you we're going shopping."

"I'm your bodyguard and I should be going, not that bitch."

"Her name is Vera."

Gina took an aggressive step forward, surprising Paulie.

"You hate to go shopping, Paulie. I thought I was doing you a favor."

"I don't trust her."

Gina laughed. "I'll be fine. Now I've got to go."

Paulie narrowed his eyes as Gina walked away, and he growled when she tossed the car keys toward the other woman. "You're driving." The words made his insides seethe and his jaw tense when the Porsche Boxster Spyder started pulling away.

No one but Gina ever drives that car. How dare that woman take over my job? Watching out for Gina is my *responsibility. When we signed on with Antonio to infiltrate Leonid's organization, we were a package deal. Obviously Gina seems to have forgotten that.* He balled his fist at his increasing rage and needed to strike out and make someone pay.

"Two can play that game, Gina," he growled.

It was time he took back control. He'd make sure both the bitches paid. He'd seen the way Gina looked at her bodyguard; she was clearly attracted to Vera. If Paulie had seen it, then, unless he was blind, Leonid had too. He'd make his sister's little crush work to his advantage. He and Gina had faced many challenges together while growing up, but he put those thoughts out of his mind. It was time to part ways and make a name for himself.

Paulie had plans. Once Antonio destroyed Leonid's gang, he would move in and take control. He'd leave the human trafficking to someone else and become the newest drug king. All he needed was to become Leonid's confidant. Over the last months he'd already made inroads into Leonid's inner circle by being a courier for sensitive information. Of course, he had to wear a body camera and was timed when making deliveries, so he had no opportunity to investigate what he was carrying, but he'd figure out a way to take over.

He rubbed his jaw as the Porsche disappeared from sight, surprised at how little emotion he felt at the thought of selling Gina out. The more he thought about how badly she was treating him, the more enraged he became.

"How dare she do this to me after all the times I watched out for her growing up?" he grumbled. He was the one who'd protected her when their alcoholic father tried to force himself on her. The one time he got close, Paulie beat him to a pulp, soon after he left home with Gina.

Now she was betraying him. For what? Some bitch with a gun?

Vera had thwarted two attempts on Gina's life. The first was a woman Leonid saw a profit in and sold into slavery. The second, a man, she killed. That gave her high marks with Leonid, so Paulie would have to devise a plan that would cast the Vera woman in an unfavorable light. It would take time, but he was willing to wait until the perfect moment arrived, and then he'd pounce and make the woman regret ever crossing him.

Paulie sneered. "You'll both pay, I promise you that."

†

Leonid pushed the heavy bar above his head and grunted. After he finished with his routine with free weights, he intended to punch the bag a few times. He would imagine the *pizda*'s face. Soon, very soon, he would have his revenge.

The little bitch would pay for his father's demise. He'd been patient and had waited a long time for this, and he wouldn't be satisfied with her complete destruction; he wanted the whole organization to pay for helping her after the slow deterioration of his father's business. Letting a *sooka* escape had been a fatal blow to his father's reputation in the lucrative business.

Leonid had to admit he was at least thankful Viktor was no longer a competitor and that this mysterious organization had done him a favor by eliminating the competition, but that wouldn't derail him from his primary mission—to obliterate the woman in a way that would leave no question about his family's superiority in the human trafficking business.

It was time to let his little brother in on his plans. Leonid would call Alexei later and provide him the details. He was carefully baiting the trap for the rats. He'd smoke every last one of the rodents out, then his path would be clear.

Chapter Nine

Leonid leaned back in his office chair as he waited for his computer to boot up after going through the complicated security protocol he'd established for communicating with Alexei. When Alexei's smiling face appeared on the screen, Leonid moved closer to the small camera on the monitor.

"Good evening, brother. You look like you've just returned from an evening out. I trust you had a beautiful woman on your arm, so I am sorry to disturb your evening entertainment."

"No, it's all right. I've asked my companion to wait for me while I attend to business. Do not worry, the brief delay will hopefully intensify the experience for her. Sometimes keeping them waiting is a good thing. I assumed it was important for you to send me a message earlier."

"You remember the *pizda* who escaped and ruined our father's reputation?"

"Yes, how could I forget? I was not so young that I do not remember the pandemonium her treachery caused our dear father. I blame his heart attack on that little cunt."

"Yes, and so do I, little brother. Fate is a good thing and it has shined upon us. Remember when I informed you that my plans were well under way to smoke out our enemies?"

"*Da.*"

"The *pizda* came to us, and everything is falling into place. My unsuspecting wife is making things easy for us." Leonid leaned back in his chair and laughed. "I never thought her shopping trips would produce such good fortune for us. They may cost me a few thousand, but the return in my investment will be much greater than I had expected."

Alexei's handsome face smiled. "What are your plans for your wife?"

Leonid sighed. "Ah, I had hoped to keep her around long enough to produce a son, but her blatant flirtations cannot be ignored. Do you wish to use her before I take out the trash?"

"Hmmm, tempting. She is a beautiful woman. Perhaps. How quickly do you anticipate a resolution? Shall I make the arrangements to travel to the United States within the week?"

"It will be nice to have you by my side when we prevail and take our rightful place."

Alexei lifted a tumbler of amber liquid. "To our father, may his blessed soul finally rest in peace."

Leonid picked up his glass of juice. "*Da*, yes, to Father. We shall toast again when you arrive and both of us are able to drink Russian vodka and not the substandard scotch you have in your hand or the juice from my breakfast."

Alexei leaned back and laughed. "Ah, so you noticed the color in my glass. I never drink vodka with anyone but you, my dear brother. We must always savor the traditions of our youth. Father would be pleased by that."

"I will look forward to your visit and will save you the honor of joining me as we annihilate our adversaries as a united front. Be well, little brother."

†

Gina watched as Vera expertly drove down the freeway. There was no denying there was an attraction between them, but the problem was Leonid and all his spies. She needed to go somewhere he wouldn't expect her to go.

"Get off at this exit," she ordered. "After that, take a left at the next light, then pull into the parking lot of the first store you see."

When Vera turned into the parking lot and gave her a quizzical look, Gina laughed.

"This store doesn't seem quite your style." Vera glanced over at Gina again before pulling into an empty spot.

"Get out." Gina looked around and grinned before exiting the vehicle. Target was the last place Leonid would expect her to be. She waited for Vera to join her. When she did, Gina whispered, "He won't have any of his spies here."

"Don't be so sure about that. Certainly you know he has a tracking device on the car. It's only a matter of time before they show up."

Gina laughed. "I know, but I'll take this small bit of freedom and make the most of it."

Vera narrowed her eyes. "Look, Gina, I know you're not exactly well versed in this kind of work, but surely you've figured out I'm the undercover operative my organization sent to work with you. Your cavalier behavior is going to blow our cover. I need you to stop playing your little games and think before you act."

"You worry too much."

"And you don't worry enough. This *is* a dangerous game we are playing."

"Do you think I don't know that? Of course I do. You're not the one who has to let him paw your body and take you. I do, Vera. I do. Right now I need some distraction before I have to go back to him." When Vera's expression softened a bit, she grabbed her hand. "Come on. We'll call a cab and go to town and shop." She laughed. "Can you imagine his goons traipsing through Target looking for us?"

"I need to know our final destination. I have some friends that plan on providing us with a very handy device that will enable us to speak more freely. She'll be the one with overly dramatic makeup. After that, I'll welcome your flirtations." Vera winked.

"Hmm, who says I want to flirt with you?" Gina took her phone out of her purse and threw it in the car. "I'm sure he's tracking that too. There's a small coffee shop a block down. We can call a taxi from there. Staying here very long is dangerous."

Vera's eyes shifted to a spot on Gina's right side. "Too late. Goon at ten o'clock. I suggest you let the professionals follow through with the original plans. I'll grab some hand cream at Target so it's not so obvious that we were trying to shake a tail. We'll pick up the device at your favorite boutique, and then I promise we can talk."

"Fair enough. I see my other bodyguard has arrived to save me from your clutches." She shook her head. "I'll deal with him while you shop."

Vera raised her middle finger at Paulie before pivoting on her heel and walking into the store.

"What the hell do you think you're doing?" Paulie yelled as he exited the black SUV.

"I might ask you the same question. Vera needed a special hand cream, so we stopped to get it."

"And she left you out here unprotected?"

Gina grinned and pulled a handgun from her purse. "Does it look like I'm unprotected?"

†

Val was growing more concerned about the chances Gina took when they were together.

"Char just arrived, thanks for the hint of a detour to Target. I'm sending her to find you now," Sophie alerted her.

Maybe this side trip to Target wasn't a bad thing. With Gina distracting her brother and the other foot soldier, now would be the perfect opportunity to make the switch. Char was good at blending in; her disguise might not be as obvious in Val's current location. An exclusive shop had far fewer people to enable Char to fade into the crowd.

The store was bustling with tired mothers and their screaming brood, but Val caught a glimpse of another one of Leonid's men out of the corner of her eye. She suspected he was trying his best to remain inconspicuous, but her trained observation skills picked him out in a manner of seconds.

"One of his goons is in the store, so be careful," Val whispered as she pretended to look down at folded sweaters so Leonid's man wasn't able to see her lips move.

"Fuck. Just stall for five more minutes, please, so Char has a chance to make the exchange. You have to make this more difficult for us, don't you?"

Val gritted her teeth and turned away from the man lurking in the men's athletic wear aisle. "When I'm finished with this assignment, I'm going to break every single one of your bones, Sophie. Haven't you ever considered that Tammy Faye fits much better into the Target crowd? Tell her to be careful. It's up to three goons and counting."

95

"Two more minutes. You think you can handle waiting that long? Or are you about to blow your cover by making smartass remarks to me?"

Val growled but didn't respond as she saw yet another of Leonid's men slink down the other side of the aisle.

She turned the corner and walked toward the cosmetics section, thinking a person who wore too much makeup might not stand out in that particular part of the store. Since Val didn't wear makeup, the hand or body lotion was a perfect choice. How about some natural product with a citrus or lavender scent? She used lotions because she liked the way they felt going on her body and how she smelled after putting them on following a shower.

A fleeting look to her left revealed the large man awkwardly standing in front of the feminine hygiene products. Val smirked, and then she felt someone brush against her side. "Watch it," she growled giving the woman with heavy eyeshadow and false lashes a glare.

"Oh, I'm terribly sorry. I wasn't watching where I was going," Char said.

"Just watch where you're going the next time." Val glared at the Tammy Faye lookalike.

"Some people have no manners at all," Char grumbled before shuffling away.

Val watched as Char continued down the aisle hoping Char was convincing enough for the two goons watching her. They had narrowed their eyes and watched the interaction with an intensity that made her insides shudder.

Val grabbed the tube of lavender-scented lotion and continued browsing the shelves so the exchange wouldn't be obvious. She even managed to bump into someone else before eventually pivoting on her heel and turning away from the penetrating scrutiny of Leonid's men closing in on her.

Years of living on the street and a practiced sleight of hand allowed her to adjust the new watch to ensure it was securely attached to her wrist without anyone taking notice.

She decided to activate the scrambling device just in case Leonid had placed a video and audio bug in the car in addition to the tracker. She thought doing this might be for naught, because they'd already engaged in risky behavior, but better late than never.

It was time to get the hell out of the store and back to Gina. Her gut told her the reckless woman was digging herself an early grave. Gina needed more than a bodyguard; she needed a protector who would keep her from being her own worst enemy.

†

"You're playing with fire, Gina." Paulie pounded his fist into his hand. "And if you're not careful, you will pay with your life for crossing him."

"You don't own me, so get off my back and let me have some fun for once," Gina snarled. She saw Vera approach and admired her confident stride as she closed in on Paulie

Vera growled in his face. "You're getting on my last nerve, Paulie boy, and the last person who did that lost one of his balls."

"You don't scare me, bitch. Leave my sister alone, because if you don't, you'll be sorry."

Gina grinned and ran a finger down Vera's arm. "You're so hot when you're angry."

Vera smacked her hand away. "Let's just get this fucking shopping trip over before I decide it's time to cut my losses and go on a massive shooting spree."

"You heard my bodyguard, Paulie, so why don't you make yourself disappear. We have more important things to do than stand here talking to you."

Vera shook her head and stalked back to the car, where she punctuated her exit by slamming the door.

"Get lost, Paulie." Gina grinned at him and followed Vera to the car and climbed inside. "Today is going to be fantastic," she gushed and squeezed Vera's thigh.

Vera gave Gina a sideways glance. "Not that I don't appreciate your hand on my thigh, but soon I'll be seeing what this car of yours can do and I'd hate to get too distracted. I've got a new watch with a very high-tech chip that'll allow us complete privacy. We need to figure out a way to break whatever code he has protecting his assets. Any ideas? You do know we're supposed to be working together on this?"

"Aw, you take all the fun out of trying to make that husband of mine go crazy. He's such an ass. I can't stand to be around him, but I'll do what I can to help you."

Vera glared at Gina. "We have a biodevice that allows us to track him, but I think at this point that's secondary to finding a way into his computer. I'm not going to let you attempt to have him ingest the agent. No sense in taking unnecessary chances. Does he suspect anything about your involvement with Antonio? I picked out three men not including Paulie. That seems like overkill even for a paranoid bastard like Leonid. Has he ever hurt—"

"No." She ground her teeth. "If he had, I'd be out of there after the first slap."

"Well...then I'm amazed at his self-control. Leonid isn't known for his gentle and loving care of women. The moment he decides you're no longer useful to him, it will get ugly. I swear I'll tear his fucking arm off if he ever lays a hand on you." Vera turned her head and captured Gina's gaze as her jaw clenched before she swung her concentration back to the parking lot and began to back out of the space.

"My hero." Gina sighed. "He beats up the girls he sells when he's angry, but not me...he wants me to have his baby. Not going to happen, I can tell you that."

"I'm no hero, Gina. In fact, I'm such damaged goods that after this is all over, you need to make a wide arc around me. Just be careful, okay? It would be a pity to see your beautiful face marred by that asshole if he loses his temper."

"Not to worry, I've got him wrapped around my finger. What Gina wants, Gina gets."

"For the record, I'm not on the menu. Listen, my gut is rarely wrong and major bells are going off for me. Don't underestimate Leonid. I get the sense he's biding his time and when whatever falls into place occurs, your days are numbered. Don't think for one minute that someone like Leonid can be wrapped around anyone's finger. He isn't motivated by love, he's motivated by hate and revenge. That makes him dangerous because passion is a strength when it's twisted toward violence. He and I are probably more alike than I want to admit."

"Duly noted. But if you're trying to scare me, it isn't working. I've lived on the streets, so I know how to take care of myself." She caressed Vera's cheek. "I know exactly who he is and what he's capable of, and I never underestimate him." She lifted a shoulder. "He should never underestimate me."

Vera shifted her eyes from the road and looked at Gina with a puzzled expression. "A street rat, huh? I learned a lot on the streets too. I guess that makes me feel slightly better about your abilities. Who knows? Maybe we crossed paths at some point. That was a lifetime ago for me...."

Gina sighed and touched Vera again. "Yes, it was, and believe me, if I'd met you, I'd remember. I'm glad to have you on my side. Now if only I can get Paulie to stop acting like a dick and play nice, things would be perfect."

"I know Paulie is your brother, but he's another one that's activating my Spidey sense. I think he'd roll on you to save his ass. When this blows up, and it will very soon, you need to find me, and I swear I'll get you out in one piece. Promise me you won't depend on your brother to do that. In this case I would say that blood is not thicker than water."

"He won't betray me. We've been through a lot together." She frowned. "He wouldn't, would he?"

"Unfortunately I believe he would." Vera pulled into a parking space in front of Gina's favorite boutique and glanced quickly in the rearview mirror. "Showtime. While Leonid's men are tailing us through the store, you need to be more reserved in your interactions with me. I plan on making a big show of my distaste for you and shopping. We can talk later about how to annihilate Leonid, because we will bring him down."

"I'm glad we're on the same side." Gina looked out the window and saw one of Leonid's men standing in front of the boutique with his arms folded over his massive chest. "Showtime," she said as she got out of the car.

Chapter Ten

Char glanced in her rearview mirror for the third time in less than a minute. Something tickled her cheek, and she briskly lifted her hand to brush away the bug or whatever it was. The false eyelash fluttered onto the console between the passenger and driver's bucket seats.

She was irritated that she had a tail and decided Leonid's men were a lot smarter and more competent than The Organization had given them credit for. She wasn't sure how they made her, but it was time to teach them a little lesson.

Char pushed the button on the steering wheel. Seven beeps later, Ronda answered.

"What's up, buttercup?"

"You're in a good mood; you musta just gotten some. Well, I'm about to interrupt your little lovefest. Get your ass outta bed and give a lady a hand."

Clap clap clap

"Oh you're a real comedian. Listen, I have a car with two unwelcome admirers on my tail, and I suppose I could shake them, but they've pissed me off enough that I'd prefer a more permanent solution."

"Maggie's gonna be pissed. How'd you manage to attract that kind of attention?" Ronda asked.

"Don't start with me. Listen, I got a bad feeling about this whole operation. They had three guys tailing Val. Don't you think that's just a little suspicious?"

"Hmmm. I suppose so. Okay, I'll intersect with you in about twenty minutes. Enjoy the wild goose chase you're about to take these guys on before I send the little fuckers straight to hell." Ronda laughed.

"Hey, can you be a little…uh, subtle when you take them out? I don't think Maggie would be happy to watch this on the ten o'clock news. No explosives, okay?"

"God, you're no fun. You got it. Besides, it's harder to use explosives on a moving vehicle, so I'll do things the old-fashioned way. Sophie can drive while I get in some target practice. Can you at least lead us to a road less traveled?"

"Piece of cake. Tell Cindy I'm sorry I disturbed you guys. I really am happy you two finally got together."

Char could almost see the blush on Ronda's face. "Hang tight, we'll be there as soon as I grab Soph."

Char grinned. She marveled at how far Ronda and Sophie had come since their initial meeting. She supposed she wouldn't have taken too kindly to a gun against her head and even worse, one pointed at the woman she loved. It didn't help when Sophie had misinterpreted Ronda when she had said she just wanted to "shoot them all" and be done with it. Of course, Ronda had been talking about the bastard Viktor, but Toni and Sophie didn't know that. Ronda and Sophie were cut from the same cloth, and Val was at the head of the class. Not too many people rattled Char, but Val was by far the most lethal agent in The Organization. She made Ronda look like a pacifist.

✝

Leonid leaned against the steaming tub of water as the jets swirled around his muscular torso. He was smiling as he envisioned wreaking the ultimate justice on the whole lot of them. He felt certain there would be an attempt to make contact with their agent, and then his men would follow her back to the hidden complex. A tentative knock on the door interrupted his fantasy.

"I'm sorry to disturb you, sir, but our men have been stationary for over an hour in a remote area outside of Maryland. None of our attempts to call them have been answered. Would you like me to send someone out to the site?"

Leonid rose from the whirlpool, then grabbed a towel and patted himself dry before donning a robe. "Perhaps they have found what we are looking for and the area has intermittent service. Have you tried to obtain satellite pictures of the location?"

"*Da*, there is some interference that will not allow us to penetrate."

Leonid frowned. "They must have more advanced technology than I suspected. It would make sense they would wish to use technology to camouflage their base of operations. I will inspect this location personally. I want three men ready to accompany me in five minutes. Not one second more or I will take that as a sign of incompetence, and you know how I abhor ineptitude."

"Yes, sir. We'll be ready."

✝

Toni and Dani were slouched in their chairs sharing a bag of chips. Toni looked up when Char entered the lab. She didn't like the frown on Char's beautiful face. Something told her things were going sideways, fast. She worried the device she and Dani had just refined had somehow malfunctioned and that Val would remain at risk.

"Hey, hon, how did the handoff go?" Toni asked.

Char pulled off the row of fake lashes on her left eye and sat heavily in the chair across from them. "Well…we ran into a tiny problem. Ronda and Sophie are dealing with it."

"Oh?" Dani raised her eyebrow. "Care to expound?"

"There's something we're missing, because Leonid had three guys watching Val and two of them tailed me." Char rummaged in the large handbag she'd set on her lap, pulled out some tissues, and began wiping the heavy makeup from her face.

"Maybe we should talk to Maggie about pulling Val out and finding some other way." Dani sat forward in her chair.

"What about Gina?" Toni asked.

"She's Antonio's. Not our problem to deal with." Char pulled the wig off and ran her fingers through her long red hair, untangling the thick strands.

"That's harsh. From what Sophie tells us, there's something happening between Val and Gina. Can't we have Maggie make sure Antonio pulls her from the fire?" Toni asked.

Char shrugged. "Why don't you find Maggie while I take a shower. By the time I'm finished, I'm sure Sophie and Ronda will have come back from their cleanup mission." Char stood, grabbed her bag, and walked out of the lab.

†

The tinted window in Leonid's black sedan slowly and soundlessly rolled down as the vehicle came to a stop behind the stalled SUV. His gaze traveled to the deflated back right tire.

His driver pulled on the lever, and the ding of the opening door merged with the click of Leonid's seat belt as he emerged from the car. He peered into the vehicle and noted the two bodies, one slumped against the steering wheel and the other with his head awkwardly resting on the passenger-side window.

"Check to see if they are dead," Leonid directed.

Leonid's driver lumbered to the car, opened the driver's-side door, and pressed his fingers against the man's neck. "He is unconscious, but alive." He reached inside and repeated the assessment on the other man. "Both are alive."

Leonid slowly made his way toward the SUV, took out his gun, and pulled the trigger, making a neat hole in the side of the driver's head. He aimed his gun at the passenger and deftly executed the other man. "Now they are not."

The large man blinked once before asking, "Do you wish me to arrange for retrieval of the car?"

"Leave it and find me competent replacements. I want to find these women, and my patience is growing very thin."

Leonid was in a cold fury. Normally he would wait out his enemies and strike at just the right moment. It had taken years to position himself for sweet revenge, and the opportunity to destroy his enemies was so close he could taste the rewards, but they had managed to elude him once again. It was a pity he had to make an example of two of his best men. They'd never failed before, and this puzzled Leonid. Perhaps this mysterious organization was better than he'd suspected. Vera had certainly surprised him, and her caution to not underestimate her skills served as a dire warning. Perhaps it was time to take a different tack.

†

After the fiasco at Target ended, Paulie scowled while watching his sister provocatively run a finger down the bodyguard's arm. He heard her tell the woman how hot she was and sucked in a breath. He knew how many spies and cameras Leonid had, and the chances that Leonid had seen Gina's outrageous antics too were overwhelming. He needed to cut his losses, and that meant throwing Gina and her guard under the bus.

He straightened his shirt and looked down to make sure his clothes were pristine, then knocked on the door to Leonid's office. A tall, muscular man, Sergei, opened the door and glared at him.

"Do you have an appointment?" he asked in a brusque tone.

"No, but I need to see the boss immediately. A situation has happened that he needs to be aware of."

"Send him in," Leonid said from the office.

Paulie brushed past Sergei and strolled confidently toward Leonid's desk.

"What is it that is so important?" Leonid demanded.

"It's about Gina and that woman you hired to protect her."

Leonid glared at him. "Enough. I am tired of your petty jealousy."

"There's something going on between the bodyguard and your wife," Paulie blurted out.

"What?" Leonid stood and balled his fists on his desk. "That woman has touched what is mine?"

Paulie swallowed hard. "No, it is more like Gina is coming on to her." There, he'd said it, proving to Leonid that he was loyal and ready to move up in the ranks.

Leonid stood and came around the desk. Paulie gulped at the force of the strong hand squeezing his shoulder.

"Loyalty is something I value, Paulie," Leonid said in a measured voice. "For without loyalty a business cannot run effectively."

Paulie let out a breath. His time had come, and now Leonid was going to reward him. It was so simple. All he'd had to do was sell out his sister. She and that bitch Vera would pay for their disrespect. Triumph bubbled up in him and he let out a satisfied sigh.

"What is more important," Leonid continued, "than loyalty to the business is loyalty to family." He pressed the shoulder under his hand harder. "Family is everything."

Paulie was suddenly confused. "But she's dishonored you, and with a woman."

"Do you think me stupid, Paulie?" Leonid's voice was cold.

Confusion was replaced with an overwhelming feeling of dread. "No. No, not at all. They are being sneaky, and I wanted to warn you."

"Now you have, and you will pay for that." Leonid let go of his shoulder. "Get him out of my sight," he ordered.

Paulie began shaking. He'd miscalculated, and now he was certain he'd pay with his life. "Wait. There's more."

Leonid was in his face, and the stench of cigar smoke assaulted his nose. "There's nothing you can tell me that I don't already know." He took a step back. "Get rid of him."

A warm stream ran down Paulie's leg.

Chapter Eleven

Antonio had suggested a late lunch and called Maggie earlier to see if she was available. She'd invited him to join her in her living quarters.

Ludwig van Beethoven's *Symphony No. 9 In D Minor* played in the background as Maggie brought the glass of wine to her lips. The buzz of Antonio's phone barely registered with the symphony filling the empty space, but Maggie's acute hearing picked up the sound. She focused on Antonio as he pressed the Answer button.

"How long ago?.... Ah, I see.... Anything else to report?.... Thank you, my friend, it is good to have contacts in high places.... Yes, we will need to get together soon...." Antonio chuckled. "Ah, we shall see. I am making progress." He glanced in Maggie's direction before ending the call.

Maggie raised her eyebrow. "Why do I get the feeling this call has something to do with me or the current operation?"

"You always were very astute and incredibly beautiful. Such a wonderful combination."

"Stop trying to schmooze and tell me what's happening."

"Apparently the police found two of Leonid's men on the side of some country road with an extra piece of lead in their heads. The tire of the car had been shot out. Preliminary investigation concludes a different gun was used to shoot out the tire. Execution style on the men. Could this be the work of one of your overzealous agents?"

Maggie frowned. "Unfortunately, yes. I better head to the lab where I can get some answers. If I had to take a guess, it's either Ronda or Sophie. The two of them try my patience sometimes."

Antonio chuckled. "Sophie may not approve of our collaboration, but I do appreciate her direct approach, and as for Ronda...personally I think she is a delight."

"Sure, you say that now, but if you're in her line of sight when she decides to go on a rampage, you may be singing a different tune."

"Ronda doesn't strike me as the type to be all that concerned about a little bit of gambling. I have removed myself from the other more distasteful businesses. Surely that counts for something."

"With me, yes, but Ronda has a tendency to hold a grudge. I'm not sure on her feelings about drugs. You wouldn't be here if you'd ever dabbled in the sex trade business, though. I might have eliminated you myself." Maggie grinned.

"Ah, that is the Maggie I remember. Feisty as ever. I do regret my past ties to drugs, although I may amend that slightly. Marijuana does have medicinal properties that prove very beneficial to people who struggle with cancer." Antonio shrugged. "If I can make money and provide a valuable medicine, it's a win-win. Don't you agree?"

"Perhaps. Come on, let's go see if any of my rogue agents were responsible." Maggie sighed. "I think I'm getting far too old to control them. Perhaps it's time for a change in leadership."

"I don't think it's time to put you out to pasture just yet." He winked at her.

†

Ronda was crunching on a potato chip in the main lab while she waited for Char to return. She didn't want to call Maggie before everyone was in the room. Ronda hated having to repeat herself. Sophie was fidgeting in her chair, and Ronda suspected she wanted to go join Kim. Sophie always seemed slightly discombobulated without Kim. Her lover had a way about her that grounded Sophie and softened her edges, a lot like what Cindy did for Ronda.

The lab door swung open and Maggie and Antonio gracefully entered. They did make a stunning couple, but even though they appeared to be the epitome of calm, cool, and collected, something was off. Ronda wondered what prompted their rigid postures and grim expressions.

She was proud of herself for thinking ahead and using the darts to subdue Leonid's men rather than outright killing them. Maggie would have been pissed at her for executing them without consulting her first, so that couldn't be the reason they seemed tense. It had to be the same concern Char had. Ronda agreed this mission was going down a bad road quickly. Flashbacks to Viktor and some of the missteps they'd all made when attempting to shut him down resurfaced, causing Ronda to shiver with that creepy-crawly feeling she always got before something catastrophic happened.

110

Maggie didn't waste any time. "Two of Leonid's men were found on the side of the road in Maryland. Anyone care to share what might have happened?" She pointed her laser-like stare on Ronda before shifting to Sophie.

"Can we wait for Char? I don't want to have to repeat anything and she has some information to add." Ronda leaned back in her chair and popped another potato chip in her mouth.

The deathly silence in the room created an air of uncertainty. Ronda was used to Maggie's steely gaze, but Toni squirmed in her chair and kept looking at Dani, who shrugged. After what seemed like an hour, but was probably only five minutes, Char strolled into the lab dressed in a worn pair of jeans with her wet hair hanging loose down her back. At one time, Ronda thought she might be in love with the beautiful woman, but then Toni came along and Char was a goner. Ronda had felt a twinge of jealousy in the beginning that soon turned to respect and admiration as she watched the couple's love grow. She was thankful she'd finally opened her eyes and heart to Cindy. Getting shot by Viktor's man was probably the best thing that had ever happened to her, as she basked in Cindy's loving attentiveness during her rehabilitation.

Char's gaze rotated around the room, making brief contact with each of the occupants. "So, did I somehow miss it was someone's birthday? Where's the cake? You know how I hate to come late to a party," she drolly observed.

"Let me get straight to the point. I am curious how two of Leonid's men ended up with a bullet in their heads, execution style. The police came across their vehicle on a sparsely traveled road in Maryland." Maggie paused as she sat in the chair Antonio pulled out for her.

"Wait. What? I swear, Maggie, they were alive when I left them. Char had a tail and I thought you'd be proud of me when I used restraint and shot them with darts versus lead. Sure, I might have used a heavy dose to ensure they remained unconscious for a while, but honest I wasn't the one to place those bullets there. Soph, tell her."

"She's telling the truth, Maggie. I went with her so she could shoot out the tire. I'll admit we did briefly entertain the idea of a permanent solution, but then we thought these men may or may not have deserved to die. We didn't have definitive evidence that either one of them deserved elimination because all they were doing was tailing Char," Sophie explained.

"We have bigger problems than who decided to off the goons. My guess is Leonid did it himself. He's a true sociopath and seems to eliminate anyone who performs less than perfectly for him. There were three men at the store tracking Val, and Paulie, Gina's brother, was in a heated argument with her in front of the store. I don't like any of this one bit. I know Val can take care of herself, but perhaps we should cut our losses, pull her out, and think of another way to get inside the operation. Maybe our brilliant scientists will discover an electronic solution?" Char smiled and took a few steps forward to stroke Toni's arm. "I don't like how risky this operation has become."

"I agree. Something is definitely off. Sophie, make contact with Val and tell her to extricate herself at the first opportunity," Maggie directed.

"What about Gina and Paulie?" Antonio asked.

"How much do you trust them?" Char asked.

"Gina is a pain in my ass sometimes, but I trust her far more than Paulie. She presents a very different persona than who I know her to be inside. In many ways, she is still that scared little girl who lived on the streets. I feel a certain sense of protectiveness toward her. She is like a daughter to me. Paulie is a coldhearted bastard who I suspect would turn his own grandmother in if he believed it was to his advantage. Can Val manage to ensure her safety?"

"Our first priority is Val. We shall see what can be done, but you need to be prepared to ensure Gina's safety with your own resources. I won't subject Val to any greater risk than we already have placed on her," Maggie responded.

"Can you at least get a message to her through Val? She needs to learn about your suspicions that everyone's cover might be blown," Antonio argued.

"Sophie, make sure Val puts the scrambler to good use and updates Gina. Anything else I need to know about?" Maggie asked.

"I still say we smoke the bastard out and shoot him," Ronda interjected.

Maggie sighed. "We've been over that. All it will do is bring the brother or some other thug into power. We have to find where he holds his wealth. It's been impossible to track. Leonid is much smarter with his resources than Viktor, and he has them buried so deep in multiple offshore accounts, we've not been able to penetrate his endless layers of protection. It's something more than a sophisticated biometrics system. Leonid being dead at this point does us no good."

"While we've got our thumbs up our asses, he's continuing to kidnap these kids and put them through a terror that is a million times worse than hell," Ronda argued. "At least if we kept picking off the bad guys, we'd interrupt their operations. You're wrong that doing that would only bring the other baddies out of the woodwork; it'd make me feel a whole lot better. Instant gratification, even if it is short-lived, is still satisfying. It'd be like having multiple orgasms every time I eliminate another sick fuck." She grinned.

Sophie rolled her eyes. "As much as I hate to agree with Ronda. I think we ought to reconsider the whole mission, and we can't afford to take another six months of putting those kids at risk to shut him down," Sophie added. "Let's get Val and Gina out and go on the attack."

"We're no better than they are if that's our go-to position. Antonio, back me up on this."

Antonio shrugged. "I'm sorry, my dear. You know that we deviate from one another on fundamental beliefs regarding how to take out the trash. It is what caused the rift so many years ago. I want to play by your rules, because I do wish to show you the respect you deserve, but I cannot always agree with you. However, Maggie, you are the head of this organization, and ultimately if your agents wish to remain, they must agree to do only the things you are comfortable with, or they need to decide to part ways." Antonio paused to make eye contact with Sophie and Ronda. "Do you wish to leave The Organization?"

"No, that's not what I was saying, and who the fuck are you to suggest we don't support Maggie?" Ronda questioned.

"I've pledged to abide by the group's wishes, and I know Char, Kim, Toni, and Dani are all in agreement with your..." she lifted a shoulder "...code, for lack of better terminology. I just wanted it on record that Ronda does make some good points," Sophie clarified.

Maggie took a moment to look at everyone.

Ronda chuckled. "It must be snowing in hell."

Sophie slung her arm around Ronda. "You're growing on me...like a wart, but you're still growing on me."

"Such a sweet-talker. Now get your ass in gear and make contact with Val. She at least agrees with me most of the time and adds her twisted spin on things. I like that about her, she's more devious than I am." Ronda gave Sophie a gentle shove toward the lab's exit.

"Fuck." Toni stood so abruptly that her chair rolled away and crashed into Char.

"Ouch!"

Toni turned around and gave her a quick kiss. "Leonid is diabetic, right?"

Ronda and Sophie stopped walking toward the exit, turned, and rejoined the group.

Maggie nodded. "Our intel has revealed that he checks his blood sugar several times a day. Why?"

"Maybe we should force-feed him some chocolate," Ronda joked.

"Damn, it's been right under our noses," Dani said.

"Will you two stop talking in code and tell us non-geeks what the hell you're talking about?" Sophie crossed her arms over her chest.

"I don't think you were right about his system not being a simple...well, not exactly simple...but I'd bet our little cubicle home that he's using a drop of blood to access his systems. His DNA is the only thing that will allow entry," Toni explained.

"Perfect. I'd love to spill a little blood. Can we shoot him now?" Ronda asked.

Sophie raised her hand. "I vote for that option."

"Not so fast. I'm sure that's just one layer of creative protection. He's bound to have more. We need a camera right above his computer to see everything he does. I can get one to Val that's so small and easy to connect that she'd only have to figure out a way to place it on his ceiling. Dani tweaked it and it's virtually indiscoverable by the best bug-sweeping equipment. We have the most advanced detectors on or off the market and they've not picked it up." Toni patted Dani on the back. "You're an ingenious little shit, and I love it."

"There is no way she'll be able to plant that. Leonid has everything video and audio bugged in his mansion. We need something to loop an empty office and whatever route she plans to take to get to his inner sanctum," Char said.

Dani leaned back in her chair and grinned. "As a matter of fact, Toni and I have just the device, don't we?"

"Yes, we do." Toni lifted her hand and connected with Dani's in a quick fist bump. "She just needs to slide it under her watch. The magnetized device, which by the way is as thin as a single piece of paper and smaller in circumference than the tip of an eraser, can be activated at the same time she activates the scrambler already embedded in her watch."

"Why didn't we just use that device to begin with?" Char asked.

"Because Leonid isn't stupid and those replacement feeds have to be used sparingly. Each has a different purpose," Toni clarified.

"How fast can we get both contraptions to Val? I still don't like how this is evolving. I think she's really at risk right now and the danger grows every minute she remains in the lion's den," Sophie stated.

"Agreed, but this may be our only window of opportunity since she's already inside," Maggie answered.

"I hope you also have replacement video of Gina's bedroom too. Val won't be able to resist checking on her," Sophie said.

"We do, we suspected that would be needed," Dani answered.

"What about Gina? Can't she place the video bug? Or whatever the hell you're calling it?" Ronda asked.

"No, it has to be Val. First, she's trained for this and Gina is not, and second, she already has the hardware installed into her watch to activate the new device," Toni explained.

"Sophie, tell her she has twenty-four hours to plant the camera, and then I want her out of there. Tell her she needs to find some excuse to leave his mansion tonight. I want that device in her hands before nightfall. Understood?"

"You're not going to have any more Tourette's moments, are you? We were just about to head out and give Val some direction before your outburst." Sophie grinned at Toni.

Toni stuck up her middle finger. "Nope, none from me." She glanced at Dani. "Dani?"

"Nope, I'm good."

"Why do you two poke each other so much?" Char asked.

Toni shrugged. "Because it's fun."

Sophie chuckled as she exited the lab.

Chapter Twelve

Val was trying not to pace the room, which would surely tip off that she was agitated. Gina kept acting like an amateur earlier in the day before Val had a chance to activate the scrambling device. She had a sneaking suspicion their cover was blown and wondered why Leonid hadn't already made his move. Every muscle in her body was taut and ready for action because she was sure the moment was imminent.

"Hey, lover girl. New plan. The natives are getting restless, and you have twenty-four hours to plant a new video/audio bug on the ceiling above Leonid's computer. We have a second device that will make you invisible to Leonid's cameras. You'll need to attach that paper-thin disk to your watch. The audio/video bug is red, and the new device, which is magnetized, is blue. Don't confuse the two. Just slip the blue disc under your watch, and it activates the same way you've already been activating the scrambler. Find a way to get out tonight and we'll get you the prototype, which the eggheads guarantee is completely undetectable. After you place the bug, you need to get the fuck out, pronto."

Val pushed the button on her watch and pretended to look at the time while activating the scrambler. She hoped Leonid wouldn't consider it odd if he saw her talking to herself. It was all so confusing to her—the scrambler changed the audio but did nothing to change the video feed. She was eager to get her hands on the new device that would make herself invisible to Leonid's numerous cameras. She wasn't sure how long the technology would keep her hidden and hoped it provided enough time to plant the bug and get her and Gina out safely. She chanced asking, "Are we compromised?" She hoped the current scrambler would mask the question.

"Char seems to think so, and the rest of us agree. Ronda took care of the two goons tailing Char after the exchange but insists she wasn't the one who executed them. We suspect Gina's beloved husband was responsible. Do not play hero by trying to get Gina out. She's on her own, and besides, she's Antonio's responsibility."

Val decided it was best not to answer—too much talking to herself would cause suspicion. She planned on taking matters into her own hands and wasn't about to extricate herself without Gina. Ask not for permission, but rather for forgiveness. It had worked for her in the past, and she was sure Maggie would understand when all was said and done, because she did not plan to fuck things up.

"Don't think I don't know exactly what you're thinking just because you didn't fire back an argument. Don't do it, Val. I don't care if Gina ends up being the love of your life, it's too risky. Let Antonio handle it. He's got plenty of resources. It's why we joined forces to begin with."

Val pressed her watch again to turn off the scrambler. "All this money and power and no good ice cream in the freezer. I do believe it's time for a quick trip to the store. You hear that, Leonid? I know you're bugging my room, so feel free to send a few tails, but I'm going out to get some Ben and Jerry's and they better not get between me and my addiction. I've killed for less."

"Clever. I do love your bravado. See you at the grocery store in thirty. Do a little stalling. We need Kim to do her thing. I'll let you know what to look for. On second thought, I think we should send Dani and Kimiko. I don't think they'll be recognized."

Val was irritated about their decision to involve Kimiko and activated the scrambler to issue a warning to Sophie. "If you let them harm one hair on Kimiko's head, I'm holding you personally responsible, and Dani better not suffer any consequences either."

"There will be more backup for those two than you can imagine. We would never let any harm come to either of them. Char would beat you to my skinning."

†

A dim light blanketed the office in an eerie glow as Leonid sat in front of a wall of security monitors to the right of his computer. Any minute now Sergei would undoubtedly knock on the door to ask about the latest development. He leaned back in his chair and waited.

When the knock came, he responded, "Enter."

Sergei crossed the room and stood rigid in front of the desk. "Shall I intercept Vera and keep her from leaving the house?"

Leonid pierced Sergei with his cold stare. "No. She will undoubtedly make good on her threat and force me to put another lame animal out of its misery. I've almost grown fond of you, Sergei, and would hate to have to shoot you myself, considering you've been in my employment the longest. Send six men this time, and I want every single

120

person she interacts with, bumps into, or merely glances at followed. If they lose who they're following, eliminate them. I abhor incompetence." Leonid waved his hand in dismissal.

Sergei's face remained blank as he pivoted and exited the room.

Leonid had to admit a certain amount of admiration for his employee who never seemed to be rattled. He was sincere in saying that terminating Sergei would be a waste, but he had no doubt Vera would not hesitate to put a bullet in his most loyal bodyguard. Leonid begrudgingly acknowledged her skills. Under different circumstances she might have made an excellent addition to his organization. She was like a shark—a killing machine without emotion. He respected that.

Leonid was quickly reaching the end of his patience for learning more about the organization Vera worked for. If tonight didn't provide the information he needed, he would proceed tomorrow and make the *pizda* pay for what she'd done to his father. He hadn't yet decided what to do with Gina, but she would pay as well for her blatant attentions to Vera and the embarrassment it caused him. The more he thought about it, the more he wanted to teach that lesson to her tonight. His anger began to boil over, hot and sticky, an oozing, putrid substance that reeked of hate and revenge.

†

Like a tightly strung violin, Val's body tensed as she made her way through the mansion. She'd tucked Gina's car keys in her pocket without thinking and was surprised no one had asked her to relinquish them. It didn't really matter because Val had learned long ago how to hotwire the older autos in a matter of seconds. She still enjoyed the old classics, but thanks to Toni and Dani, new cars with their enhanced technology weren't an issue either. The twin geeks had invented a device that could calibrate to any of the fancy new vehicles that started with the press of a Power button. She hadn't needed to dig that impressive gadget out of her bag with Gina's keys in her pocket.

Sergei stood in the hallway, impassive and immobile as she walked out the front door. She winked at him in passing, suspecting Leonid had ordered him to stand down. That was a wise move. Val also anticipated Leonid would send an army of men to tail her to the store. That was fine with her. None of the other agents would be at risk since they'd be long gone by the time she reached the store. She'd take them on a wild goose chase, just for the fun of it, then stroll into the store and pick up the goods. She was looking forward to her favorite ice cream treat. She wanted to reward herself for not getting snuffed while in the lion's den. Val was good, but she knew her luck wouldn't last forever. She'd never expected to live a long life, but hoped she would at least get Gina to safety and bring down Leonid before her time was up.

The sleek car chirped when she pressed the button on the key fob, and she slid her tall body into the soft contours of the seat. The engine purred to life and Val enjoyed the subtle vibration as she took a moment to breathe in the experience of relative quiet. She eased the car onto the main road, teasing it like a woman before deciding to open it up. The power beneath her was a bit like having a woman under her, waiting for Val's touch to ignite her.

Val gave herself plenty of time to reach her destination as she took a few of the back roads and snaked around the curves at an accelerated speed. She surmised that the goons would think she was trying to ditch them, but that wasn't her intent at all, and she smiled to herself as she thought about the real purpose for deviating from her route.

She needed to make sure Dani and Kimiko were long gone from the store. The hired help probably thought they were hot stuff as they nearly glued themselves to her back bumper. The absurdity of the situation made her laugh.

When she finally pulled into the grocery store and climbed out of the car, she realized she was in an excellent mood. The drive had done her a world of good. She flipped her wrist to glance at the time and frowned when she realized getting here had taken her sixty minutes instead of thirty.

Her entourage followed her into the store, and she stalked to the freezer section. Flanked on all sides by the six men as they lingered on the periphery, she noticed a middle-aged woman holding a pint of Ben and Jerry's Chocolate Chip Cookie Dough ice cream. Her ice cream. She knew her outburst at Leonid's mansion about her preference for that particular flavor would have clued Sophie into what they needed to do to plant the devices.

Val didn't consider the consequences when she smoothly withdrew her gun and pointed it at the woman. "If that's the last pint of Chocolate Chip Cookie Dough, you need to put that right back in the freezer case." Her growl punctuated the seriousness of her directive.

The startled woman dropped the sweet treat and gasped. She scurried out the door, and two men followed her.

Val bent to pick up the pint of ice cream and grinned at one of the men standing at the end of the aisle watching her every move. When she turned around she bumped into a balding, potbellied man looking at the frozen options stacked neatly side by side. She scowled at him as she placed her revolver back in her pants. "Watch where you're fucking going. I coulda blown your balls off by mistake."

The man scrambled away, looking over his shoulder as two more men peeled off and followed him.

Val smirked. *I'd love to be a fly on the wall when they find out they've followed those two back to their depressing little hovels in the burbs.*

With the ice cream in her hands, Val strolled to the "fifteen items or less" line. She ran her hand along the underside and felt the two minuscule bumps. She gently set the carton on the conveyor belt, let the clerk scan the side, and handed her a twenty. After scooping the change from the silver dispenser and grabbing the paper money from the clerk, Val sauntered to her car as if she didn't have a care in the world. She turned her head around and flipped off the remaining two goons who'd followed her out.

One more task, then she and Gina could fly the coop and wash their hands of the whole bloody mess. Perhaps Maggie would let her shoot the bastard after they broke his web of security. She'd ask her about that as appropriate compensation for a job well done. That was the type of incentive payment that provided the perfect motivation to continue working for The Organization, but Maggie rarely let her take that final action. Pity. It was the reward she always looked for at the end of the day.

†

Val swung by the kitchen and grabbed a spoon before returning to her room. She wondered where Gina had gone. She worried about her and could sense that a storm was brewing.

She leaned back against the soft pillows on her bed and pulled the top off the container of ice cream. Priorities. She would eat her treat first, then retrieve the prototypes, which she hoped would do the job intended.

Dipping her spoon into the container repeatedly, she finished devouring her favorite dessert and dumped the spoon into the empty cardboard. As she leaned over to place the container on her nightstand, she removed the red and blue discs from the bottom and folded them into her hand. Her trusted gun remained on the bed beside her, pressed up against her thigh within easy reach.

Performing magic shows for money when she ran the streets in her youth made doing this without detection easy. When she was bored at night these days as an adult, she would continue to practice this skill. It came in handy with this mission. She wondered if Maggie knew about this and if that was why they'd chosen to plant the devices rather than making an exchange.

It was child's play for her to slip the blue disc under her watch at the same time she slipped the red disc under the battery charger and placed the watch on top. Pretending to remove her watch as she did every night before turning in was a habit they would find routine, so they wouldn't closely scrutinize it.

She swiveled her legs off the bed and stepped on the wood floor. Her bare feet padded on the hard surface as she pulled off her T-shirt and tossed it on the chair. She slipped off her jeans and added them to the pile. Lifting the sports bra and pulling it over her breasts, she grinned, flung it toward the chair, and raised her middle finger. She bent to retrieve her gun and held it loosely in her hand as she stood there in her underwear.

"Are you getting a good look, you fucking perverts?" Val lazily strolled into the guest bathroom, where she raised her hands above her head—the gun an almost natural extension of her hand—and stretched before completing her nightly routine of brushing her teeth, washing her face, and using the toilet.

When she returned to the bedroom, she slipped under the covers, placed her gun by her pillow, and leaned over to

125

press the button on her phone as though she was checking the time. She knew the new device would soon show her settled back in her bed peacefully sleeping as the video and audio feed was replaced with what Toni and Dani had created to throw Leonid's men off track.

"Hey, Soph, thanks for the neat gadgets. I'm incognito right now. I need to know they didn't do anything to the poor slobs who had the misfortune to interact with me in the store."

"What's the deal? Are you actually developing a conscience?"

"I might have overreacted a bit and pulled my gun on some mousy housewife who was about to purchase my ice cream. You know how irritable I get when someone gets between me and my nighttime treat. I think the goons thought that poor woman was my contact."

Sophie laughed in her head. *"We saw that. Ronda made sure they didn't act rashly with the innocents. You really should control your temper. I bet they both had to change their underwear after their little exchange with you. I think Leonid's men recognized as soon as they reached suburbia that neither of them were worthwhile targets."*

"Here's my plan. I'm going to wait a few hours until about one, when they do a change in shift. The new device had enough of a feed showing me turning over a few times in my sleep, right?"

"Yeah, don't worry, it will look like you've settled in for the night."

"Okay, that's good. There's extra security precautions on the office door, but I think I've figured out how to deactivate them. I'll carry a few darts in case I have to incapacitate a guard for a few hours, and I'll hope and pray someone doesn't stroll into their area until morning. The dumbasses will probably think they just fell asleep."

"I don't know how the new device works, but I was assured it'll give you the ability to move through the house undetected by their security cameras. It won't mask any sound from the live bodies around you, so be careful."

"Stealth is my middle name." Val pushed the button again to deactivate the new device, then pulled the pillow under her head as she rolled over and settled in for several hours. She would periodically shift her position in bed as she normally did while sleeping.

Her thoughts traveled to Gina and how beautiful and innocent she looked today. It was an uncomfortable feeling. Gina was starting to worm her way inside Val's hard shell, and that was not a good thing. Emotions tended to cloud her reasoning. She was a killing machine, not some lovesick weakling. Fueled by hate and anger, she was lethal; conversely, driven by love she was ineffective. She was surprised that her mind considered that love was even a possibility for how she was feeling.

A door slammed and Val wondered what that was about but decided to lay low until she was ready to plant the camera. Then she would worry about finding Gina.

✝

Leonid shook the glass of scotch and the ice clinked against the sides. His irritation was growing. An hour had passed and still no word from Sergei. Leonid did not wish to appear anxious or weak, so he remained glued to his leather chair sipping his drink. It was getting late, and he wondered where his traitorous wife had gone after her day of shopping.

He hadn't bothered to summon her for dinner because he'd had some business to attend to and couldn't be bothered with inane conversation with an empty-headed woman. Holding back on his baser instincts had been hard. He'd wanted a son, and making him legitimate required a wife. Fortunately he had others to satisfy his needs for rough sex.

His father had taught him that men didn't leave marks on their wife for others to see because that showed a weakness in one's character. The difference between Leonid's marriage and his father's was that his mother had never dared to show any disrespect toward his father. She had been an obedient, demure woman who knew her place. Gina did not understand the rules, and he needed to use a steady hand to correct that if she was going to survive long enough to produce his heir.

Leonid looked up when Sergei entered the room. His footsteps were soft on the wood floor, but Leonid had a natural ability to pick up on every cue that revealed another person had entered his space.

"I apologize for disturbing your peace. There were two individuals who interacted with Vera, but neither appears to have any connection to the mysterious organization. It looks as though her trip to the store was for the purpose she said—obtaining her precious pint of ice cream. I do not understand the American love affair with that dessert."

"Hmmm. Have you watched her since her return? There is nothing unusual in her behavior?"

"*Da.* She is lounging in her bed with a spoon that she grabbed from the kitchen on her way back to her room, eating what she purchased. She did not even bother to put it in a bowl. She is an uncouth, despicable representation of her gender." Sergei's face showed a rare expression of disgust.

"I do not trust that this trip was without purpose. I want her watched closely all night long. Do not take your eyes off her," Leonid directed.

Sergei nodded. "I will make sure we watch her every move."

"Where is my wife?"

"She is out in the gardens. Alone. We will track her as well."

"Bring her to me. She has had enough alone time. I believe I have been too lenient with her and it is time she learned her place. My generosity has limits." Leonid took a sip of his drink.

"I will bring her to you." A small smile formed on Sergei's lips as he turned and began to leave the room.

"Never mind. I'll find her later after she's retired. I've not finished my drink and she's not worth interrupting my tranquility until I'm ready to deal with her. Let me know when she goes to her room."

Sergei turned around and nodded.

†

Gina sat on a wooden bench in the garden, breathing in the scent of the flowers that surrounded her. She hoped being here would calm her nerves but it had the opposite effect. Her thoughts were scattered. One second she'd think of Vera and her growing attraction for the woman, and the next she'd focus on her present predicament. The pregnancy test had turned pink, and that was definitely not what she wanted to see.

She'd had enough of Leonid and his controlling ways and was ready to tell Antonio she wanted out. Paulie, who was usually constantly nearby, was curiously MIA, and that worried her. Yes, he was a loose cannon, but he was family.

Her actions toward Vera had been playful at first, but as her attraction grew she'd begun flirting in earnest. *Why? I've been reckless and blatant and there's no doubt that Leonid has witnessed my behavior.* He had been cool toward

129

her of late, and she needed to leave before he killed her. And he would, of that she was certain.

Perhaps if I tell him about the baby he'll keep me around long enough for me to get away. Vera had said something about escaping, but Gina's thoughts were so jumbled that she couldn't remember the conversation clearly. She yawned. *I guess that's why I've been so tired lately.* After stretching her arms above her head, she stood and walked back toward the house, grateful Leonid had stopped coming to her room at night.

✝

Leonid, dressed in a robe, slammed open the door to her bedroom and snarled. From the look on his face, Gina knew she was in trouble.

"It has been too long since you've visited me in my room," she cooed, hoping to soothe some of his anger.

"Don't say a word," he growled as he opened his robe and dropped it to the floor.

Gina gulped back her rising terror. He had never been so enraged at her, and for the first time she feared she might not survive. She watched as he approached, his erection jutting out like an exclamation mark. She shivered at the sight of it. With palpable anger he savagely tore at her clothes before slapping her hard and pushing her back on the bed. In anticipation of what was to come, she closed her eyes.

"You will never embarrass me again," he screamed before hitting her.

Gina refused to cry out or touch her burning cheek. She wouldn't give him that satisfaction. He punched her in the stomach so hard that it knocked the air out of her lungs.

Even though she feared for the child growing inside her, she lay motionless.

"*Pizda*," he growled as he rammed himself into her. He ferociously pounded her body until he collapsed on top of her.

Gina sent up a silent prayer that he was finished and would leave her alone, but he wasn't.

Again, he took her, all the while repeating, "I'm going to kill you and that bitch."

When he was finally done, he slapped her again. "Your days are numbered, just like that bitch of yours." He looked at the blood on his hands and sneered.

Gina watched him go into her bathroom and heard the water run, then he left the room, slamming the door so hard it seemed to shake the house.

Terrified he would come back, Gina placed her hands over her abdomen protectively before lying there motionlessly. Her thoughts went to Vera. If only she'd listened when the bodyguard told her to be careful, neither of them would be in Leonid's crosshairs. She needed to go to Vera and warn her, but how would she do that? He had cameras and spies everywhere, and after what he'd just done, he'd said he would be watching. She closed her eyes and passed out from the pain.

†

Val had honed her skill for estimating time. She'd first developed it when they'd held her captive so many years ago. She shuddered as her thoughts briefly returned to that time in her life. A quick touch and go, like a butterfly landing on a flower. She put that visual in her brain to erase the other, more gruesome vision. Her innate sense of time was a major factor in the success of her escape. She'd timed her assault perfectly. She learned over the years that timing is everything. She knew when to squeeze the sniper rifle, when to land the perfect blow, and when to sit patiently for just the right moment.

She rolled over and pressed the button on her watch at one o'clock on the nose. She crawled out of bed, grabbed her gun, and felt settled in the knowledge that she was currently invisible. A loop of her patterned sleep would continue to replace the actual footage in the camera that was recording her room.

Not bothering to put on her bra, Val quickly donned her T-shirt and jeans and stuffed her gun into her pants. She crept out of her room without making a sound after grabbing the pen containing the darts and the device that would disrupt the laser protection on Leonid's office door. Earlier in the night she'd taken the time to retrieve the disrupter from her electric toothbrush. She was glad that when she'd first arrived, they hadn't given her pen or toothbrush a second look. She'd kept the pen on the nightstand the whole time right in front of their noses. The hard feel of the metal against her stomach provided a feeling of security and reminded her that her gun was a natural part of her. She would never give that up without a fight.

Val didn't worry about Leonid's guards intercepting her because she didn't plan on leaving any of them standing and she'd be long gone by the time they came out of dreamland. Sending her first dart down the long hallway caused the first man to slump against the wall. One down, three to go. She'd done her own reconnaissance and established how many she would have to put out of commission before reaching his office.

She had just the right number of darts to eliminate those obstacles, so it was imperative that each hit its mark. Val wasn't sure what to think as she easily picked off the next two, but the third somehow managed to avoid the final dart.

Fuck. She hated having to kill the man, but she had no choice now. Her agile reflexes kicked into gear as she engaged him. After a quick twist that cracked his neck, she eased him to the ground.

Standing in front of the office door, she pulled out the disruptor and deactivated the laser beam that would send a jolt of energy into anyone daring to cross the threshold into his office. It took Val less than two minutes to hop onto the desk, remove the red covering, and place the minuscule disc above Leonid's computer. It was virtually undetectable to the naked eye. A person would need to carefully inspect the ceiling to discover the camera. Like a chameleon, the device was designed to blend into whatever substance it was placed upon. Dani and Toni were such clever little minxes.

It was time to get the hell out of Dodge, so she crept along the path to Gina's room. She was prepared to do whatever it took to leave this place with Gina, even if that meant killing Leonid and pissing Maggie off. She thought she'd be able to render him unconscious without having to resort to a permanent solution if he was in the bedroom with her, but she shrugged when she considered the fatal alternative.

†

Outside the door to Gina's bedroom, Val paused before placing her hand on the round brass knob and listened intently for any noise. She turned it carefully, pushed the door open a sliver, and peeked inside. Her sigh was nearly audible as she looked at Gina curled up on the bed—alone. She quietly closed the door behind her.

133

She wasn't sure what had tipped her off, but she knew something was very wrong. As she crept closer, she saw the spatter of blood on the sheets and quickly went to rouse Gina.

She brushed her hand lightly against Gina's forehead and Val moved her hair aside as Gina remained curled up on her side in the vulnerable fetal position.

When Gina turned over and Val saw the results of what was clearly a beating, her blood ran cold and she gritted her teeth. Her emotions warred with her. She wasn't sure whether she should take care of Gina first or rid the earth of the bastard who'd done this to her.

Gina's heartbreaking moan interrupted her thoughts.

"We gotta get you out of here. Let me help you up." Val continued to stroke her face. A trickle of blood marked a path down Gina's chin.

"I…I can't…he'll find me and kill me."

Val's jaw stiffened. "Oh, honey, what did he do to you? Did he…?"

Gina looked away. "I'm pregnant, and he was so brutal I'm afraid I might lose the baby," she cried.

Val kissed Gina's forehead before the cold fury crept into every single cell in her body. "I'm going to take care of some unfinished business, and then I promise I'll get you out of here."

"I don't think you can, Vera. There are too many of his men for you to fight alone."

Val let her fingers slide down Gina's battered and bruised face. She wished her touch was magic and would heal her pain. "You let me worry about that, baby. I told you not to underestimate me."

"If anything happens to you, I won't be able to forgive myself for playing such a dangerous game when I knew he'd be watching. I'm so sorry." Gina began to weep.

Val was fighting a war inside her head. She desperately wanted to seek retribution for what Leonid had done, but Gina's tears pulled at her heartstrings, and that won out. She gently lifted the covers and pulled Gina into her arms before stroking her back. "Shh, nothing is going to happen to me. Everything is going to work out."

"You can't be sure of that. Look at me." Gina put her hand on her face. "He did this to me. I can only imagine what he's going to do to you. He told me he'd kill you. Get away while you can. Please. For me."

"There is no way I'm leaving you behind. Don't ever suggest that again." After putting a small amount of distance between herself and Gina, Val leaned in and touched her lips to Gina's. Val reluctantly left the warmth of her embrace and crawled off the bed. "Rest for a little bit, and if I have to, I will carry you out of this place."

"My protector."

"Always," Val whispered as she turned and left the room without looking back. She had unfinished business to take care of.

†

Val wasn't thinking clearly as her rage completely overtook her actions. Slamming Gina's bedroom door behind her, she went on a rampage with only one thought in her mind. She was going to kill that bastard, but only after making him pay. Anyone stupid enough to get in her way would find themselves in an early grave.

Two quick shots and two men were down, never to rise again. In a swift motion, almost too quick to witness, she shoved one of the downed men's guns into the waistband of her jeans and grabbed the gun from the second man. She proceeded with her double-barreled assault on the men

135

rushing to the site of the disturbance, and five more crumpled to the floor. She was picking them off like ducks in an arcade.

Soon she found herself on the other side of the door leading to her main target. She figured Leonid had already heard the commotion, but she didn't believe he had a chance in hell against her rage and deadly aim. Val rarely missed her target. Two quick shots at the doorknob was all it took to push the door in and rush into the room.

"Shit, the laser beams."

It was too late; they were already activated. Enhanced emotions were never a good thing, and she wondered if it was her hate or if it was love that caused her demise just before a jolt of energy ran through her body, crumpling her to the floor. The force of the electricity coursing through her hurt worse than any pain she'd ever experienced. She wondered if this was what a sophisticated Taser felt like. Her last thought before she saw black was *Gina*.

Chapter Thirteen

The trickle of blood from her mouth was the most irritating thing about her current predicament. Hanging from chains secured to walls was old hat for her. Just as before, Val disassociated herself from the biting metal on her wrists. The blood that tickled her cheeks reminded her of the cockroaches that used to scamper across her skin. She hated those disgusting bugs and had fantasies of becoming an exterminator who specializes in cockroach infestations. She supposed in a way she had become an exterminator of a different kind of cockroach.

Ah fuck. Right about now she would welcome Sophie chirping in her ear. Val looked down at her naked body. The angry red marks would leave permanent scarring, she'd have a few more reminders to contend with, but they left her legs free. *Big mistake.* The Organization was probably going berserk. She guessed it was already morning. She was supposed to be back at the compound by now.

Val smiled as she thought about how Maggie hated to lose an agent. She knew they'd put every available person on this, but Val didn't plan to wait for any women on white horses. She'd gotten herself into this mess and she was going to make damned sure she got herself out of it.

Patterns.

Timing.

It was all about patterns and timing. She'd escaped before, and she'd do it again. Breaking away wasn't what worried her the most. Gina concerned her more. She needed to find a way to get Gina out, but first things first. Her unfortunate situation needed resolution.

She wondered why they'd taken the blindfold off. They had to know that taking away her sense of sight was one more way to put her at a disadvantage. Not that it had stopped her before, nor would it stop her now, but she was curious.

✝

Leonid brought the rich, dark liquid to his lips and took a large sip. The aggravation of the previous night with alarms sounding continually hadn't changed his internal clock that caused him to wake at his normal time. When another alarm went off a few hours after Sergei had taken the *pizda*, he'd almost emerged from his bedroom to check on the new irritation, but it was quickly silenced and he returned to sleep. As he set the cup down next to his mouse, the quick knock on his door announced an imminent update from his most loyal servant. He hadn't wanted anything to disturb the few short hours of sleep he might managed to salvage, so he'd waved Sergei away after removing the garbage and securing her in his tightly controlled holding pen. It was the location for all his possessions, where he broke them before offering them up to the free market so they would be malleable to their new lot in life.

Leonid shifted his eyes to Sergei, who stood in front of his massive desk waiting for acknowledgment. "How many?"

"Ten dead, two just waking up."

He liked that about Sergei. He was succinct and to the point. "Where were you when this shitstorm happened?"

"On the other side of the mansion. When I heard the first shots, I came quickly. By the time I arrived, the *pizda* was a pathetic lump of garbage on the threshold of your bedroom."

Leonid nodded. "Gina?"

"She has not emerged from her bedroom. Do you wish for her to have an accident?"

"No. Bring the doctor. No one is to lay a hand on her. I learned something interesting last night. My heir is growing inside her. Once she has given me my son, you may arrange the accident."

"Are you sure she is telling you the truth? Perhaps she lies to save herself," Sergei stated.

"I saw the evidence in her bathroom when I went to wash my hands of her blood. She did not tell me the news. It is a pity she failed to share this with me before I taught her the lesson. I will be disappointed if she caused a miscarriage.

"I will finish my breakfast before paying a visit to Vera. I want the pleasure of killing her myself. No one is to lay a hand on her. Her death will be excruciatingly slow and painful. We will need to find another way into this mysterious organization. Please dispose of the two men who had the bad sense to nap on the job. I abhor incompetence. Good help is so hard to come by these days. Who is watching Vera right now?"

"Dimitri."

"I sure hope he is better equipped to deal with her than the rest."

"She is chained to the wall as instructed with solid steel links that allow ten feet of movement. A toilet is within that range. The same setup as all the others without the cot."

"Are her legs and arms secured?" Leonid asked.

Sergei furrowed his brow. "No, just her arms."

"Idiots," Leonid yelled. "Now I will need to disturb my breakfast. Move Gina to a secure location. Now," he ordered. "You better hope Vera is still securely fastened to the wall, or I may choose to forget your many years of loyal service and that would pain me. I will deal with Vera this morning. No more delays."

†

Bang bang bang bang

The loud knocking on their door startled Sophie and she sat up in bed.

"What the hell?" Her gaze shifted to the clock on her nightstand. Five thirty in the morning. She'd stayed up late last night making love with Kim, and this abrupt disturbance of her sleep made her especially irritable.

Kim shifted in bed and rubbed her eyes. She scooted to a sitting position with her hair sticking out in all directions. Sophie's eyes softened when she looked at her lover. Even with her hair in disarray, she was still the most beautiful woman Sophie had ever laid her eyes on.

"I think someone desperately wants to talk to us. My guess is Dani or Toni. They're the only two people I know who don't seem to get the concept of sleep," Kim grumbled.

"I'll get it. Go on back to sleep, hon."

Kim slid back under the covers and pulled a pillow over her head.

Sophie padded to the door, yanked it open, and glared at Ronda. "I sure hope you have a damn good reason for waking me up at oh dark hundred."

"Val's dot isn't anywhere near the compound. When Dani went into the lab at five, she wanted to make sure Val had made it back. She not only didn't sneak in last night, but she's at least twenty minutes away in some remote part of Virginia."

"Val's dot? All she had to do is use the wire in her underwear. I would have heard her." Sophie waved Ronda inside.

"Not if they stripped her, so the twin geniuses put in their own plan B. I guess they learned from Maggie never to expect that everything will go as planned. Toni snuck her biotracking device in the red cover on the camera. Or was it the blue cover—"

"Who gives a shit about the color coding. So what you're telling me is that Toni engineered the same little device she used on Char? I guess after Val removed the video feed gadget from the bottom of the ice cream container, that nasty little biobug burrowed into her skin and now we have a GPS location on our crusty little pal. That's why she insisted on putting it there herself. Ooh, Val is gonna be so pissed that we can track her for six months, give or take a day."

"I doubt she'll care when we save her ass. Come on, we've been elected to go get her." Ronda grabbed the keys sitting on the dresser. "I'm driving."

Sophie grabbed Ronda's wrist and put pressure on the most sensitive point until she dropped the keys. "No, you're not. Besides, while I'm driving you can lean out the window and shoot at the bad guys, because I guarantee there will be bad guys to shoot at. She might not be able to communicate with us, but I'll let her know we're on our way."

Ronda shook her hand out. "Shit, you didn't have to squeeze so hard. All you had to do was mention shooting the bad guys and I woulda given the keys back. Fucking brute."

"Shut up. Let me throw on some pants and a shirt, and then we'll get on the road. I may need to push the speed limit, so I hope you don't get carsick. If you do, that'll be another reason to stick your big head out the window, because you better not puke in my car."

Ronda crossed her arms over her chest. "I can take whatever speed you dish out, pantywaist."

Sophie glared and stalked back to the bedroom, calling over her shoulder, "We're wasting time. Why I let you drag me into your infantile behavior...." She shook her head. "You're worse than Toni."

†

Maggie grabbed the towel hanging on the hook and patted herself dry. She'd carefully slid out of bed so she wouldn't wake Antonio. Maybe starting up again with him wasn't the smartest thing, but he'd made resisting his charms very hard, and she'd never stopped loving him. She couldn't worry about that now. Val was her top priority.

Val hadn't reported in, and that worried her. They had an understanding. No matter how late it was, Maggie expected her to check in after a mission. Neither of them ever verbalized the reason they'd established this rule, but Maggie knew this was Val's roundabout way of letting her know she both cared about and respected her. Maggie wasn't any better at showing her emotions, but she knew it would tear a hole in her heart if something happened to Val.

She hurried through her morning routine, anxious to receive an update from Dani or Toni. She suspected that one, if not both of them would be glued to the monitor, hoping to learn something from the sensitive camera. It was still early, but she was anxious to find out why Val hadn't made it back to the compound.

When she opened the door to the lab, she was surprised to see Char gathered around the monitor that Toni and Dani were staring intently at.

"Shit," Dani exclaimed.

"Ooh, that's not good," Char chimed in.

Toni scrunched up her face, and Char's eyes went wide.

"Perhaps you can tell me what is so fascinating on that screen."

"Hiya, boss." Dani glanced up. "Um, Val was successful in placing the camera. Leonid is pissed. He lost ten men and just stalked off...and, um...." Dani glanced at Toni with a sheepish expression.

Maggie raised her eyebrow. "The rest, please."

"I initiated plan B. Ronda and Sophie left about a half hour ago to retrieve Val. I snuck my biotracker on the camera device. We have a location for her, but it sounds like they have her chained up."

Maggie furrowed her brow. "How come you only sent Ronda and Sophie? What if Leonid has an army protecting his captive?"

"I don't think he has an army left. Besides, it sounds like he had to split his crew and move Gina to another location," Char explained.

"I don't suppose you found a way to track her?" Maggie asked.

Toni shook her head. "No, sorry. Maybe we'll learn something when Leonid returns. I can watch the monitor all day if you want."

"I want round-the-clock shifts on that monitor. I know it isn't our responsibility to get Gina out, but I feel a sense of duty to help Antonio. Agreed?"

"Hey, the dot is moving kinda fast. Val's on the move." Dani pointed to the second monitor.

Maggie smiled. "That's my girl. Get Sophie and Ronda on the phone. I want them to intercept and get Val out of there. Tell them not to kill Leonid. We need him alive for now."

Char pulled her phone from her pocket. "I'm on it." She punched in a number and leaned in to brush a kiss across Toni's lips. "I love your plan B, and Val will too once she has a chance to cool down."

Toni grinned.

"Hey, Ronda.... Yeah, so you see it moving too.... Great.... Maggie says don't kill Leonid, but if you get a chance to maim him...."

Maggie shook her finger, but her lips curved in a small smile.

Chapter Fourteen

Val leaned against the cold, rough cement with her head bent forward. She felt a small vibration in her head and wondered if Sophie was trying to contact her. The hits to her head had surely dislodged the device, and she couldn't make out any sounds, only something that resembled a sort of droning pulse. She supposed the men had taken out their frustrations on her while she was unconscious. What a bunch of assholes, feeling the need to beat on someone who wouldn't fight back. She slowed her breathing and waited patiently.

She heard the man before she smelled him. His odor was rank, but she couldn't react.

"The bitch is still out cold.... We made sure she wouldn't wake up.... No, I swear she isn't moving.... No problem. I will chain her legs, but she is no threat.... Don't worry, she will be more than secure by the time you arrive."

Timing. The seconds ticked by as the click of his shoes inched closer. *Wait for it, wait for it....* She was a deadly cobra ready to strike.

145

When he entered her sphere just a few feet away, Val jumped up and looped the chain around the unsuspecting man's throat. It didn't take her long to choke him to death, grab his gun, and shoot the steel chain to release her hands.

She didn't believe it was in her best interest to remove his clothes to cover her naked body. Besides, his smell was almost enough to cause her to vomit on the cement floor. If she had to flag down a car in her birthday suit, so be it.

What a stupid dickhead. He hadn't locked the door behind him, and she slithered through the opening, checking right and left for any guards she might have to eliminate. When she reached the top of the stairs, she cocked her head and listened intently to the sounds around her. The crush of gravel from a car's tires was an unmistakable sound. *Shit, time to leave this little party.*

Val pushed open the back door and ran for her life. She heard two gunshots but kept her eyes focused on her escape route. She needed a little more cover before she could think about shooting back. Two more shots. Something was not adding up, because they sounded too far away.

The leaves, pine needles, and sharp branches tore into her skin as she moved through the dense foliage. When she heard the car crash through it, breaking branches and navigating down the narrow pathway, she thought for sure her luck had ended. She started to weigh her options. Climb a tree and take aim. Jump to the side and shoot her way out. Both were viable depending on how many goons Leonid had sent. She only had one gun and would have to make that count.

She chose the latter. Jumping into the brush, she rolled and crouched, aiming her gun at the oncoming car. It looked vaguely familiar.

A recognizable dark head popped out of the window. "Don't even think about it."

The car skidded to a stop. "Get in," Ronda ordered.

Val scrambled into the car. "'Bout fucking time you got here. Wait, how the hell did you know where I was?"

"We'll explain later. Just sit your naked ass down and enjoy Sophie's expert driving," Ronda directed.

"Let me guess, Toni put her tiny Frankenstein's monster on one of the devices. I don't understand why we haven't shoved one of her biobugs up Leonid's ass. You didn't have any qualms about letting that little miracle of science burrow into my skin," Val grumbled.

"Hey, don't blame me, it wasn't my plan B. But I'm glad she took the initiative, so stop your bitching, and don't get blood on my leather seats. Besides, we gave you the vial with her biobug. It isn't our fault neither one of you were able to deploy it. There's a blanket back there you can wrap yourself up in." Sophie turned her head. "You okay, Val?"

Val pulled the blanket around her battered body and nodded. "Never better. At least I won't have your nagging voice in my ear. A few well-placed kicks to my head took care of that. It probably sent the little bugger all the way to my gut. Tell me you got Gina out."

The silence in the car was deafening.

"Soph? Ronda?"

"We're working on it," Ronda answered.

Val slumped in the seat. The wheels in her head were already turning. She wasn't about to let Gina rot under Leonid's roof. "Wish Toni's fucking plan B had extended to Leonid. We'd be tracking him right now. Eventually he'll go to Gina because he won't be able to trust that someone else will take care of his property," she spit out.

"Tracking him has always been a means to the ultimate goal. We need to get into his computer system, not

147

track him for elimination. You know that's not our style," Sophie answered.

"Yeah, well, I thought the little nerds were good at chess, and we should have anticipated his next move," Val argued.

"I guess you have a point, but don't count us out just yet. Toni and Dani are very creative. We'll find a way, don't worry. Oh, and this should make you happy." She grinned. "I'm pretty sure I clipped Leonid. We were told not to kill him, so I made sure to aim for his leg." Ronda laughed. "He's going to need medical attention and it'll probably hurt like a bitch. Couldn't happen to a nicer guy."

"Good. Wish I had been the one to do it, but I probably would have aimed a little higher and either shot his dick off or killed the son of a bitch. I want in when we put together a rescue mission," Val stated.

"Of course you do," Sophie answered.

"What's that supposed to mean?" Val asked.

"Admit it. You have feelings for her." Sophie glanced into the rearview mirror, and Val met her gaze.

"I need a nap, so if you don't mind, a little peace and quiet would be nice. It wasn't exactly a picnic hanging out in Leonid's chamber of horrors." Val shuddered and laid her head against the window as she stretched out across the backseat. She was thankful Sophie and Ronda didn't continue to pursue the conversation. She closed her eyes and tried to let the past few hours wash over her.

A new set of nightmares was just around the corner. She knew that, but maybe her exhaustion would kick in and she'd have at least one hour to relax and not remember. Her memories just kept poking at her and she felt like every time she turned around, her past resurfaced after some vague trigger that she couldn't put her finger on. Of course, being chained to the wall again wasn't exactly an elusive impression; it was nearly a full-blown repeat of the terror she'd endured so many years ago. Ten minutes after Val closed her eyes, the dream began.

It wasn't daylight anymore and she was crashing through the dense forest, scraping her arms and legs, tearing up the tender soles of her feet. The murkiness of the night disoriented her. The wind was whipping through her hair and howling as if it were in excruciating pain. Through the sound, she heard the desperate plea. "Vera, help me, please."

Gina's voice sounded far away, yet she felt like it was blasting inside her head. She stopped running and turned her head right and left. The sound of a large vehicle moving quickly through the forest was all she could hear besides the painful cries of the wind. She had to find Gina.

The bark scratched her body as she scrambled up a tree, and she looked down and was surprised to see she wasn't wearing any clothes. The branches began to thin as she climbed, and she knew she wouldn't remain stable for much longer, but she now had an expansive view of the surrounding terrain.

An ugly cement building sat in a wide clearing with a gravel path leading to the main road. The building was close, and Val could see several vehicles and a large contingent of armed soldiers swarming around it like wasps on a slab of meat. Instinctively she knew that was where they had imprisoned Gina. She had to get there and save her.

The clouds began to move over the bright full moon, and suddenly the inky-black night made the building nearly invisible. Val scrambled down from the tree, and as she got closer to the cement prison, she saw ten men snaking around the building in slow motion, bumping into one another as if they'd lost their sight. Each one had a bullet hole in his head, and their vacant stares reminded her of Hollywood zombies. She recognized them as the men she'd killed in her earlier rampage and wondered if any of them had family. Did they have little girls to protect? She brushed past them undetected as they continued their unorganized shuffle.

The moaning from the woman chained to the wall increased incrementally until the sound overtook the room.

"Oh Gina. I'm going to get you out of here. Trust me," Val promised.

Gina raised her head and Val recognized the same bullet wound as the men had. Blood oozed from the hole and the coppery scent assaulted her nostrils.

"I trusted you. You failed me," Gina wailed.

Her body morphed into that of a young girl with golden hair and a dirty face. Blood tears trailed down her cheeks. Val knew this girl. When the girl morphed into an adolescent with blonde hair and steel gray eyes, Val heard herself scream as she recognized herself at age twelve.

"You never let me escape. I trusted you. You failed me."

"Hey, Val, wake up, buddy. Come on, wake the fuck up."

Val startled awake and looked into Ronda's concerned eyes.

"I'm okay." Val glanced at the rearview mirror and saw Sophie's skeptical gaze.

She needed to get her shit together or they wouldn't let her go after Gina, and she needed to be on that extraction team like she needed to continue to breathe.

Chapter Fifteen

Ever since the first alarms sounded, they kept randomly going off, Gina heard doors banging and hurried footsteps outside her room. Her adrenaline started to kick in. It had only been a matter of minutes after Vera left her room before all hell broke loose. Gina heard several gunshots and hoped none of them had wounded Vera. She recalled the rage in Vera's eyes when she stormed out of her room after realizing Leonid had beaten and raped Gina. After spending several anxious minutes listening to the commotion, Gina thought it prudent to dress quickly and be ready to go when Vera returned.

If she returns. Vera had been gone for too long, and that concerned her.

The bedroom door banged open and she instinctively pulled the sheet up in a protective gesture. Two men with guns drawn came into the room. One was Sergei, Leonid's main lieutenant and a mountain of a man who leered at her before opening her closet door.

"Where is she?" Sergei pushed the bathroom door open with his gun before looking inside.

Gina was frozen in place. Vera was in trouble, and when they found her, she knew they would kill her.

Sergei approached the bed and leaned in close. "I asked you where the bitch is."

His breath was hot against her cheek and she couldn't help trembling. "I don't know," she cried.

He grabbed her chin and twisted her face around. "When I find her I will kill her, and then I will come for you."

Rage suddenly filled her and she slapped his face. "Get away from me or I will tell him that you manhandled me, and we both know you'll be the one that's dead."

Sergei stepped back and laughed. "Don't be so sure about that." He turned and looked at the other man. "You go and stand outside the door. If you see the bitch, shoot her but don't kill her. The boss wants to have his fun with her." Sergei snarled at Gina before the two men left her bedroom.

It had been several hours since Vera left her room, and the sinking feeling that Leonid had killed her made bile rise to her throat. She looked at the clock and saw the sun wouldn't be up for another two hours. If she was going to get away from Leonid, she needed to rely on herself and leave sooner rather than later. While waiting for Vera she'd formulated a plan, and the time to put it into motion was now.

She got out of bed and locked the door. It wouldn't stop anyone for long, but she didn't need much time. She'd been through too much in her life to sit by and let thugs kill her. In the back of her mind, she hoped Vera had gotten away and that when she made it back to Antonio's she would discover Vera was there. It was a small kernel of hope, but that was all she had to cling to. They were on the same side, so she reasoned it wasn't impossible.

She switched off the light and made her way to the walk-in closet. She changed into black jeans, a black shirt, and black boots, then rummaged around for a moment before pulling out the backpack she'd had when living on the streets. She opened it and went through the items. Some she'd acquired during her time on the street, some were mementos of her earlier life, and others Antonio had given her in case she needed to leave quickly. She had to leave everything behind except for the essentials—a gun, a flashlight, night goggles, money, ID, survival gear, and the extraction button Antonio had given her.

After exiting the closet with the backpack in place, she reached under the bed for the rope ladder Leonid insisted she have in case of fire. She'd use the fact the alarms kept sounding to her advantage. Once the window was open, another alarm went off. She waited five minutes for it to stop before inserting a device that would help her later in her escape into a wall socket. After making certain no one was outside, she let the ladder unfurl down the side of the house. Taking a deep breath, she scampered down the rope's rungs to the ground and yanked at the ladder. It fell.

More alarms sounded and she waited. She stood in the shadows and after watching several of Leonid's men run by, she took another deep breath.

"Now to make my escape."

She edged away from the house toward the nearby wooded area.

In the time she'd been living in the house, she and Paulie had mapped out the route they'd need to take to escape. The last time she'd seen her brother was in the parking lot at Target, and her heart sank with the certainty that he was dead. She would have to mourn for him later. Right now all she could focus on was getting away. Gina made her way in the shadows on the path that she hoped would take her away from danger.

Three and a half minutes later, she was two hundred yards from the house and almost to the property's boundary. From this point on escaping would get sticky since she was certain there was an underground alarm system. She pulled a small device from her jeans pocket that would connect with the device she'd put in the wall socket to shut off all the electricity on the grounds. She pressed the button and watched until the house and grounds went dark. She had forty-five seconds until the backup generator kicked the electricity back on. Gina ran for the woods.

†

Maggie hesitated before deciding to ask Char to join her for breakfast. She figured she had about another hour before the trio of agents returned to the compound. Char was the most levelheaded, and Maggie was more than a little worried about Val and what the latest development might do to her already unraveling psyche. Char and Dani had a way of compartmentalizing things, and that had served them well. Perhaps she'd made an error in judgment sending Val into the field so soon after asking her to witness the horror of those poor young girls chained together, but she'd thought Val also had an ability to separate herself from the experience. Clearly that had not been the case of late.

Maggie turned her cool gaze to Char. In a voice barely audible above the chatter in the room, she asked, "Would you like to join me for breakfast while we wait for Ronda, Sophie, and Val to return?"

A subtle nod was Char's only response as she disengaged from Toni. She protectively draped her hand over

154

Toni's shoulder. The physical connection seemed to ground both of them.

Maggie didn't wait for Char before turning to leave. She trusted that Char would follow her into the garden room. The room wasn't an actual garden, but was as close as Dani could make it. It had live plants and a bubbling fountain, but the open sky and fresh air weren't luxuries they could afford in the secure compound. Despite its false nature, Dani had managed to replicate all the sights, smells, and sounds to near perfection. What mattered was that it felt like a real garden.

The glass doors slid open and Maggie inhaled the sweet aroma of lilacs, her favorite bush, that never failed to calm her. She wondered what brought a calming peace to Val; for Char it was either Toni or Dani—the two prominent women in her life.

The small patio had four chairs clustered around a round table with a glass top. The coffeepot, four cups and saucers, cream, and sugar sat on the table, waiting for someone to enjoy the addictive elixir. Maggie hadn't stopped for a cup prior to heading for the lab, so she made a beeline for the pot and poured two cups. She'd already made a quick call to Kimiko, who had set up the garden. She wasn't sure how many people would join her for an intimate breakfast, so she'd asked for four settings, just to be on the safe side. Off to the side stood a folding table with pastries, yogurt, and her favorite fruit.

Char hadn't said a word, waiting patiently for Maggie to speak as she followed her to the folding table and selected an array of items, placing them artistically on her plate. They sat at the glass table, and Char raised her eyebrow before spearing a piece of fruit and delicately taking it into her mouth.

155

"I want you and Toni to take it easy on Val when she returns. No teasing or poking the bear, please." Maggie lifted her cup, blew on the black coffee, and took a small sip.

Char set her fork on the table. "Val isn't exactly made of glass. Why the warning?"

"Val's experience in Leonid's secret holding location is very likely the epitome of déjà vu, with stunning clarity. I suspect they chained her to the wall after a serious beating. She narrowly escaped the same treatment twelve years ago when she was just a child. Her nightmares had started to come back before she left for this undercover assignment. I've already started to see signs of deterioration in her mental stability, and this will likely either put her over the edge or cause her to tiptoe precariously on the line. I know more about her past than she realizes, and I shouldn't have placed her in this position. I regret my decision. I wanted so badly to nail Leonid that I didn't act with prudence. Your Russian is good enough. I believe you might have been a better choice."

"My Russian is not anywhere near Val's. Your choice was based on fact and limited options. She got the job done and she will survive this." Char leaned back in her chair.

"Dani seems to have a connection with her. Do you think she might tear herself away from the lab to assist?" Maggie asked.

"You're really worried. Hmmm. Val must be very good at hiding her weaknesses. I do recall Dani saying something about Val being upset lately, but I just passed it off as Dani being Dani. You know how she has a soft spot for strays and women who are bat-shit crazy."

Maggie glared.

Char held up her hand. "I was kidding. Of course we'll be cautious and treat her with kid gloves. Contrary to popular belief, I do have a conscience, and I genuinely like and respect Val. I'd lay my life on the line for any of the women you've recruited. You know that."

"I do. Please keep this conversation in confidence. I don't wish to embarrass Val, but I thought you should know. You can give Toni the broad strokes, but not the details, please."

"Consider it done, and, Maggie, for what it's worth, we're going to get this bastard and stop him from doing this again to someone else. It will all be worth it, and I'm betting Val will agree with me."

†

Maggie and Char had barely returned to the lab when Ronda, Sophie, and Val stumbled inside. Dani shook her head when Antonio stepped inside thirty seconds after Maggie crossed the room. Dani was starting to feel claustrophobic with everyone crowding into her sacred space. She felt as if some hidden siren were calling everyone to the lab.

"Jesus Christ, don't you all have some conference room you can go to?" Dani grumbled. "At least Kim decided to sleep in and stay out of the melee."

Toni kept her head bent, snickering in her chair.

Val limped to Dani and stood behind her screen. "Have you found out where they took Gina?"

Dani shook her head.

"Christ, Val, you look like shit," Toni noted as she glanced over at Val.

Dani took a good look at Val. She was obviously naked underneath the blanket wrapped around her, and her face looked like she'd gone twenty rounds with Muhamad Ali when he was in his prime. Sophie and Ronda looked uncharacteristically uncomfortable as they tossed a quick look in Maggie's direction.

"You should go to the infirmary and have Cindy check you out," Dani said quietly.

"I tried to tell her that, but she made a beeline here," Ronda said.

"Val, this is not up for debate. March yourself to the infirmary right now. I will personally come to see you when we obtain more information on Gina, but I'll shoot you with one of Dani's darts myself if you don't heed my order. I promise we'll find her. Now go," Maggie directed.

"I want in on the extraction." Val's steely gaze met Maggie's, and Dani thought if the invisible energy of their silent battle were ever harvested, it might start World War III.

"We'll see." Maggie turned to Antonio, who moved to her side. "Good morning, Antonio. Do you have any information to contribute?"

"I received a present delivered to my doorstep last night," he added dryly.

Maggie raised her eyebrow. "Can you please be a little less cryptic?"

"Paulie is dead, and I believe we can safely assume they've figured out Gina and Paulie work for me. I can't say for sure how much else they've determined. I suppose it would not be much of a leap for them to extrapolate that we are working together."

Maggie glanced over to where Val was still standing. "Why aren't you in the infirmary already?"

"Fine, but I want a full report sooner rather than later." Val hobbled to the exit.

"Hey, I hear something," Dani said as she looked up from the computer. "It's muffled, so it's probably happening outside of the office. From the sounds of it, something major is going on. I hear yelling, but I can't quite make out what they're saying. This is all being taped, so maybe we can enhance it later and decipher what's happening."

"Sophie, Char, Antonio, and Ronda, come with me, please. Let's get out of Toni and Dani's hair so they have the space they need to work. I suspect we're disrupting them," Maggie directed.

"About time," Dani mumbled.

Char chuckled. "I think my sister hasn't gotten enough sleep lately. It's making her usually sunny disposition turn decidedly gray."

"Ha-ha, now get the hell out like Maggie said," Dani retorted.

"I need to swing by our pod and tell Kim we're all fine and don't have any extra holes in our bodies to contend with," Sophie said.

"Yes, of course. She'll worry if you don't let her know you're back," Maggie responded.

The group followed Maggie and Antonio out of the lab, and Dani started punching the keys to increase the volume and sharpen the sounds. She heard the keyboard next to her alight with action as Toni began her own staccato with their newest program—an algorithm to predict movement of funds in the various bank accounts organized crime syndicates and crooked politicians managed. If The Organization could anticipate the transfers, they would be able to steal the money before they occurred. It would save hours of field work.

†

Even wearing the night goggles, Gina still stumbled through the wooded area. She could no longer hear the intrusion sirens from the estate, but she didn't slow down.

Everything seemed to be happening in slow motion. She felt like she was some cartoon character who was running as fast as she could, but going nowhere as big drops of sweat leaped from her forehead. A quick look at her wrist made her realize she hadn't brought her watch, so she had no way to know how much time had passed since she escaped. Had it been fewer than five minutes since she'd heard the last alarm or longer? When she'd looked back at the house after she reached the woods, the mass confusion of the previous evening was still going on, but she never got a clear view of anything and didn't have the luxury of waiting to scrutinize what was happening.

She had no doubt Leonid would use dogs to track her when they discovered she was missing. While she'd lived at the mansion, she'd used her phone to open Google Earth to map out her escape route and immediately deleted the search. She came upon the wide creek she'd expected to find and entered the cold water and began running. When she found the road about ten miles from the house, she'd engage the panic button and wait for Antonio.

Just as she knew it would, the stream became deeper, and she had to exit the water.

The cold water had seeped into every pore and she was shivering. She stopped only long enough to pull on a lightweight jacket from her backpack and take out a small bottle of water before she continued running toward the lake. She wanted to at least make it to the alternate extraction point at the campground.

Once there, she ran in the water at the edge of the lake, then ran out for about a hundred yards before backtracking and running in the water again. She did this several times. Hopefully that would confuse any dog Leonid had tracking her. Back in the water, she ran toward the way she came and continued for another two hundred yards.

There, she came upon what looked like an abandoned row boat resting half on the shore and half in the water. She pulled it farther into the water and waited. When it didn't sink, she got in, set the oars, and rowed away from the campground.

I sure hope Antonio has a helicopter.

She rowed toward the middle of the lake and headed for a small cove that would afford her more cover. Once there, she activated the device to alert Antonio of her location. The sun was rising, and dogs barked in the distance. She lay down between the seats on the bottom of the boat and pulled an old tarp over her, hoping they wouldn't spot her.

†

Leonid held the makeshift compress against his leg as he hobbled into the house. The bleeding had stopped hours earlier, and now the injury was more of a nuisance than anything. The entire night had tried his patience and his quiet fury suffocated everything around him, including conversation. The remainder of his men waited patiently in the wings, standing stiffly as their gazes traveled to where their boss held Sergei's shirt against his wound.

"Where is the doctor?" Leonid asked, barely controlling his rage.

"He is on his way," Sergei responded.

"Why is he not here already? Is he tending to Gina?" Leonid rubbed a hand over his face to settle his anger. With all the commotion Gina was never taken to a secure location. "I ordered the doctor to be brought several hours ago, before that clusterfuck that I blame you and Dimitri for. Consider yourself very lucky, Sergei. I am too shorthanded to dispose of you, and in consideration of your many years of loyal

161

service, I am giving you a second chance. Do not disappoint me. And get those tires on the cars replaced. Fucking *sooka*s are good shots, I'll give them that."

Sergei nodded, and Leonid was impressed that he didn't show any emotion when faced with the looming threat.

"When he arrives, send him to me. I want this fucking bullet out of my leg before he examines my two-timing wife. If he discovers she has miscarried, bring her to me. I want the pleasure of putting the bullet in her head, but not before I force her to tell me where I can find that bitch Vera," Leonid spit out.

The bell to the front door chimed, and Leonid thought he saw a flicker of emotion on Sergei's face. Relief? So the man wasn't made of stone after all. Leonid wasn't sure if that was a good or bad thing.

Sergei quickly opened the door, then stepped aside as the doctor crossed the threshold.

"Where's the damn fire? You interrupted my morning coffee, and I'd planned to spend the day on the golf course, Sergei." The tall, thin man with graying hair entered the foyer, carrying a black bag. His gaze landed on Leonid and the flicker of fear in it was almost instantaneous. "I apologize. If I had realized when Sergei contacted me that this was an emergency, I would have come sooner." He rushed over and pointed to the couch. "Sit while I examine the wound."

"No, I don't want to get blood on the leather. We can go into the bathroom. It will be easier to clean." Leonid hobbled down the hall. Sergei followed him and the doctor, and stood in the doorway of the enormous bathroom as Leonid sat on the edge of the tub and the doctor crossed the room before kneeling next to him.

"You really should have gone to the emergency room for this." The doctor shook his head as he pulled the makeshift compress from the wound, ripped open Leonid's pant leg, and palpated the area.

"Just get the damn bullet out and then go see my wife. She is pregnant and may have lost the baby. If she is still carrying the child, I want her given the best care to ensure she carries him to full term." He looked at Sergei. "Go check on her. I don't care if you have to wake her up. I may have been a bit too stern last night to the mother of my son."

Sergei nodded and moved away from the doorway.

The doctor removed a large needle from his bag and quickly jabbed it into the muscle close to the wound.

Leonid winced but didn't say a word.

"I find that when I give people notice before sticking in the needle, they tense up and that makes the pain worse. The numbing should kick in shortly, and then I'll flush and irrigate the wound before removing the bullet. It shouldn't take too many stitches to close it up, but you will have a scar as a reminder of whoever crossed your path today."

Leonid glared down at the doctor. "Just do your fucking job and forget making any snide comments."

"I'll give you another shot with a boost of antibiotics, and then you need to take these for ten days, twice a day, after food." He rummaged in his bag and pulled out a prescription bottle that he set on the marble edge of the Jacuzzi tub.

Leonid leaned back against the wall while the physician attended to his wound. Heavy footsteps hurried toward the bathroom, and Sergei entered with a rare look of panic on his face.

"What the fuck is it now?" Leonid asked.

"Gina is not in her room. We've search the mansion. She does not appear to be in the house."

"Well, check the fucking gardens. You didn't think to check on her when those damn alarms were malfunctioning in the middle of the night. I knew I should have personally attended to that. Fucking imbeciles. Do I have to think for you as well?"

"We'll scour every inch of the grounds, sir." Sergei left the room quickly.

Leonid turned his quiet, barely controlled rage on the doctor. "As you can see, I don't have time for your incompetence. Get the fucking leg stitched up and get out of my sight. If they find my errant wife, I will attend to her myself, but somehow I doubt she will turn up," he added with disgust.

The physician pulled the needle through his flesh one last time, finished the stitching, and dressed the wound. He then tossed the remains of the suture kit and the rest of the partially used supplies back into his bag and scurried out of the house like a rat from a drowning ship.

Leonid needed the peace and quiet of his office and the calming influence of his younger brother, who at this point was the only person he trusted or cared about. He slowly made his way to the lush office and looked around it. Something felt off, but he couldn't quite put his finger on what. The mouse by his computer was slightly askew, but he couldn't find anything else out of place. If Vera or Gina had found their way into his sacred space, that would be the final violation.

His carefully designed world was crumbling, brick by brick. In a rare moment of introspection, he wondered if this was what had happened to his father. The demise of his father's reputation all started with one small act of defiance, and now that very same person was at the center of this implosion. There wasn't enough pain in the world to inflict on this *pizda* to right the wrongs she was responsible for.

Chapter Sixteen

The faint hum of the top-of-the-line computers and the clicking of keys on Toni's keyboard were the only sounds in the lab. Dani looked up when the lab doors swung open and was irritated for a moment that the group was coming back into what she felt was predominantly her and Toni's space. A feeling of relief settled in as she watched Kim open the door, juggling a box. The petite woman was freshly showered, as indicated by her wet, slicked-back hair. She was dressed casually in jeans and a T-shirt, but somehow she managed to look elegant. Sophie was a lucky woman. Kim was both kind and beautiful, and she had a kind of quiet, subtle, intelligence that seemed to leak out effortlessly.

"Where is everyone? I brought something healthy for breakfast." Kim set down the box filled with yogurt parfaits on the nearly empty table next to Dani. The cups of yogurt beautifully layered with fresh blueberries, strawberries, and kiwis sat lined up in the box in neat rows. Several spoons lay alongside them.

Dani grabbed one of the healthy treats, scooped up a heaping spoonful and placed it in her mouth. "Conference room," she mumbled.

"Is Val okay?"

"She's in the infirmary. Looks like she's been to hell and back. She looked a bit rattled but insisted on being involved in the extraction." Toni looked up, reached across Dani, and grabbed her own yogurt. "Thanks, Kim. I had some Crunch Berries earlier, but this is so much better for me."

"That sugary crap is gonna kill you someday." Kim shook her head.

"Um...I think we're all in far more danger as a result of our chosen career," Toni wryly added.

"What extraction?" Kim asked.

"Gina got left behind," Dani answered, then focused her attention back on the monitor.

"Gina wasn't with Val?" Kim sat on the corner of the table and picked up her own yogurt.

"Shh. Leonid just came into his office. He looks irritated and...he's looking around like something is amiss. He's limping and has a large bandage on his leg. I'm guessing Sophie found her mark. I'll bet that hurts." Dani laughed.

Toni craned her neck to look at Dani's monitor, and Kim hopped off the table and walked up behind Dani. Dani felt her warm breath and could just barely detect the mint from her toothpaste.

Leonid sat heavily in his chair and pressed his finger against a drawer before opening it. He pulled out his testing kit, pricked his finger, checked the results, and frowned. He grabbed a granola bar from the drawer after pressing his pricked finger on a spot in the center of the keyboard. The monitor came to life, and he moved his face close to a circle

167

that appeared on the screen. He placed his right eye to the screen, a red light blinked, and then he put his left eye in the same spot. A green light blinked, he placed his left thumb against the circle on the monitor, and the red light blinked again. He placed his right index finger on the keyboard. The monitor flashed twice and a wide array of icons Dani had never seen before appeared.

"Wow, that is some security protocol. Only a paranoid bastard would set up something as complicated as that," Toni remarked. "You're getting everything on tape, right?"

Dani nodded and placed her finger against her mouth. She wanted to catch everything he said, even though she knew she would be able to watch it again later. She was grateful Val had managed to place the camera slightly behind the monitor and she could rotate the tiny device to capture a perfect image.

"Activate security protocol alpha 6315, beta 216," Leonid said. The screen changed again, and a new set of icons splashed across it. He pressed on a small picture of a handsome man in his thirties. Dani assumed this was Leonid's brother because of the resemblance.

The screen filled with a live version of the tiny icon. "I am glad you called, brother. I wanted to let you know I've made arrangements and will arrive tomorrow. Do not worry about picking me up from the airport. I would prefer to rent a car. I do like the fast American automobiles. They are enjoyable to drive."

"*Da*, very good. I was hoping your arrival would be soon. Unfortunately, we have a situation. The *sooka* has escaped, and I am waiting to hear about my wife. That *mudak* Antonio has his fingers all over this. I did send him a message. Gina's brother and his whining got very tiresome, so I delivered him to Antonio's doorstep. If I have to hire a new army to swarm his castle, I will. When you arrive, we shall work together to right this wrong. I believe Antonio is working with that *pizda* organization, and perhaps by attacking his home we shall…how does that American saying go?…kill two *sooka*s with one stone."

Alexei laughed. "I think it is two birds, big brother, but I like your version better."

"I want Gina kept alive when we find her."

Alexei raised his eyebrow. "Do not tell me you have a soft spot for your wife now?"

"No. She is carrying my son—at least I hope she is still pregnant. Perhaps our coupling the other night was a bit rough and it is possible she miscarried, but until I know for sure, she will not be harmed. If she miscarried, I suppose it is for the better. I do not wish inferior genes in my son, and if she was unable to endure a bit of rough sex, she is too weak."

"*Da*, that makes sense. I am not anywhere near prepared to marry and have a son, but I will be sure to find someone who will contribute to the strength of our ancestry."

Knock, knock, knock.

Leonid's hand hovered over a glass square on his desk, and a series of red and green lights began to flicker. He moved his left eye, then his right close to the square. "Come," he ordered.

A behemoth of a man stepped close to the desk. "Gina is not in the gardens. We have the dogs tracking her scent."

Leonid leaned back. "I wish an update on this every hour. Understood?"

"*Da*." Sergei nodded.

"Hire replacements for our fallen comrades and double the number of employees. I wish to be prepared. We will find my wife and her *pizda* lover. Go. My brother will arrive tomorrow, and I want a full contingent ready for action."

Taking her attention from the screen, Dani asked, "Do you two mind letting the rest know that Gina escaped and is in the wind right now? I'm still a bit slow." She glanced at the metal leg braces next to the desk.

"I'll go. You two keep watching and focusing on whatever you're working on. We need you here in the lab more than as information runners," Kim answered.

"Thanks, and also we appreciate the healthy breakfast." Toni grinned.

Kim turned and waved over her shoulder. "Gotta keep you two supplied with protein versus sugar. Protein is brain food; ice cream and Crunch Berries aren't."

Dani looked at Toni and laughed when Toni's shrug mirrored her own. They were definitely two peas in a pod. They both returned to their monitors, but despite Toni's intense focus on her own computer, Dani knew she would hear every word uttered in Leonid's office. She was a master multitasker.

†

Kim knocked lightly on the conference room door. She always felt a little out of her element with the rest of the agents. She didn't have any mad computer skills, nor was she an expert fighter, sniper, or munitions expert. All she contributed to the group was her theater knowledge and the ability to transform anyone into a completely different person that not even their own mother would recognize. Sophie had always insisted her set of skills was invaluable to The Organization, particularly her ability to act a part to absolute perfection when called upon, and Maggie had agreed. Still, she felt powerless to help her recalcitrant friend, Val.

They need to add a licensed psychiatrist to the group. That's a skillset that's really needed.

Val stood rigid next to her, quieter than normal if that were possible. Val normally had a small smile for Kim because unlike Sophie, Kim seemed to bring out Val's softer side. Dani always teased that out of her as well, but today Val was particularly surly, and Kim worried about her.

Val was like a quiet sentinel, always doing her job and making sure that if necessary, threats to the other agents were eliminated quickly and efficiently. She'd saved their bacon before, and Kim had no illusions that she'd do it again, but at what cost? Surely Maggie knew Val was slowly unraveling. The signs were subtle, but they were there, and now it looked as if Val seemed to have developed real feelings for Gina. That could either be a blessing or a curse. Right now, she wasn't sure which.

Kim had collected Val before going to the conference room because she wanted to update everyone and knew Val would want the information first. Val hadn't shown much of a reaction, but when Cindy suggested she hang back and get some rest before charging off, her quiet fury came through loud and clear with just one look and a quick "You know I can't do that."

When the door to the conference room opened, Char raised her eyebrow. "News?"

"Dani and Toni sent me to update you on the latest developments."

"Aren't you supposed to be resting, Val? You'll only be a hindrance to us if you're not 100 percent. We'll come get you when we're ready to move and can fill you in on the way," Char said.

Val's only response was a growl.

"Whatever. You, Sophie, and Ronda are all cut from the same female Neanderthal cloth. To think I was beginning to like you." Char waved them inside the room.

Maggie, Antonio, and Ronda sat around the large oval table with two detailed topical maps spread out on the wood. Kim didn't recognize either location, but she was rarely involved in this part of the missions, so she wasn't surprised.

Maggie's eyes lifted to meet Kim's. "Please tell me Gina has managed to escape."

"How'd you know?" Kim asked.

"Antonio is rarely wrong about people. He's placed his faith in her ability to survive, and I believe she had some supplies at her disposal that might have upped the odds," Maggie answered.

Val moved closer to the table and peered at the maps. She pointed to the one on her right. "What's that?"

"That is my compound." Antonio frowned. "I was quite disturbed by Leonid's ability to penetrate my security and dump his gift on my doorstep. I was looking at the building's weaknesses and the possible entry point."

Val nodded. "That's a lot of territory around Leonid's place." She placed her finger on the blue line on the other map. "That's where I would go. The waterway. Can we get a satellite view close enough to detect a person?"

"We can, but so can Leonid. If she's using the waterway, she'll stick close to the edges and travel along the brush. She'll find a way to this road." Antonio placed his finger on the far edge of the map. "We just have to wait until she activates the panic button again, and then we can safely extract her."

"Fuck that. I'm not waiting for Leonid's men or dogs to track her. Maggie, please, we need to send a team in. If you're not willing to send anyone else, I'll go myself."

"I'm in," Ronda interjected.

"Me too," Sophie added.

"Oh what the hell, I've been picking up weight and getting soft with all the inactivity. Count me in," Char said.

Maggie sighed. "Very well. Char, you are team leader. Val, you need to listen to her. She doesn't have the same..." Maggie paused "...distractions you have."

Val barely nodded to indicate her agreement.

"Go get your gear ready. We leave in ten," Char ordered.

Kim ran her hand down Sophie's arm. "Not that I don't love your enthusiasm for the job, but do you really have to volunteer for every risky mission?"

Sophie looked up, and Kim could see the love in her eyes. "I do, but I'm damn impossible to kill. I'll be back. I promise." Sophie pecked her on the lips before jogging out of the room after the rest of the extraction team.

In an uncharacteristic moment of irritation, Kim turned her attention to Antonio. "Gina is your agent. Aren't you going to send some of your resources?"

"They've already been sent." Antonio leaned back in his chair and grinned. "Double the firepower is never a bad idea. We thought the signal was activated, but then it flickered off. To be on the safe side, I sent a team to check things out in the last location we registered the signal." He leaned over the map of the land around Leonid's compound. "The waterway may be her escape route, but the panic button is not waterproof and may either send an inaccurate signal or none at all. We won't be able to track her progress if it is disabled. I've sent my best people, and clearly your best team will have boots on the ground in less than thirty minutes."

Chapter Seventeen

Gina shivered as the dogs' baying grew louder. She fumbled in her bag and took out the gun before dropping it. A thud pierced the air. She was glad the rowboat was wood and not metal. She'd activated the extraction alert and there was no sign of Antonio or anyone else coming to her rescue. She pressed the button again. The device was wet, and she hoped the water hadn't shorted the damn thing out.

It must have gotten wet when I was splashing through the water attempting to throw off the dogs. Dammit.

Where are you? You promised you'd keep me safe. How had she allowed this to happen? One day she and Paulie were working the streets picking pockets and scamming anyone who would fall for what they were selling. She'd found she was a natural at luring men and some women into their trickery by offering them things she and Paulie could not deliver. Often she'd go back to the two-room apartment they rented in a seedy part of town high on the pure joy of fleecing someone.

It was an exhilarating feeling, and one that made Antonio's offer so easy to accept. It was simple, really.

174

Ingratiate herself into Leonid Petrov's life and seduce him into marrying her. She understood that meant having sex with him, but she was never averse to using her body for profit. Leonid wasn't easy to convince, but she loved the rush the game gave her and eventually she won him over.

But when Gina learned that Leonid's business ventures included prostituting and selling girls, his touch repulsed her. Gina was grateful he was a minute man and never stayed after he'd gotten what he wanted. That was, until the night before when he'd beaten her before raping her.

Where are you, Antonio? The sun was rising and she could hear that the dogs were getting closer. She could only hope all her backtracking would confuse them, and their handlers would give up. She heard loud voices and tried to get lower in the boat. With the daylight approaching she needed to stay close to the shoreline where the brush would camouflage her location. She knew Leonid had satellite surveillance with pinpoint accuracy.

Maybe Antonio's organization does too. At least I hope he does. Her situation was dire and she couldn't take any chances on a maybe. She needed a plan if she was going to make it out alive.

†

The leader of Antonio's elite team, Alberto Armani—Al to his friends—held up his hand and signaled for the five-man team to take cover. He crouched in the brush, watched, and listened as two large men with assault weapons slung over their shoulders came crashing through the dense foliage.

"I'm telling you, we have a better chance of survival far away from that crazy son of a bitch. Men are dropping like flies. Haven't you noticed there aren't many of us left?"

"Leonid despises deserters. He will track us down and...." The smaller man with reddish-blond hair shuddered.

"He'll kill us regardless of what we do. You knew when you found that ladder and we realized Gina had flown the coop that our days were numbered. I don't even think Sergei will survive his wrath."

"At least we know she came in this direction." The other man pulled a pack of cigarettes from his pocket and lit one with a trembling hand. "Mexico sounds good to me. Do you think your brother can help us leave the country?"

"It's our only chance. I wish we'd found her; then we'd be heroes." He shook his head. "I think it's only another mile, maybe less to the road, then if our luck holds up, we can flag a ride."

"Not with these guns. Nobody's gonna stop with AK-47s hanging off our shoulders."

"I'm not giving up the only chance we have against whoever else Leonid has working for him until we're on the blacktop. We can lose the guns when we get to the road and not one second before that."

"Good point. Come on, let's get a move on. If we're lucky, he hasn't discovered his wife's absence yet and we have a bit more time."

"I doubt it. Don't you hear the dogs?"

"They're always like that. He has over twenty of the nasty little beasts, and a whole contingent of them that patrol the perimeter with their handlers."

"All the more reason for us to get to that damn road and get the fuck away from this whole mess."

Al watched the two men pass, then nodded to his team. He checked his GPS.

"The target should be fifty yards ahead," he said into his commlink. "Spread out, and when you're near the water, take up defensive positions." He hoped Gina had been the one who'd discovered the missing rowboat. He didn't really want to take down the dogs, but they could be a damn nuisance if he didn't. Oddly enough, he didn't share the hesitation about eliminating their handlers.

When they were in view of the small cove, Al watched as the team stopped, scattered, and blended in with the dense underbrush. He crouched on the ground, inwardly cursing when he heard the snick of the branch. *You'd think I was an amateur.* He took out his binoculars and looked at the boat. The water around it was still, and no one appeared to be inside. He checked the coordinates again and confirmed the signal had come from the rowboat, then he saw the water ripple slightly.

"Mark, two hundred yards west, target is in the boat. Circle around and come at the boat from the east. Assume she is armed," he whispered into his commlink.

†

Exhausted, Gina had nodded off, but her eyes opened at what sounded like a twig snapping. She held the gun next to her cheek, wanting to peek out from under her cover but knew better than to give her location away. She took a breath and waited, gripping the gun tighter. Because she'd dozed off, she worried the boat had drifted into the middle of the lake, which would make her a sitting duck for sure. If they were coming for her, she'd fight and kill as many as she could and save one bullet for herself—that was her only option.

†

Al turned when he heard the barking just behind them. He watched as ten dogs scampered frantically onto the

177

campground with their noses to the ground. They loped toward the water then away from it, only to rush back at a frenzied pace. Yapping incessantly, they continued running in circles. Al smiled, realizing Gina was responsible for the dogs' confusion. His attention turned to a tall goliath of a man who fired a shot in the air.

"Stop. She's in the water. Spread out and find her."

Al knew it was only a matter of time before they found the rowboat. He looked at the water and saw that Mark was closing in on the boat.

"Mark, stay away from the boat until we can take care of Leonid's men. The last thing we want is for her to scream."

"Roger."

"I count seven men. Close in and take them out as quietly as you can," he said into the commlink.

Al saw a tall man coming his way. He waited for him to pass before he sprung out, put a hand over his mouth, and twisted his neck.

"Hey, who are you?" someone shouted from behind him.

With one smooth, flawless motion, Al spun and threw his knife into the man's chest.

His team dispatched the rest of Leonid's men in hand-to-hand combat. Meanwhile, the dogs still frantically searched for the scent.

Leonid must be scraping the bottom of the barrel if that's the best he has. "Mark, go ahead and get the package," Al said.

✝

Gina heard what sounded like a battle, then she felt the boat rock slightly and heard the water lapping against it. They'd found her, and she readied herself for a fight.

No way will I let them take me.

She sprang up holding the gun with two hands and pointed it at a camouflaged man in the water several feet away from the boat.

"Stop. I'm with Antonio." The man raised his hands. "I'm one of the good guys."

Gina glared at him. The man didn't look like one of Leonid's men, but at this point she wasn't taking any chances. "How do I know you're telling the truth?"

"I'm Mark, and Antonio sent a team after you activated the panic button. Right now, we're waiting for a helicopter to pick you up."

In the distance, Gina heard the familiar sound of helicopter rotors. She wanted to look up but wouldn't take that chance and held the gun steady. "Do I wait here or row to the shore?"

"Al, where is the extraction point?"

Gina looked at the shore and saw a man she recognized from one of her meetings with Antonio. She sighed in relief.

At the sound of rapid gunfire, Mark yelled, "Get down."

She didn't waste any time crouching in the boat.

Mark hung on to the side of it with his gun at the ready. "Roger that." He lowered his gun. "We need to get you to the campground. Extracting you from here will make you a target when they raise you up. Can you get there?"

"Yes."

The sound of the helicopter was louder as she rowed in earnest, hoping to make a clean getaway. By the time she reached the campground, the helicopter had already landed and a man was hurrying toward her.

"Quickly. We saw a group of men heading this way."

Gina kept her head down and ran for the helicopter, got in, and barely had time to sit in a jump seat before they were in the air. She looked down and saw a group of Leonid's men firing their guns at the helicopter while running toward them. The helicopter banked to the right and within seconds was out of range. The men who had rescued her were vastly outnumbered but began firing on the newcomers anyway.

"We need to go back for them," she shouted to the pilot.

"Don't worry about them, ma'am. They'll be okay." He grinned. "We have a secret weapon."

Gina heard a loud explosion and saw most of Leonid's men fall. Coming from the road was another group, and Gina recognized one of them when the figure lost its hat.

"Vera."

†

Sophie wasn't going fast enough for Val's comfort. She worried that after the beating Gina had taken, she'd be at a disadvantage against Leonid's men and his dogs.

"Can't you push the speed a little more?" Val asked.

Sophie glanced into the rearview mirror and glared. "Nobody likes a backseat driver, Val."

The phone propped on the middle console began to ring through the car's speaker system. Sophie pushed the button on her steering wheel to answer it.

"Hello, love. What's up? Kinda busy here telling Val to stop being an ass."

"Antonio failed to provide a key piece of information," Kim said. "After you all left, he enlightened us. Apparently he sent a team in to extract Gina after they received the first signal. It sounds like they might have located her, but Leonid's men are also en route. Our satellite shows a small rowboat and a lot of different men milling about. I don't think we can distinguish who is who at this point. How far away are you?"

"We're almost to the edge of the north side of his property, the part that's closest to the main road."

"Good, that's where the action is," Kim answered.

The cacophony of sounds overwhelmed Val before she could distinguish the distinct *whup whup whup* of helicopter propellers, the *rat-tat-tat* of gunfire, and the shouts of men.

Sophie screeched to a stop.

Kaboom!

The car had barely stopped when Val scrambled out, looked up at the helicopter, and ran for the heavy brush. "Come on, get your asses moving. They might need our help," she yelled over her shoulder.

Her AK-47 kept slipping from her shoulder as she ran, and her hat flipped off in the wind she generated as she hurried into the melee. The small team descended on the fight, and Val quickly assessed which were her targets and picked off two men about to fire on Antonio's team. She swept her gaze from left to right, looking for other threats, and when the only sound that remained was her footsteps on the soft ground, she stopped to take in the destruction. She wondered why the blood and gore from the bodies littering the forest didn't cause her the least bit of discomfort.

Blinking, Val turned to the largest man, whose face was painted black and green. "Where's Gina?"

181

"Safely in the copter. Are you ready for a beer now? I am." The gigantic warrior grinned.

Val surprised herself when she laughed. "Rain check."

Sophie walked over and stood next to Val. "Where's the copter going?"

"Antonio's got a private helipad at his complex."

"Where's your wheels?" Sophie asked.

"Just around the bend close to the road."

Val was anxious for Gina to be in a secure place. In her mind, that meant The Organization's hub, not Antonio's estate. She pointed to the large man. "You're with us. Take us to the complex and we'll collect Gina."

"Those aren't my orders."

Char walked over and leveled her cold gaze on him. "They are now. Check with Antonio if you must, but I'd prefer to get moving soon."

The man seemed to consider the order and shrugged. "What the hell, riding with a bunch of smelly men or…some beautiful badass women. Not even a contest."

Chapter Eighteen

A knock at his door had Leonid looking up. "Come," he called. He had been expecting the report on Gina's capture and wasn't surprised to see a bloodied and wounded Sergei enter the room. "So, you have her?"

"Sir, um, wwwwe...ran into a problem. Everyone is dead."

Leonid stood and slammed his hand on the desk. "But you're still alive," he growled. "Tell me why that is, Sergei."

"I was in the initial group, and when we got to where the tracking device said she was, others were already there. They took us all out. I remember hearing the dogs before I passed out. I woke and I heard the sound of a helicopter just before an explosion took out most of the remaining men. After that a group of women came at us. We didn't have a chance."

"Again, why are you still alive?"

"I crawled most of the way back here to tell you what happened. Gina is gone."

Leonid came around his desk and stood toe-to-toe with his most trusted guard. "My wife is gone, many of my men are dead, but you are still alive." He kicked Sergei in the knee, making him fall. "I put you in charge of bringing her back to me, and you failed me. You know the punishment for that, don't you?"

Sergei nodded.

"Fail me again and you will pay the price. Now go get cleaned up. You look disgusting. Once you've done that, hire more men, find Gina, and bring her back to me." He fixed Sergei with a cold glare. "Is that clear?"

It took every ounce of willpower Leonid had not to kill Sergei on the spot. He needed Sergei to build his force back up, so he would not kill him now. But they both knew it was only a matter of time before he did.

"Yes."

Leonid could see the fear in Sergei's eyes. "Start by invading Antonio's stronghold. Now get out."

After Sergei left, Leonid went to the window. Everyone thought his world was crumbling now, but he knew better. When his brother arrived they would be a force to be reckoned with.

†

Val squirmed in the backseat of the SUV. "Jesus Christ, my grandma drove faster than you."

"Shut the fuck up, Val. You don't have a grandma," Sophie responded.

Val crossed her arms across her chest. "How the hell do you know anything about my family? I could have a grandma."

"Maggie pulled your punk ass off the streets. No grandma hanging around. We'll get there in plenty of time to collect your girlfriend." Sophie flipped the visor down after careening around a bend only to find the bright sunlight blinding her. She gripped the wheel tighter.

"She's not my girlfriend," Val grumbled.

"You sure act like she is. Ya know…since you're all hell-bent on rescuing her even though she's not one of us," Ronda interjected.

"Leave her alone." Char turned her head to first glare at Sophie, then at Ronda for a disapproving look.

Mark chuckled. "You guys sound a lot like my squad, but I'll bet you always have each other's backs."

"Who told you it was time to contribute to the conversation?" Ronda made a fist and pounded his leg.

"Ouch. What did ya do that for?"

Ronda grinned. "Just felt like it."

"Shit. Probably some dumbass looking at his cell phone again and everyone else has to rubberneck to try to find the gore." Sophie pushed the visor up. The car decelerated to a creeping speed as the line of cars ahead slowed.

"I told you to take the back roads. You know the highway is always a crapshoot, especially at this time of day," Ronda interjected.

"Shut up, Ronda. Just what I don't need, stereo backseat drivers." Sophie smacked the steering wheel. "God damn it. We're going to be caught in this for hours."

"Good thing I'm prepared." Char leaned forward, rifled through her bag, and pulled out what looked like a portable police siren. "Toni rigged this up for me a few weeks ago. She knows how much I hate waiting in traffic. We won't be flying down the highway, but at least we'll be able to navigate through this little cluster on the shoulder and be on our way."

"Okay, the little shit gets a free pass next time she raids my freezer," Val said. "Now slap that device on the roof and let's get a move on. I wouldn't put it past Leonid to send an army to Antonio's place. He won't take this lying down." She leaned forward and whispered, "Thanks, Char."

Maggie wasn't sure how she felt about Antonio's offhand comment that he'd already sent a team. She may not have authorized her resources if she'd known. Unnecessarily risking her agents wasn't something to get into the habit of doing. Granted, Val probably would have insisted on going whether or not Antonio had sent his team, but Maggie wasn't happy about Antonio holding back that information until her team departed.

She turned her attention to him. "I would have preferred to know that tidbit a bit earlier."

Antonio placed his hands together in a loose steeple gesture. "I wanted to ensure success, and with the combination of your elite crew and my men—"

Maggie sighed. "Antonio, if we are to trust you and work together, information must flow freely at all times. We cannot function independently from one another and achieve success."

"Exactly. I believe it was necessary to send both teams to Leonid's compound to ensure success."

"That is a decision to make jointly, not under duress because all of the information is not on the table. Don't disappoint me again. Otherwise I'll think we're back to where we were twenty years ago. I will accept nothing less than a partnership."

Antonio nodded. "My apologies. You, of course, are right. Old habits die hard. I suppose I need a good dressing down every once in a while, and you, my dear, are just the woman to do it. You must know I do have the upmost respect for you and your team. I anticipate they will wrap up the extraction soon. They've been instructed to bring Gina to my house."

Maggie frowned. "Antonio, I hope you don't take this the wrong way, but considering Leonid sent you a gruesome message, I don't believe your compound is as secure as our hub."

"No offense taken and I agree, but my place has a helipad and yours does not. I propose we go there now in anticipation of Gina's arrival, and then if you don't mind, I believe you are right and she'd be much safer here."

"I have a few more agents I can send with you, but my talents are not at the same level. I can take care of myself in a pinch, yet I suspect I won't be of much help if there is an all-out battle," Maggie clarified.

Antonio smiled. "I am more than happy to go alone. I only suggested *we* lest I offend you again. I know this sounds sexist of me, but I would prefer that you not accompany me. I do know, only too well, how good you are at taking care of yourself, but you are too precious to place on Leonid's radar."

"Hmmm, you certainly have a charming way of explaining your sexism. Please keep me informed of you and your team's progress."

†

Time was not on Sergei's side and he did not have the luxury of weighing his options. With a few quick calls, he'd shifted the men who were taking care of the merchandise onto a strike team. He knew that might leave that part of Leonid's operations more vulnerable, but the young women, if you could call them women, were so beaten down, he didn't believe it was a risk.

Sergei limped to the heavily reinforced Hummer and raced to meet up with the team. He was a loyal soldier by nature, but his loyalty to Leonid had limits. He was a dead man either way, so if the team wasn't able to bring Gina back, Sergei decided he was not about to stick around to feel Leonid's wrath. He'd already packed a bag and stuffed it into the vehicle. The only sane option was to plan on disappearing, depending on what transpired in the next couple of hours.

Having been the one to personally deposit Paulie on Antonio's doorstep, he had a good knowledge of the lay of the land and knew exactly where the helicopter would touch down. He didn't hold out any hope that they would be able to intercept the helicopter when it touched down. It was faster and had at least a half hour head start. Assuming that they would shuttle Gina into the mansion wasn't a stretch. If that were the case, they would need to use brute force to remove her from Antonio's protection.

We're screwed. There's no way this small force can do that.

✝

Toni was breathing heavily when she burst into the conference room. "They got her out and Leonid sent people over to Antonio's to invade his place. I'm assuming Gina is on her way there."

"Yes, Antonio just called with an update and so did Char," Maggie answered. "Everyone will converge on Antonio's compound. I'm waiting for additional news. You can either sit here with me or go back to the lab and continue to monitor Leonid with Dani."

"You know, Maggie, I don't know whether to applaud you or fear you. There's not a hair out of place on your head and you delivered that response as if you'd just informed me that we were having turkey for dinner."

Maggie raised her brow. "Do not ever misunderstand my absence of hysteria for apathy. Nothing could be further from the truth. Excess worry and emotion never adds to the strength of an operation."

"Okaaay. Um… I think I'll just head back to the lab and wait with Dani. Will you come and give us an update, please? There are people I care very much about putting their asses on the line, and I guess given the fact that things don't always go as planned when people are shooting at you, I do get a little emotional." Toni spun on her heel and walked to the door.

"Toni," Maggie called out.

Toni turned her head.

"There is nothing wrong with emotion. We are all wired a little differently, and that is a good thing."

Toni smiled before she left the conference room. The saying "still waters run deep" danced through her head and she was glad Maggie was on their side. She suspected that no matter the situation, Maggie was two or three steps ahead. Toni was exceptional at chess, but Maggie was better.

†

Val heard the distinctive sound of machine gun fire before the SUV came to a complete stop.

Mark leaned over her and grabbed the door handle before she had a chance to burst out into the chaos. "Don't be stupid. We need to get our bearings before we get our asses shot off. A dead hero is still dead and can't rescue the fair maiden from six feet under."

189

"He's right," Ronda added. "I'll lay some cover fire, but stay low to the ground. On the count of three, go. One, two, three, go, go, go."

Ronda rolled out of the car, guns blazing as the rest of her team scrambled out and into the war zone.

Val didn't know where to aim. She wondered if war was a lot like this and if more people were killed by friendly fire than the government ever admitted to. She tried to pick out Leonid's men, but she honestly couldn't be sure who was who, so she aimed to take them out of commission without killing them. This sudden tendency to placate her guilty conscience for executing someone who didn't deserve it was a mystery. She didn't have time to examine it like a bug under a microscope, but it did cause a bit of discomfort. Val knew she was making assumptions, but she spared the men who looked Mediterranean her bullets, while the Slavic-looking men earned some well-placed shots.

By the time a Hummer rolled into the compound, the shots had all but ended and the vehicle had more than a dozen guns pointed at the windows. Ronda had already strategically shot out both back tires.

Val recognized the Hummer even though she couldn't see who was inside through the heavily tinted windows. She strolled to the driver's-side window and smashed it with the butt of her gun.

"Hello, Sergei. Welcome to the party. You know, I don't remember sending you an invitation. If you so much as twitch the wrong way, I'll shoot your tiny dick off. Get out." Val took a step back with her gun pointed at him.

Sergei sneered. "Go ahead and try to shoot me." He pointed his gun at Val. "Maybe I'll shoot you first. Either way he's coming for you."

190

"He won't be happy if you kill me." Sergei's finger twitched. "Look around. All your men are wounded or dead and you're surrounded. Not very good odds."

The sound of a bullet rang out and the gun fell from Sergei's hand.

"Get out now," Val ordered.

Sergei slowly emerged from the vehicle holding his bleeding hand, his expression defiant. Val resisted the urge to shoot him between the eyes and be done with him. She wanted to send a message to Leonid, and Sergei was the perfect messenger.

Sergei stood rigidly beside the Hummer. "Go ahead and shoot me. I'm a dead man anyway."

Val shook her head. "I really don't understand your loyalty to that psychopath...never mind, I think I'll deliver the message myself." She glanced at Ronda, who stepped up beside her and smirked as she pointed her own gun at Sergei.

Val opened the door to the Hummer and found what she was looking for—Sergei's phone. She roughly grabbed Sergei's hand and pressed his thumb against the button to access the device. She scrolled to the contact she was looking for and pressed the Call button.

"I'm coming for you, Leonid. There isn't a rock large enough for you to crawl under. Consider this call Gina's notification of her intent to divorce you, although I told her that was unnecessary because you don't really need to divorce a dead man." Val pushed the button to end the call, threw the phone on the ground, and crushed it with her boot.

When she looked up she saw Antonio's smiling face and asked, "Where's Gina?"

†

Leonid resisted the urge to hurl the damn phone at the wall. Sergei's failure would have resulted in the ultimate discipline, so he wasn't disturbed by Sergei's capture and probable death, but not having the vessel for his heir was an unacceptable outcome.

He hadn't made it this far by letting small setbacks get in the way. After all, the long game was where Leonid excelled. When he joined Alexi, nothing could stop him. In the meantime, attending to his business was of paramount importance. It was time to check on his various assets. Each piece of merchandise was worth hundreds of thousands of dollars, and it was time again to move both the human and financial holdings.

He scrolled through his list of contacts before pressing a button to connect him with Gregor—his new second-in-command. Gregor's current role in the organization was controlling the human merchandise, which he excelled at. When Gregor didn't pick up after four rings, Leonid's frustration grew.

"I am surrounded by incompetents," he announced to an empty room. He turned his attention to his computer and went through the complicated security procedures he'd set up before he began moving his vast financial resources all over the world, like scattering seeds in the wind. The final measures would require his brother's biological signature, a special surprise he'd set up for anyone who managed to break the codes. After learning about the clever way the *sooka*s had destroyed Viktor, he wasn't taking any chances.

†

When Toni returned to the lab, she saw Dani's Cheshire cat grin and knew there was another development. "What are you smiling at?"

Dani clasped her hands behind her head. "It's all on tape. Chalk one up for the good guys. I do believe Leonid just received a very disturbing call, and if I know my sister and the rest of the team, I'd say they just delivered a crucial blow to his operations. He's running scared and just delivered to our very high-quality camera the complicated security procedures and keystrokes that we'll need to unravel his vast resources. There's only a few strokes we might have to experiment with because the angle was a little off to see clearly."

"Do you think Maggie will want to hit him right away?" Toni asked.

"Nah, she's a planner, patient and rational, never letting her emotions get in the way. She'll want to strategize for every possible contingency. It's what makes her the best. Besides, I imagine she'll want to serve up a final disposition to his brother, Alexei. Remember, she doesn't like to cut off the head of the snake when the damn thing can just grow back another."

Toni nodded. "I'm glad. I think Val needs a little R and R, and I know she'll want to be in the thick of things."

Dani lost her smile. "I'm really worried about her. She looked like shit, more so than any other time I've seen her come back from a mission. Do you think it will help to have Gina here with her, or is that going to be the final thing that unravels her?"

Toni shrugged. "Don't know. Love is a powerful thing, and from what Sophie says, our little psychopath might have fallen in love."

"Don't call her that! You don't have a clue about what she's gone through." Dani sat forward in her chair and glared at Toni.

Toni put her hands out. "Sorry, I was just kidding. So, you know her story?"

193

"Not all of it, but I've pieced a few things together. Underneath all that bluster is a very fragile spirit. She'd give her life for any one of us."

"I know. I'm sorry, really I am. Even when she's being...well...typical brash Val...I like her because I do sense the purity of her actions. I know Char loves her like a sister, and that's always been good enough for me. Char's a great judge of character; after all, she picked me." Toni grinned.

Dani shook her head. "Beautiful and humble, how could she resist?"

"I know."

Chapter Nineteen

Val needed to see for herself that Gina was all right. She nearly sighed in relief as Gina ran toward her.

"Vera, is it really you?" She stepped closer.

Val didn't care how much grief she got from her team. She pulled Gina against her in a desperate embrace. After they broke apart, Val gently trailed her hand down Gina's battered face. "Come on, let's get you back to the complex. Cindy will fix you right up."

"Not yet, I want to look at you." Gina ran her hand over Val's beaten body. "Did he do this to you?"

"I'm fine, nothing a pint of Ben and Jerry's won't fix right up." Val grinned and turned to look at her team, who stood gawking at her. "What are you all looking at? Get the damn SUV and let's get the hell out of here."

Gina clung to Val's arm. "Where are we going? I'm afraid he'll find me," she whimpered.

Val clasped her hand and intertwined their fingers while steering her toward the vehicle. "I promise you that he'll never find us, and even if he manages to stumble anywhere near the complex, Ronda has so many nasty booby traps that I almost wish he'd try. I'd love to see one of her bombs blow his dick off."

Char slung her arm over Gina's shoulder. "We all have your back, Gina. You won't find a better group of women to protect you than our motley crew."

Trembling, Gina smiled. "Thank you. If you're anything like Vera, then I know I'll be safe."

"I'm sorry, Gina. My name isn't Vera, it's Val."

Gina had a puzzled look on her face. "Val? Hmm, I never thought you looked like a Vera. It didn't fit you at all. I like Val. It's a strong name."

The five women hurried to the armored SUV, and Val helped Gina ease her broken body inside. She ignored her own pain and focused on making sure Gina was comfortable in the backseat while the rest of the crew filled in the empty spaces. Val wasn't about to give Sophie any grief for taking it slow because she imagined Gina would feel every bump in the road.

†

When the SUV pulled up to the nondescript building, Gina turned to Val. "This is it? This is where you'll keep me safe? It doesn't look very secure."

Ronda chuckled. "That's what makes it such a great hub. Deceiving, isn't it? There's an impressive underground structure, complete with all the amenities you're accustomed to—although admittedly they are on a smaller scale."

Ever since Leonid had beaten and raped her, Gina was running on fumes. Her escape from the compound had been harrowing, and no matter how much these women told her that she'd be safe, she had a hard time believing them. Compared to Leonid's compound, this run-down cabin didn't seem secure to her at all. "If you say so."

Val squeezed her hand. "Trust me."

Gina placed her hand over Val's and felt a wave of peace fill her. "I trusted you from the first time I laid eyes on you. Please show me."

Val helped her get out of the car and led her into the rustic cabin with the overgrown foliage spilling along the worn brick path. "First stop will be the infirmary, and then we can figure out where you'll be bunking."

"With you, I hope." Gina winked. "I won't feel safe anywhere else." She was trembling as the events of the last eleven hours came crashing down around her. Suddenly the world was whirling and she was finding it difficult to stay upright. She grabbed Val's arm. "I think I'm going to…," she said before falling into Val.

†

Val rushed into the infirmary with Gina unconscious in her arms. Val wasn't the panicking type, but her heart pounded as she tried to figure out what had caused Gina's sudden turn for the worse.

She imagined she was wild-eyed as she looked for the medic. When her gaze landed on Cindy's serene brown eyes, Val rushed to her. "She just passed out. I don't know what happened, but Leonid beat her up pretty bad and she's had a very rough morning. She's going to be all right. Isn't she?"

Cindy gently took Gina's wrist. "Her pulse is slow. What happened before she passed out?"

Val was frustrated. She didn't have a good answer. "I don't know, you're the professional. She was just talking, and then she went limp."

"Okay. Move away and let me check her out." Cindy took the stethoscope from around her neck and listened to Gina's heart before hooking her up to a monitor. She looked

197

at the readouts. "Slow heartbeat, low blood pressure, possible dehydration, and unresponsive…severe trauma is a likely cause."

Beads of sweat were forming on Val's brow. Ironically, as Gina's heart rate slowed, hers became more rapid. "Come on, you have to heal her. You always fix me when I get banged up," she pleaded, attempting to control the panic rising in her. "She's pregnant," Val whispered.

"Shit. That puts a whole new spin on things. I'd better take some blood and get it analyzed. How far along is she?"

"I don't know if she's still pregnant after Leonid's beating…."

"Listen, Val, I'll take good care of her. If need be I can call in a doctor, but let's first give her a few more minutes. I see her heartrate is increasing, so I expect her to be conscious soon." She patted Val's hand. "Does that sound like a plan to you?"

Val took Gina's hand and looked at her pasty-white face. She felt out of control, but when Gina's eyes slowly opened and she groaned, Val knew no army in the universe could get her to move from the spot next to Gina. "Hey, beautiful, glad you decided to wake up from your nap."

"What happened?" Gina asked. "Where am I?"

"Things were starting to become too boring for you, so you checked out for a little bit. Cindy's our nurse practitioner, and she patches us all up when we decide to stick our noses into something that others might not appreciate. I'll stay right here while she does her magic."

Tears trickled down Gina's cheeks. "Don't leave me. Please, don't leave me."

Val sat in the chair next to the bed. "Not a chance, you're stuck with me now. I'm like superglue."

"I like the sound of that." Gina closed her eyes and fell into what looked like a restful sleep.

†

Maggie had decided to wait for the team's return in the privacy of her own domicile at the farthest end of the complex. She didn't feel guilty about choosing the largest three-room setup for herself, and none of the other agents seemed to mind either. Maggie enjoyed her creature comforts.

Antonio had been hinting for several days that he wanted Maggie to move to his estate, and she had to admit the offer was very tempting. After the situation with Leonid and Alexei was resolved, she thought she might be able to give the proposition serious consideration. The Organization had kept a low profile ever since dismantling Viktor Borsky's empire, and she was confident that after taking care of Leonid and his brother, they wouldn't be on anyone's radar.

They would still have work to do, but she could manage that anywhere and didn't necessarily feel the need to reside at the central complex anymore. Yes, it was an extremely alluring offer. She hadn't lost her love for Antonio although he could still push her buttons sometimes with his opposing views on the world. She was older now and could not only accept, but perhaps appreciate those differences.

Antonio sat to her right sipping his second Americano of the day. Maggie was nibbling on a pastry when she heard the quiet knock on her door. She stood and swung it open and motioned Char inside.

Char looked unscathed, and Maggie assumed the extraction had gone well and everyone was settled back in the complex unharmed. "I presume everything unfolded

199

smoothly. Would you like some coffee or tea, or perhaps a fancier beverage? Antonio has managed to tame the elaborate espresso machine Dani purchased for me last Christmas. I'm sure he can make you a latte or Americano."

"Actually I think I'll have one of your special teas. Thanks, Maggie. Yes, everything went well. I'm confident we've very nearly decimated Leonid's ranks. Dani has most of the information needed to access the majority of his accounts, but I suspect you'll want to wait until his brother arrives. We have one small wrinkle, though, and I don't know the extent of the concern just yet." Char took the empty seat in front of the tea set and helped herself to a package of orange spice tea from the ornate wooden box.

Maggie frowned. "Please continue."

"Shortly after we arrived at the complex, Gina fainted and Val took her to the infirmary—"

"Oh dear, that must have rattled Val." Maggie picked up the teapot and poured hot water into Char's cup.

Char smiled. "Yeah, we're all seeing a side of the ice queen that we haven't ever seen before. Cindy is taking very good care of Gina, and it might just be dehydration combined with the trauma she's been through in the last day, but Val mentioned that she's pregnant."

Maggie nodded. "Mmm, that is a bit of a complication. The complex is Val's comfort zone, so she won't want to leave, but this is no place to raise a child. As far as seeing a softer side of Val, she only shows that side to your sister, Kim, and Kimiko. She'd never show her weakness to another alpha."

"Oh, is that what I am? An alpha?" Char chuckled.

"Most definitely." Maggie glanced over at Antonio. "You're being awfully quiet there. I suppose we should all go to the infirmary and see how Gina is doing. Of course, we can finish our tea and coffee first. I don't think a delay of a few minutes will make much of a difference."

†

Maggie walked briskly down the corridor and quietly entered the makeshift medical unit. Cindy was sitting at her desk quietly typing on her computer and looked up when the trio entered. She glanced over at Val and Gina and placed her finger to her lips.

Maggie smiled when she saw Val's head next to Gina's on the bed as their hands remained clasped. She walked to Cindy and whispered, "How are they?"

"I'd rather Val have her own bed to sleep on, but at least she's getting some rest. Gina probably has several broken ribs and the hematomas are very severe, but I don't believe she has any internal damage or that her lungs are punctured. The most important thing at this point is for her to receive fluids and rest. I'll do a more complete workup shortly, but I can't do one with the leech attached." Cindy smiled. "Val has decided to, and I quote, 'stick to her like superglue.'"

"I heard she might be pregnant," Maggie said.

"Oh yeah, there is that. I won't know until the bloodwork is analyzed. I'm afraid that even if she was pregnant, with the beating she took, she might have lost the baby."

The rustling of sheets caused Maggie to look over at the two injured women.

Val's head popped up and she blinked a few times. "We aren't planning to launch a final assault yet, are we?"

"No, nothing like that. Val, I know you want to stay with Gina, but I need you to be completely rested and healed when we make our move. You need to let Cindy do her job and conduct a complete examination. She can't do that with you in the way. After she's done, if you insist on remaining close to Gina, we can assign her to your quarters. That will actually work out well because we don't have an open space at this complex."

"I made a promise and I don't break my promises," Val ground out.

Maggie ignored Val's angry response. "I understand Gina may be pregnant. For the short term, this can certainly be her home, but the complex is no place to raise a child—"

"Bullshit. I grew up here, and what about Kimiko?" Val glared at Maggie.

"Through the years, I've brought teenagers here, but never young children. Kimiko had nowhere to go when we found her last year. You've both had the experience of adulthood being thrust on you at an early age. Surely you would not wish to force those same realities on a child," Maggie explained.

Gina began to stir. "Where am I?" She looked at Val and clutched her hand tighter.

Cindy approached the bedside. "How are you feeling right now?"

"I'm a bit groggy and sore."

Cindy smiled and patted Gina's free hand. "That's to be expected." She turned her focus to Val. "I need to do a more thorough examination, and you people are cramping my style. I need every last one of you to go find some bad guys to beat up and leave us be. Val, I promise when I'm done we can transfer her care to you. I'm assuming you'll allow her to bunk with you."

Val's eyes swiveled to Gina's.

"I don't like hospitals and want to get out of here." Gina moved to get up.

Val gently held her back. "Whoa, I don't like hospitals either, but the sooner we let Cindy have her way, the sooner you can break free, and then I'll take you to my place and get you settled."

"Wonderful." Cindy pointed to the door. "Okay, everyone, out." She turned back to Gina. "I promise this will be quick. I just need a little blood from you and a few X-rays and to let you take a shower. Once that's done I'll call Val to come get you."

Gina scratched her head. "I could use a shower. My body feels like it has creepy-crawlies everywhere."

†

Gina looked around the rather sparsely decorated room, then back at Val. "You must have been overwhelmed by how the rooms were decorated at Leonid's place." She grinned. "'Minimalist' comes to mind here."

"Yeah, well, I've never been one for collecting things. It just gets in the way."

"Hmm. You said you lived on the streets when you were growing up too?" She moved to within an inch of Val. "That home of his overwhelmed me, but I had to play the part or die."

Val tilted her head and scrutinized her. "Come on, I promised Cindy I'd take good care of you. I may not have many belongings, but my bed is extremely comfortable. It's the one item I did splurge on. I don't really have a guest bedroom, because I've never needed one, so...." Val's face turned a lovely shade of red.

"I didn't expect anything other than staying with you. Will that be a problem for you?"

203

"Oh…um…no…I didn't mean to suggest anything…um…we don't ever bring guests to the complex…that wasn't what I meant…," Val sputtered.

Gina looked at Val's lips and lightly touched them with her fingers. "I've dreamed of you." She leaned in and kissed Val.

Val succumbed to the kiss as she explored Gina's enticing mouth. She stretched her arms around Gina and pulled her close. The overwhelming feeling of love as she embraced Gina began to cause mild panic, and she broke away before they headed down a road she wasn't prepared to take.

"We need to stop. I…uh…come on, let me show you to my room."

"I don't understand. I thought this is what you wanted." Gina turned away with confusion written on her face. "Sure, why don't you show me the room." She took a step backward. "I can't wait." Her tone was icy.

Val grabbed her hand and turned her back around. "I'm sorry, I suck at this. Most everyone tells me my social skills are shit. Look, I'd like nothing more than to take you to bed, but not now, not like this while you're all battered and bruised. Cindy says there's not much she can do for broken ribs, but I know how much they hurt, and bedroom gymnastics definitely don't help. God, you are so irresistible, and if you push just a bit more, I won't be able to stop, and that wouldn't be right."

"I wasn't asking you to stop. Since I've been with Leonid, I've learned to live with pain. I know you'll be gentle with me." She pulled Val to her and kissed her again.

Yielding to Gina would be so easy, but she couldn't let Gina's impulsivity get in the way of what Val knew was the right thing to do. She pushed her away again. "So, so tempting, but just between you and me, Cindy is the real badass in this troupe, and frankly she scares the crap out of me. I'll come to bed with you because I could use the rest, but no hanky-panky. Come on." Val took Gina's hand and pulled her toward the bedroom.

"Fine, but I can't guarantee I'll be able to keep my hands to myself." She shrugged. "I guess I am tired too, and you certainly look like you're dead on your feet." She squeezed Val's hand. "Come on, show me the rest of your place."

"Do you want me to find you something to sleep in?"

Gina smirked. "I sleep in the nude."

Val laughed. "T-shirt and shorts it is." She led Gina to her bedroom and pulled an oversized, plain, black T-shirt and a pair of loose gym shorts from her pine dresser and tossed them to Gina.

"What, you're afraid of seeing me naked?"

"Yes, yes, I am." Val smiled. "Please have pity on me and put on the sleepwear."

Gina took the offered clothes. She lifted her shirt over her head, and after unzipping her jeans, she dropped them to the floor. Her boots were a bit more obstinate as she pulled on them and set them aside. She yawned. "I think I will sleep for a while," she said before putting the shorts and T-shirt on.

Val groaned and turned her head away from Gina, but only after getting a good look at her. "I'm a fucking saint," she mumbled. *I sure hope good karma comes my way for not taking what is clearly being offered to me.*

Gina crawled under the sheets. "Are you going to join me?"

Val stripped down to a T-shirt and underwear and slipped under the covers. She brought her long arms around Gina's body and sighed as Gina's head found its way to her chest. Soon her eyes closed and she surrendered to sleep.

†

Val smiled in her sleep as her dream began to take shape. She pulled Gina tighter against her as the blurry edges began to emerge.

The blonde street urchin with the smudge on her cheek kept moving, making items appear and disappear. The crowd gathered, and she spied a skinny, fair-haired girl hanging around at the edges of the cluster of tourists.

The young magician winked at the new-to-the-streets youngster, who smiled in response. She pulled a fake bouquet of flowers from out of nowhere and pushed through the crowd to hand them to her admirer.

"For you, beautiful lady," she said with a thick Russian accent, and the girl blushed. "When's the last time you had a meal?" she whispered in her ear.

The newbie shrugged.

"Show's over," the seasoned ragamuffin announced. "What's your name?" She grabbed the hat full of money and took the girl's arm.

"Gigi."

"I'm Val. Come on, let's get you some food. I can almost see your ribs poking through your rags."

"I can't. I'm supposed to meet my brother—"

"Well, he isn't here now, is he? You can find him after you get something in your belly. My treat. I'm gonna take care of you, 'cause your brother is clearly doing a shitty job."

Val shifted in her sleep as the dream morphed and Gigi hung from the cement wall. Blood poured out of a wound across her naked chest. The cockroaches crawled on the floor and her body. A large man laughed as he put his flaccid penis back into his pants. Purple, yellow, and green bruises covered over half of Gigi's emaciated body. A small trickle of blood ran down her thigh.

Gigi looked up and a single tear traversed her cheek. *"You were supposed to take care of me."* Gigi's vacant stare implored her.

Those eyes, she knew those eyes.

Val jolted in her sleep and yelled out, "Gigi, oh Gigi, I'm sorry."

Her eyes sprung open and all the pieces fell into place. Gina was staring at her in a combination of concern and confusion.

Chapter Twenty

Maggie was sitting in her favorite chair pondering the current situation. On the one hand, she preferred to contemplate her next strategic move in silence, but Antonio had proven a brilliant strategist in the past, and Maggie had also conferred with Char on occasion. She was about to bounce ideas off her guest when he broke the stillness of the room.

"It is not that I mind the quiet, but I do wish to have a ringside view of what is spinning in that beautiful head of yours. I thought we had decided collaboration was necessary to take down Leonid."

Maggie smiled. "I was contemplating whether to strike now or wait for Alexei's arrival. Perhaps you would like to weigh in on the pros and cons of both. Generally I prefer not to eliminate the enemy unless we have no choice. I'm worried if we send in a team to take on Leonid while he is vulnerable, Val will not suppress her desire for retribution. This will start a war, which I would prefer to avoid. I believe it is possible to incapacitate him without resorting to violence."

"Ah, I see you are still an idealist. How has that worked for you in the past? I seem to recall that Viktor did not escape permanent elimination." Antonio crossed his legs. "For the record, I applaud what I suspect you ordered."

"Viktor did not leave us an alternative," Maggie defended.

Antonio held up his hand. "It was not a criticism, my dear. Far from it."

"You know I have never felt good about excessive violence."

Antonio chuckled. "Yes, I know. It is one of the reasons we parted ways so many years ago. I have no such hesitation. In my opinion, Leonid does not deserve to live. While I understand your philosophy on cutting off a head only to have one grow back, that does not mean we shouldn't find a way to permanently eliminate the snake. Even a snake like Leonid with no fangs is still a vile creature."

"How do you recommend we proceed?" Maggie asked.

Antonio shrugged. "If this were my operation, I would have already sent a team to eliminate Leonid. Since Dani has learned the security protocol, Leonid would remain alive only long enough to use his blood and other biometric controls to access his accounts. Because Alexei is on his way, I'd have another team ready to deal with him upon his arrival. Leonid is at his weakest right now. I say we strike while the iron is hot."

"Val needs rest."

"Don't send Val. Send a rested team along with some of my men."

"Something tells me this is too easy and we're missing something."

"Just say the word and I will send my men to tie the loose ends in a pretty bow for you."

Maggie nodded. "Thank you for the offer, and I will give it serious consideration after I confer with Char."

"Maggie, my dear, now that Leonid is crippled, may I show you my estate? I would love to prepare a dinner for you. This nasty business has turned my mood foul. I wish to share the beauty of my world with you before we proceed with whatever plan you concoct for us."

"I'd like that. Give me a few hours."

Antonio stood. "Wonderful. I will send a car for you. I need to get back to my home and begin the preparations. I plan to cook the meal myself. It is my way to impress." He smiled.

Maggie stood and walked him to the door. "I trust you can find your way out."

He took her hands and kissed her cheek. "I will see you tonight."

†

Dani's scowl alerted Char to a possible snag. When she looked at Toni's dour expression, she knew something was up. Earlier they'd seemed elated by what the camera in Leonid's office revealed, but now their joy seemed tainted by something on the screen that had captured their undivided attention.

"What's wrong?" Char asked after leaning over, attempting to understand the gobbledygook scrolling across the monitor.

Toni lifted her eyes. "The funds are in some kind of holding pattern. It looks like we only have the first part of the security protocol and Leonid isn't moving forward. It's almost as if he doesn't have the rest of the codes at his disposal. Maybe it's like the double security on nuclear

210

weapons—they won't allow that kind of power to be in just one person's hand."

"Alexei," Char and Dani said together.

"It makes sense that Leonid's brother would hold the key, but how in the world do they achieve that when they live thousands of miles apart?" Dani asked.

"Can you find out when they've moved their funds in the past and crosscheck that information with the dates Alexei has either come to the States or Leonid has visited Russia?" Char grabbed one of the chairs and pulled it close to Toni.

Toni's fingers flew across the screen. "Bingo. Good thinking, Char. It's a perfect match. They need one another to accomplish any major movement of their resources. I suppose that settles the debate regarding when we hit Leonid's compound. We'll have to wait for little bro to arrive."

Char nodded. "Anything else I should know before I update Maggie?"

"I'd like to check a few more dark corridors to see if I can bypass this latest wrinkle. Can you give me another hour?" Dani asked.

"Sure, one hour, and then I need to catch Maggie before she heads out for her big date."

"Oooh, the boss is finally letting herself have a social life. How'd you find out about that?" Toni grinned.

"I caught Antonio on his way out and pumped him for more info. Maggie is a steel trap when it comes to releasing any personal stuff, but Antonio is an open book. He doesn't feel the need to keep their relationship a secret. In fact, I think he reveled in telling me his plans. Maggie will probably rail on him for leaving her so exposed." Char wiggled her eyebrows.

"Oh, do tell," Toni encouraged.

"It has something to do with his grandmother's famous chicken cacciatore and tiramisu. He thinks he'll win her heart with his home cooking." Char chuckled.

"Hey, don't be so sure that he won't. Maggie loves a good meal. She's a foodie, you know." Dani poked her sister. "Besides, have you seen the way they look at each other? I don't think either one of them ever got over the other."

"Speaking of the emotionally stunted, how are our little lovebirds? Has anyone heard from Gina and Val?" Toni asked.

Dani smacked her. "Hey, don't be a jerk, Toni, or I'll stop thinking of you as some kind of wonderful genius. Val is probably the most misunderstood agent we have, besides my sister."

"Sorry. I really would like to know if they're okay," Toni responded.

"They're still resting, and I'd like to leave them the hell alone while Gina settles in. I think they both have earned a rest," Char said.

Toni and Dani nodded.

"Okay, you two get back to whatever you were doing and I'll come see you in an hour." Char stood and walked to the door.

†

Dani heard the door close as she sat hunched over the computer watching the lines of code dance across the screen. She shifted her eyes to the other monitor, where the minuscule camera captured the comings and goings in Leonid's office. Monitoring both screens nearly caused her eyes to cross, and she was beyond exhausted. She leaned back and rubbed the back of her head.

"You got anything yet?" she asked Toni. She wasn't hopeful. After they'd discovered the added layer of security, they knew finding a way to bypass the protocols would be like finding a needle in a haystack. She knew in her gut that Alexei was the key, and if they could just be patient long enough for him to arrive and unlock the door, they would be done with this whole bloody nightmare.

Toni rubbed her eyes. "No, I've tried every trick in the book to hack into the back door, but I think you're right, we probably need Alexei's bio signature and some additional security protocols when the two brothers come together."

Dani pushed her chair back and stood to stretch. She was about to go get some snacks when Toni leaned forward.

"Uh-oh. Take a look at this."

Dani sat and craned her neck to look at a third monitor Toni had recently activated. "How the hell did you get video of that?"

"I wasn't sure it was going to actually work." Toni smiled. "Damn, sometimes I surprise myself."

"Hey, stop patting yourself on the back. I'm afraid we're going to have to pull the troops together and Val and Gina won't get that rest after all. You should go; you're faster than me."

Toni nodded and jogged out of the lab.

†

"I can't believe I'm here with you," Gina whispered. "I thought it was a dream when I woke and saw you next to me."

"Gigi?" Val blinked.

"How do you know that name?" Gina pulled away.

"I'm sorry. I should have stayed. I should have waited for you. If I'd done that, you never would have

213

married that bastard. Maggie, she…she saved me, but I abandoned you." Val pulled Gina back to her. She felt some initial resistance before Gina seemed to collapse into her.

"Is it really you?"

Val stroked Gina's back. She didn't trust her emotions, so she simply used her touch to convey her feelings.

Gina pushed away before punching Val in the arm. "You left me to fend for myself. How could you do that to me? Do you know how terrified I was?"

"I'm sorry. We were both just kids, but I could have told Maggie about you."

"You think?"

"Growing up on the streets tends to change a person."

"Yeah, and you left me to perfect my hustle." Gina smiled playfully punching Val again.

"Ouch. Somehow I don't see you as a wilting violet." Val chuckled. "I'm glad the universe decided to put us together again. We'll make a great team. After you heal, I know Maggie will find a spot for you here."

"You're assuming an awful lot, aren't you? Maybe I have other plans." She grinned. "I used to play a mean guitar and sing for handouts. Maybe Nashville is in my future."

"Mmmm, you're kinda cute when you get all feisty." Val gently eased Gina on her back and hovered over her. She contemplated kissing Gina, but stopped inches from her lips and grinned.

"Are you going to kiss me or not? I've waited a long time for one, so stop fooling around and kiss me already."

"Hmmm. I'm thinking about it. You know, I gotta weigh all my options."

Gina put her arms around Val's neck and pulled her in so that their lips met.

Val allowed Gina to probe inside her mouth, and the kiss intensified as their tongues swirled together.

Breaking away, Gina closed her eyes for a moment. "God, ever since we met at Leonid's, I've wanted you." She ran a hand down Val's cheek. "All my life I've dreamed of that special someone coming into my life, and now that I know who you really are, I realize it was always you. It's so—" Gina kissed her hard as Val ran her hands over the luscious body below her.

Knock, knock, knock.

"What the hell. Go away," Val snarled.

"Val, sorry, bud, but you need to put some clothes on and open the door. We've got news," Char yelled through the door.

"Unbelievable. First Leonid and now your friends." Gina pushed Val off her.

"Oh for fuck's sake, Char," Val growled. She jumped from the bed and yanked open the door. "This better be important."

Char raised her eyebrow. "We can go get Leonid on our own if you'd prefer."

"I know you," Gina said from the bed. "You were there and rescued me." She frowned. "If you're taking that bastard down, I want in."

"Sorry, we're not hitting his place just yet, but at least I got your attention." Char grinned. "We have some new information, and the rest of the team thought you'd like an update."

"You're not funny, but yes, I do want an update. Can you give us a few minutes, please?"

Char nodded. "I'll see you in the conference room." Before exiting she tossed over her shoulder, "Don't take too long."

Gina scrambled off the bed and picked up her sodden clothes as soon as Val shut the door. "I can't wear these. Look at them."

Val looked her up and down. "You're probably about Kim's size. I'll get you something to wear, don't worry about that, but...I'm not sure I'm comfortable with you being a part of any takedown mission...."

"I think you know me well enough to know I was going whether you wanted me to or not."

"We'll talk about this after the briefing or I won't bring you any dry clothes."

Gina leaned into her. "Oh, I love it when you get all tough-sounding."

Chapter Twenty-one

Leonid sat in his limo that was parked along with two cargo vans on the tarmac of a private airport. Alexei's planes were late and that had him worried. When he saw a plane with wheels down landing, he let out a sigh of relief. The first plane held twelve of Alexei's mercenaries who would help Leonid reclaim what was his. He sneered at the thought of his wife and her bodyguard before a feral smile curved his lips.

The twelve men were loading into the vans just as the next plane landed and taxied toward the convoy. Leonid got out of the vehicle and walked rapidly to the lowering stairs. Alexei smiled down at him from the doorway before descending the steps.

"My brother, you are here at last." They embraced before kissing each other's cheeks.

"Look at you, Leonid. What has happened?"

"Now that you are here, brother, my fortunes will change for the better." Leonid took Alexei's arm and led him to the limo. "Great things are in store for us."

"What of the wife? Have you found her yet?"

217

"No, but I have a good idea where to find her. Once we have your men in place, I am planning on getting her back." Leonid got into the vehicle. "No one takes what is mine."

Alexei followed his brother into the limo. "We are invincible, and with us working together, they will not see it coming. Do you have enough arms?"

"*Da*. I got a new shipment this morning."

"Good, good. My men are like an army. No one will defeat them." Alexei grabbed himself. "It was a long trip and I am in need of a young one."

"I have been saving two for you, brother. They are untouched." He waved at the van in front of them. "They will have none until their mission is complete." Leonid laughed. "Something for them to kill faster for."

"Perhaps you can parade them so my men will see their reward."

"That can be arranged."

"Excellent. It is good to be here with you." Alexei poured glasses of vodka and passed one to his brother.

Leonid nodded. "We need to move the money from the Cayman accounts to the new one we have in Belize."

"*Da*, we will once I've had the young ones."

†

Maggie was sitting with Antonio on the veranda enjoying a glass of exceptional Pinot Noir he had paired with the meal, when a black SUV careened into the circular driveway. Her nearly imperceptible movement forward was the only indication that something might be amiss.

"One of yours," Antonio noted.

"Coming in hot is never a good sign." Maggie sighed. "I suspect they have something important to share with us. It was a lovely dinner."

Antonio stood and held out his hand. "Shall we greet our guests?"

Ronda, Char, Sophie, Val, and Gina barreled out of the vehicle, each equipped with heavy-duty firepower.

Maggie accepted Antonio's hand. "They do look insistent on bringing us whatever news has transpired in the short time we've been away from the compound."

After Antonio led Maggie to the front door, he released her hand. "Why don't you go ahead and greet your team while I round up my men. I suspect we will need more than your agents to deal with whatever storm is heading our way."

Maggie nodded and pulled the door open as Antonio disappeared into another part of the mansion.

"Leonid and Alexei are likely on their way, and I believe they intend to launch a frontal assault with twelve of the meanest-looking mercenaries I've ever seen. I recognized one of them—he'd slit his own mother's throat for a dollar," Char reported. "I'm not sure how many of Leonid's men are still around, but we can count on the twelve they've hired to give us a run for our money."

Maggie turned to the side and gestured for the small team to enter the mansion. "Antonio is rounding up his men. This seems like a rash move for Leonid, but I suppose desperate men will choose unwisely. We need both Leonid and his brother alive. Do you think you can manage that?"

Val growled. "As much as I would like to put a bullet in Leonid's head, I understand what's at stake. I'd worry more about Antonio's men. Men don't always seem to have the same level of patience or finesse that we do."

Maggie smiled. "Agreed, but how to communicate that to Antonio without causing a blow to his ego—"

"I'm sure you have your ways," Char blurted.

Antonio entered the room with the same team he'd sent to extract Gina from Leonid's complex. Maggie thought they looked especially eager to engage in battle.

Antonio looked from Char to Maggie. "'Have your ways'? Why do I feel my ears burning?" He smiled. "Let me guess, you believe my team will stomp around like elephants in a dense forest."

"We need Leonid and Alexei alive, and not for the reasons you might suspect. This is not a noble gesture; their bio signatures are the only things we suspect that will unlock their assets," Maggie explained. "Both of them," she added for clarification.

Antonio nodded and looked each man in the eye. "Understood?"

Al crossed his massive arms over his chest and glared at the women. "We do know what we're doing. You want them alive, then that's what you'll get."

"I believe we have at most another hour to prepare. Alexei was momentarily sidetracked. I really wish we'd been able to stop that distraction from happening, but our priority was coming here to set up our defense and end this thing." Char repositioned her weapon. "Can we go sit and make some plans?"

Maggie glanced at Val when Char mentioned the distraction and saw how her face paled. She really needed to get Val into some form of treatment, because her defenses were slowly loosening as her cool exterior crumbled bit by bit. She watched Gina touch Val's arm and hoped Gina might be the salve for her reopened wounds.

†

220

Dani and Toni's eyes remained riveted to the screen, and finally they had to turn away in disgust. They kept their communication devices open so they could alert the team of an estimated arrival time. Dani decided she would rather distract herself and asked Toni, "How did you manage to get this camera feed that's now recording every gory detail?" Her stomach turned at Alexei's brutal behavior toward the young girl, and Toni squirmed and looked away too.

"I didn't think it would work because it was such a long shot. The bullets in Ronda's gun were equipped with a camera that on impact was designed to travel through the host's body until finding an opening. It moves around seeking light and won't stabilize until it finds it. I don't exactly know where that opening is, but I suspect it traveled up Leonid's ear canal. I kept testing it, and most of the time it would end up irritating my eye, but I guess this time it went somewhere else."

"Hmm, that's why we're getting that weird view of the events. Jesus, where do you come up with these ideas?" Dani asked.

Toni shrugged. "If you can imagine it, you can invent it. Who would have thought it was possible to reach the moon? Nanobots and bioelectrical combination devices are the next truly unknown frontier, and I plan on leading that expedition."

"Will you teach me more about that?"

"Of course. You balance my knowledge base. Some of the things you've invented are far more ingenious than my bio devices."

"I don't think so, but I'm so glad you do." Dani beamed.

"We make a great team." Toni glanced back at the screen. "I think it's safe to watch now."

221

†

Leonid had experienced a slight bout of dizziness prior to meeting his brother at the airport, and that unsettled him. He was sure his wooziness was probably related to that *sooka*'s bullet, but he couldn't afford to let his leg injury affect him. It was a lucky shot, and he was furious she'd been able to leave an indelible mark on him.

The nearly imperceptible buzz in his ear caused him to rub the spot again. After leaving the holding cell where his latest merchandise huddled in fear in the corners, he'd been incessantly rubbing or scratching it.

"What is wrong with your ear?" Alexei narrowed his eyes.

Leonid brought his hand back to his lap. "Nothing. It is nothing. Perhaps a bug bite. I suppose we will have to take the chance that my whore of a wife will get caught in the crossfire. After the rocket launchers do their job, send the men in to at least try to salvage her life. I would like my son spared if at all possible."

"Ah, so you believe she is still pregnant?" Alexei asked. "How do you know the child is yours? From what you have described, she was not a faithful wife."

Leonid's eyes went dark. "There is only one she has messed with, and that filth cannot produce a baby. She is an aberration. When the time is right, I will have the doctor cut out my son and leave the *pizda* for dead and screaming in agony for her life and my son. It shall be a fitting punishment."

"*Da*, that would be a fitting punishment." Alexei smiled. "I am glad you arranged for us to have a ringside view of the hell we will rain down upon our enemy."

"I would not miss this. It is unfortunate we will not witness how those rocket launchers will wipe the smug smile off Antonio's face. There will be nothing but rubble left of his estate when we are through with him. We shall strike hard and fast, not unlike when the Americans launched their shock and awe campaign against Iraq. I did not like that bastard Bush, but I did respect that show of power."

Alexei leaned back in the limousine, then picked up his drink. "We can follow the men inside after they have cleared the path. Perhaps you will be lucky and find your errant wife. I suspect they will wish to move Gina to a safe zone once the assault begins."

"*Da*, that is what I am counting on." Leonid rubbed his ear again and thought that after this was all over, he might want to check out the irritation that didn't seem to want to subside.

✝

Maggie looked at Antonio as he closed his phone, then at the group awaiting her orders.

"My men tell me a military-type convoy of seven armored vehicles are leaving Leonid's compound now," Antonio said in a low voice. "They think there are about thirty heavily armed men."

"Good intel. That gives us enough time to get everyone in position." Maggie's phone chirped and she looked at it. "Antonio, please brief the others about our strategy." She glanced at her phone and began to read the flurry of text messages.

"Okay everyone, listen up. I have some of my men located in these positions outside of the gate." He pointed to the map of his compound and the surrounding area, which he'd laid out on the table. "Once Leonid's men pass them,

223

they will attack from behind. The rest of you will be in the locations indicated on the map. Once we have them surrounded, we can attack from—"

Maggie looked up from her phone. "That was Dani." She shook her head. Although she had certainly been involved in some very dangerous situations in the past, rocket launchers and weapons designed for combat weren't in her usual repertoire. She doubted the majority of her agents were prepared for such a battle.

"It appears Alexei has not only brought twelve very qualified mercenaries, but he has also invested in massive arms." She caught each team member's eye as she relayed the information. "Dani thinks there are about thirty rockets and three launchers. This changes our original strategy."

"It does to a degree, but our basic plan is solid," Antonio interjected.

"Agreed." Maggie looked over the group. "Val, you have the most skill as a sniper. Did Dani finish her adjustments to your weapon, and did you bring it with you?"

Val nodded. "That and a few other specialty weapons are all in the back of the SUV, but we aren't prepared for the firepower that seems to be coming our way. We'll need to be precise with our shots or get some additional assistance from other trained snipers. Ronda is good backup, but it would be better if we had a third person. If any of the three men with the rocket launchers manage to—"

Antonio held up a hand and sent his cool gaze to a short, wiry man with a menacing glare. "Quinn will provide the support required to take out the third man. He has never missed a kill shot in his twenty years of service to the Army. He has a personal interest in shutting down Leonid's business. I believe you will find him quite motivated to get the job done."

After assessing the man's posture and grim expression, Maggie breathed a small sigh of relief that the sniper team would even the odds. "Char, will you please work with...." Maggie smiled at the giant man with arms the size of tree trunks. "I'm sorry, I've forgotten your name."

"Al, ma'am."

"Ah, yes, Al. I should have remembered. I trust that you and Char can arrange the team that is not already in position around the estate for maximum efficiency. I do believe it would be best to spread out our sniper team, as I suspect Leonid and Alexei's men are very well trained." Maggie frowned. "We have a limited amount of time to get into position since Leonid's force is on the move. Val, please provide me with one of the weapons, as I plan to take arms along with the team." She held up her hand as Antonio opened his mouth. "This is not up for debate, Antonio."

"Very well. I won't argue, because I know how stubborn you are." Antonio touched Maggie's arm and kissed her cheek.

"I'm not going to be the only one without a gun," Gina said.

Maggie smiled as Val opened her mouth to protest and then quickly closed it after Gina scowled.

"Any chance I can provide some additional assistance with a few well-placed explosives?" Ronda asked.

Char tilted her head and gave a quick nod. "Maybe, but you'll have to be quick. We don't have much time." She pointed to Mark, the other member of the team Antonio had sent to extract Gina. "Mark, can you work with Ronda to see if we can set the explosives quickly, and then both of you get your asses back here. Ronda can take her position on that relatively flat section of the roof covering the right side of the estate." She squinted, placed her hand above her eyes as she looked out the window, and gave a curt nod. "Yes, that will be a good location. Val, Ronda, and Quinn, most likely the first vehicle will have the rocket launchers, so be prepared to take them out before they can get in position. Everyone check your weapons and be ready for action within the next five minutes."

Maggie watched as her team and Antonio's men bolted into action. She was surprised to see Al, the team lead, acquiesce to Char's directives as they huddled quickly and moved all the players into position.

Val bounded out of the room quickly on Ronda and Quinn's tail with Gina trailing behind. Maggie watched as they hurried to the SUV and began removing the cache of weapons, including Val's special sniper rifle.

✝

A bead of sweat trickled down the side of Val's face next to her ear as she lay down on the rough shingles covering the roof of a building that was maybe 300 yards from the main compound. She saw that Ronda and Quinn were also in position. The rockets would be fired from a distance, and that meant they needed to hit their targets square-on to be successful.

She was in an awkward position lying there, but she'd made the shot under worse conditions. She slowed her breathing and heart rate, trying to remove every thought but the mission from her brain. The hurt look on Gina's face when she'd barked at her earlier to remain with Maggie and Antonio because her presence was a distraction flashed through her mind, but she quickly dispelled it. This was not the time for that.

Clearing her mind was proving more difficult as she took deep breaths, expelling the air as if she were removing all the toxicity from her body and creating a pure space to accomplish her mission. She envisioned Gina's bruised and battered face as she whimpered in the chains holding her to the cement wall, which created an unwanted distraction. It was the vision in her recent nightmares, but today she was wide awake. She needed to focus and couldn't let her nightmares get in the way. Shaking her head, she removed the images and placed her eye on the scope as Leonid's army came into view.

The loud explosion startled her, and her eye scraped against the scope. She quickly adjusted and forced herself not to let any of the noises divert her attention. She had to focus on the Humvee barreling toward the estate in her zone. She needed to do her job while trusting the rest of the team not to let her down.

Boom boom boom
Rat-tat-tat-tat

The sounds resembled those of a war zone, and Val knew by instinct that Ronda's explosives weren't the only ones littering the air waves with their deafening music.

A smoking Humvee careened to the right and hit one of Ronda's special welcome gifts. The implosion and complete destruction of the vehicle caused a tiny smile in Val, but she didn't take her eyes off the second Humvee as it entered her field of vision.

The sturdy tank managed to miss all the other booby traps and came to an abrupt stop turned to its side about one hundred and fifty meters from the house. In this position, the Humvee provided protection to the two men who scrambled out, and Val didn't have a clear shot. Sucking in a deep breath, she watched and waited. Finally one of the men emerged from behind the vehicle with the launcher on his shoulder and took aim in a standing position.

Val set her sights on his forehead and gently squeezed. The man and the launcher tumbled to the ground.

Two seconds later as she peered through the scope waiting for the second man, her focus wavered as she felt a direct hit to the building.

"Fuck," she hissed. She brought her attention back to the second man and watched in horror as his fingers wrapped around the trigger while he took aim on one knee. The second bullet found its mark, but not before the rocket barreled in her direction. She braced herself for the impact and barely managed to hang on to her rifle as she rolled across the roof.

When she gained stability, she scrambled across the shingles, listening for more noises that might indicate whether Ronda or Quinn had finally disposed of the other bazooka-toting mercenaries. She saw the third man fall, and after climbing from the roof, she ran toward the estate.

It was pandemonium as she made her way through some of the rubble inside the building and found Maggie sprawled on the floor. She crouched and placed her fingers on Maggie's neck after seeing the gaping wound in her shoulder. An audible sigh of relief expelled from her lungs when she felt Maggie's thready heartbeat. A small pool of blood was blossoming on the ground under her prone body.

Val heard a noise and looked up in time to see Leonid's maniacal face grinning at her. In that moment, her rage was greater than at any time in her life and her instincts took over. The knife in her boot was out and ready to find his heart, but a dart appeared on his neck before she had a chance to once again hit her mark.

"You're welcome." Char tossed her an automatic weapon. "There are about another half dozen men to take care of, but Alexei slipped through. Sophie is trying to find him, but so far, no luck."

"Maggie," Val whispered.

"I know. I called Cindy, but we need to secure this estate so she isn't coming into a war zone. I need you with me more than Maggie does right now."

"I'll take care of her. I know first aid. I can compress the wound until Cindy comes," Gina said.

Val swiveled and looked into Gina's intense eyes. She wanted to wrap her arms around Gina and never let go. She felt guilty for feeling relieved Gina wasn't the one on the floor possibly bleeding to death.

Gina pulled her T-shirt off and rushed over to Maggie, where she used it as a compress on Maggie's shoulder.

Val blinked once, trying to get the vision of Gina lying in a pool of blood out of her head.

"Hey, snap out of it. I need you with me now," Char yelled.

Val gripped the semiautomatic tightly and jumped up. She followed Char as they methodically searched for the remaining men so they could quickly dispose of the threat.

Chapter Twenty-two

Val felt like her face had lost all color as she tentatively pushed open the infirmary door and saw Maggie in the hospital bed. Wires protruded from her body as the steady beep of the monitor filled the silence. She was exhausted. It had taken them several hours to complete their mission. Val knew she should have been relieved that their side didn't have any other casualties, but she couldn't muster enough logic to feel that way. Char had taken over and wasn't allowing Val anywhere near Leonid. It was a wise move, but it didn't reduce Val's fury.

Gina was sitting next to Maggie, and the vision of the two women she loved melted her heart. Val had called the compound to check on Maggie after the last shot was fired at Antonio's mansion, and Cindy had relayed the key part Gina had played in Maggie's resuscitation. Gina's unwavering pressure on Maggie's wound was probably the single most important action that saved her life. No amount of chaos had drawn her away from that critical role.

Antonio stood on Maggie's other side, holding her hand. Concern was evident on his handsome features and in his red-rimmed eyes.

Cindy pushed a button on the beeping monitor and caught Val's eye. "Is Antonio's mansion secure now?"

"Yeah." Val knew the one-word answer didn't give the complete story, but she decided to let someone else fill Cindy in. She heard the door open and was relieved when Ronda and Char quietly entered the room. Val's forehead furrowed in surprise when Toni and Dani didn't follow, but she suspected Cindy had insisted that Maggie was only allowed a few visitors at a time until she was stronger. Sophie was notoriously absent, and Val knew that wasn't accidental.

Cindy rushed to steer them away from where Maggie was recovering from surgery. She pulled them into the office adjacent to the recovery room.

Val caught Gina's eye, nodded once, then followed the team into the small room.

"We still haven't found Alexei. I don't think he'll return to Leonid's place, but I've sent Antonio's men there just in case," Char reported to Cindy.

Ronda pounded on the table. "I almost had the slimy bastard and somehow he managed to escape."

"Where is Leonid?" Val asked, barely containing her wrath.

"Let's just say we're exercising a little poetic justice. The punishment should definitely fit the crime. We'll hold him there until we're able to capture his little brother," Char answered.

Val knew Dani and Toni would be able to reveal his location. They'd been somehow monitoring him since the whole shitstorm began.

Without saying a word to the small group, Val pivoted and traveled to the computer lab in haste. She wasn't planning to ask about his whereabouts. A surprise visit with a quick glance at one of their monitors would tell her everything she needed to know.

†

Dani leaned back in her chair and yawned. "Hey, Val."

"Hey," Val grunted.

Val stalked to where Toni and Dani were halfheartedly watching the monitors. Her eyes narrowed as she looked at each screen.

"You need something?" Toni asked.

Val's predatory smile appeared on her face. "Nope, I got what I need."

"Okay," Dani answered good-naturedly.

Toni shrugged when Val left the lab.

Dani got an uneasy feeling. Val had left in a hurry and looked like she was on a new mission, but Maggie was still recovering, so Dani couldn't imagine what that mission would be.

"What do you think that was all about?" she asked.

"I don't know. Who can guess what rolls around in her demented little head."

Dani glared at her. "Why do you insist on being a total ass when it comes to Val?"

Toni looked sheepish. "I don't really know."

"I think you're jealous. You wish you were a badass like Ronda, Sophie, or Val. It's why you needle them so much and leave me and Kim alone." Dani smirked.

Toni frowned. "I'm a badass with technology."

Dani laughed. "Geeks can't be badasses."

"They can too," Toni insisted.

Char burst into the computer lab. "Where's Val?"

Toni shrugged. "Don't know. She stalked in, scowled at us, peeked at the monitors, and left."

"Shit, shit, shit," Char mumbled.

Ronda pushed the door open. "Well, where'd she go?"

"Where do you think?" Char grumbled. "The smart little shit looked at the monitor and off she went on her personal little revenge mission."

"Fuck. Let's go before she chops him into little pieces prior to us grabbing his slimy little brother." Ronda hurried out, and Char jogged after her.

"Damn. This is bad. She knows the location of the chamber of horrors. She's been there on multiple occasions...."

Toni's eyes went wide. "Yesterday wasn't the first time?"

Dani shook her head.

†

The lethal combination of urine and vomit assaulted Val's nose as she entered the dank room. A hint of human excrement danced along the edges of her olfactory glands. She didn't bother to cover her face to diminish the odor because she wasn't planning to spend a long time in the dungeon. That's what she'd named it the first time, when her time in the depths of hell had been a lot longer than this past involuntary stay.

Despite his current predicament, Leonid stood defiant chained against the wall. Val wanted to wipe that confident look off his face as she approached. She wanted him to feel her wrath up close and personal. She wasn't carrying her firearm, because she preferred to finish him off with her bare hands and perhaps a sharp knife.

"Ah, you've come to finish the game we started so long ago. I suppose turnabout is fair play. You know, of all the young girls, yours was the sweetest pussy I ever had." Leonid's smug voice echoed in the cement chamber. "I'd be more than happy to fuck you again, chained or unchained." He showed his teeth, which were lightly coated with traces of blood.

Val began to perspire as a wave of nausea hit her. Her stutter step forward elicited another smirk from Leonid. She resisted the urge to throw up and leaned forward, holding her knees to stabilize her reaction to Leonid's voice.

The rape came flooding back, and Val barely held on to her thin veil of composure. She took a deep breath, willing herself to finish things.

Fuck the money. If both brothers are dead, no one else can access their vast resources.

She stood up straight and took a step toward Leonid, whose eyes shifted to a place slightly to the right of Val. Before she could spin in the direction of his focus, she felt the cold steel of the barrel pressed against her temple.

"Where are the keys to the cuff, you filthy *pizda*?" The low vibration of Alexei's cold voice reverberated in her ear.

"Fuck you," Val spit out without turning around. "I sure am glad you joined the party, Alexei, because you've just saved me the trouble of tracking you down."

She barely responded to the swift blow against her forehead from the butt of Alexei's gun, but the small trickle of blood down her face reminded her of the cockroaches that scurried over her naked body so long ago. Another wave of memories distracted her enough to allow a second blow and corresponding kick as she stumbled back.

Val needed to pull herself together, and then Alexei wouldn't stand a chance against her quick reflexes. The slow unraveling of her psyche wasn't affecting her ability to finish the mission in the manner she had decided was appropriate. She knew she'd gone rogue, but that mattered less than Alexei and Leonid's ability to break through her mental defenses.

"Your arrogance will be your downfall," Alexei said.

"Funny, I think that's my line." Val lifted her head and stared into Alexei's eyes. She grinned as she strategically allowed Alexei to connect with her head again in an attempt to pistol-whip her into submission. She pretended the harsh blow affected her more than it had and artfully crumbled to the ground, pulling the knife from her boot and slicing the front of Alexei's upper thigh down to his left knee.

The bright red fluid streamed from Alexei's body as he clutched at the deep wound with his left hand while keeping the gun tightly gripped in his right. "You fucking bitch. I ought to shoot you right now and be done with it." He sneered. "I heard you were a mighty fine piece of ass, and after I release my brother, we're both gonna fuck you until you scream." He held the gun to her temple.

Val laughed and with lightning speed, she stabbed between his scrotum before slicing upward through his penis.

Alexei clutched himself, bending over in agony and letting the gun clatter to the ground.

Val listened as Leonid's chains clanged. She turned around to watch him struggle against his metal restraints as the vein in his neck pulsed in anger. Although the gun had landed inches away from his left foot, without the use of his arms, he was unable to pick it up.

The sickening crunch of bones added to the cacophony of Alexei's moans as Val delivered a perfect roundhouse kick to his torso. In slow motion, she turned, cocked her head, and grinned at Leonid, transferring the knife back and forth between her right and left hands.

"Hmmm, perhaps I'll prepare a dick kabob for the coyotes to feed on." A feral smile crossed her lips when she saw something she'd never seen before—fear etched on Leonid's face.

"Get away from me, bitch."

Val ignored his words as she crouched next to him and cut his belt, pants, waistband, and along the zipper. Using the knife, she pushed the material aside. "Do you know what it feels like to be raped?" She sliced open his boxers and ran the knife along his flaccid penis. "No, of course you don't." She grinned. "But you will."

Leonid struggled with his restraints while kicking at her. "Get away from me."

"Hmm, I seem to remember screaming those same words." She lifted his penis with the knife. "Pleading is the first step in rape and—"

The door clattered open and Val grabbed the gun, ready to fire on whoever came in.

"Stop!" Ronda grabbed Val's downward-angling arm. "We need them both alive." She looked at the bleeding Alexei. "Take care of him, Char. Don't let the asshole die."

Char knelt by Alexei. "We need to get him back to the compound immediately. I'll call and see if they can send a helicopter...I don't think he'll make it otherwise."

"Val, what have you done?" Ronda grabbed Leonid. "I should let her have her way with you, but we need you."

"I can still cut off his balls. We don't need them," Val growled before kicking him.

"You know the plan. When we're done, you can do what you want with him. Now back off."

"The copter is on its way." Char ripped his pants and held the material to Alexei's bleeding leg. "I hope it gets here in time. He can't lose much more blood."

"Val, get Leonid's belt and use it as a tourniquet on his leg."

Val sneered at Leonid. "You're mine when this is over." She picked up the belt and went to help Char.

Ronda unlocked the chains, pulled Leonid to his feet, roughly pulled his hands behind his back and secured the handcuffs.

"What about my pants?"

Ronda gave him a once-over and laughed. "Trust me, no one is interested in your junk."

"The helicopter is here," Char said just as the medics charged into the prison.

Val thought that it was fortunate Antonio's mansion was so close, otherwise they'd both be dead.

†

Maggie slowly opened her eyes and turned her head toward the beeping sound on her right. She met concerned brown eyes. "Antonio," she croaked. She felt him squeeze her hand.

Antonio offered a sad smile. "My dear, if you wanted to sleep in, all you had to do was ask. Getting shot was a little dramatic to force a well-needed rest, don't you think?"

Antonio's attempt at humor didn't sidetrack Maggie. "My team?"

"Everyone is fine. Char called and they're bringing in both Leonid and Alexei. I'm afraid Val got to them before Char and Ronda could intervene. Alexei is iffy at best."

Maggie sighed. "Is Val okay?"

237

Antonio's brow raised. "The drugs must be very potent. You're not pissed."

"There are worse things than losing millions, even if those funds can help countless victims. Val's well-being means more to me than the money."

"Does that mean you are giving your implicit permission to terminate the brothers once we have secured their assets?"

Maggie closed her eyes. She wondered if she could admit that she was beginning to see his perspective and those of some of her more vocal agents. Did that make her as much of a monster as those her organization targeted? Could human life begin to mean so little to her? "I don't know, Antonio. It's hard to think right now." She felt his lips brush across her forehead.

"Rest now. I will make sure everything goes smoothly. We will take over those assets, and I will personally ensure they are put to good use."

A few seconds later, the commotion in the infirmary startled Maggie, and she watched as a stretcher was rolled into the small medical center. She really didn't think it was necessary to restrain the prone figure on the rolling bed, but her team was thorough and not inclined to take any chances.

She shifted her eyes and observed that one member of the team was noticeably absent. She sent up a small prayer that Val was getting much-needed support from the one person Maggie believed could soothe her wounded psyche. Gina had been a surprising gift, and from what she understood, she owed her life to the young woman. Earlier, she had opened her eyes long enough to discover Gina sitting quietly on the other side of her bed.

Antonio stroked her hand before barking at Cindy, "Why do you only have one medical facility in your

compound? Maggie does not need to be disturbed by that"—
he pointed to the stretcher—"piece of shit."

Cindy rushed over and pushed a hypodermic into the
IV line. "That should help her go back to sleep and hopefully
distance her from the commotion."

The fog overtook Maggie's body before she could
hear Antonio's response.

Chapter Twenty-three

Char slipped into the computer lab, strode over to her lover, and slid her fingers down Toni's arm. Toni looked up, and the love Char saw in her eyes caused her heart to speed up. "Hey, gorgeous. How's my little genius doing?"

"You look relaxed. I take it you were able to stop the impending train wreck from happening." Toni leaned into Char's touch.

"Well...maybe, maybe not. Is there any chance we can break into those accounts without Alexei?"

"Not doing so well, huh? We sort of saw what went down from the monitors, but then Alexei went out of view." Toni shook her head. "We need him alive. Dead eyes won't unlock the system. You know how quickly the image changes once someone is dead."

"Okay, I guess we'll just have to see what happens in the next twenty-four hours. Cindy is working hard to save the son of a bitch. How easy will it be to break into the accounts after we stabilize him?"

"Like taking candy from a baby," Dani piped up.

"Can you two keep working on ways to break in without Alexei…just in case?"

"Who do you think we are, Stephen Hawking?" Toni asked.

"Actually, no. Both of you are so far ahead of him that there's no comparison."

"Tell Cindy that if she thinks he's gonna die, she needs to call me pronto," Toni said. "I might have something that will work. It's a little gruesome, but—"

"I don't need the details. In fact, I don't want the details. I'll head to the medical room right now, because honestly I don't think he'll make it." Char grazed her fingertips against the side of Toni's face before leaving the lab.

†

Toni tossed a ball in the air in boredom. The monitors in front of her showed Leonid locked away in one of the secure rooms in his compound, and he wasn't doing anything of interest.

She suspected they'd moved him there in case Val wouldn't let things go. She might go as far as disabling her fellow agents left behind to watch him in the hellhole he created. Toni believed saving Val's sanity was more important than any sick poetic justice Sophie or Ronda insisted on. She'd talked a bit more with Dani and understood that every trip back to her worst nightmare was one more snip to the fragile thread Val was hanging on to.

"How'd they get Val to go back to her cubicle?" Dani asked.

Toni shrugged. "Don't know. You heard Char. She wasn't really a fountain of information. When she gets all stressed like that, I just wait until she's ready to fill me in completely."

"Should we call Ronda? I bet she'll give us the full scoop."

Toni grabbed the ball and held it in her right hand. "Nah, I should just wait in case Alexei is close."

"So…Ms. Bio Queen. What'd you invent to save our ass this time?" Dani asked.

Toni's eyes lit up. "Well, I started to get a little concerned that maybe Val wouldn't be able to control herself, not to mention our other resident hotheads, Ronda and Sophie, so I've been playing around with a little preservative of sorts. A little injection here and there and the computer security protocols won't be able to distinguish between biometrics from someone dead or alive."

"Wow, eye mummification? I like it. Have you discovered the secrets of Egypt?"

Toni grinned. "Something like that. I don't think they'll want to drag the dead body to Leonid's office, so if it works they can remove his hands and eyeballs. I'll also need to take some blood before expiration and add a little something to the mixture to keep it fresh enough to fool the computer."

"How come you're not down in the infirmary right now?" Dani asked.

"My special formulas don't last very long. Two hours, tops. Timing is everything."

The smartphone vibrated where it sat next to the monitor on the right. Toni grabbed the phone, pressed the Answer button, and placed it next to her ear. "Hey… okay, I'm on my way."

Shoving the phone in her back pocket, Toni jogged to the stainless-steel minifridge in the corner of the lab. She pulled the door open and grabbed several small vials of clear liquid. The door to the lab clanged loudly against the wall as she rushed to the medical center.

✝

When Toni entered the medical facility, she glanced at Ronda, who was leaning against the wall with her arms folded and a blank expression on her face. Cindy hovered over Alexei, and Toni suspected that despite who she was working on, the accomplished medical professional would do whatever it took to save his life. On numerous occasions, she'd overheard the lively debate between Ronda and Cindy. The nurse practitioner insisted that she uphold the Hippocratic Oath no matter who she cared for. Toni was glad Cindy had maintained her core values, especially today, since this might be the difference between accessing the funds and losing those vast resources.

Cindy switched her focus from her patient to Toni and waved her over. "Whatever magic you have, you better hurry."

Toni rushed to the bedside. "I need two hypodermic needles." She handed Cindy two vials. "Can you please draw up these two vials?" She shrugged. "You're a lot faster at it."

Cindy grabbed the small containers, then snatched a needle from the crash cart and expertly filled it with the liquid in one vial. She handed the device to Toni and quickly prepared the second one.

Toni didn't waste any time picking up Alexei's right hand, sticking the hypodermic into the middle of his palm, and discharging half of the contents. Before she had a chance to push in the rest of the preservative, bells started to ring on the heart monitors.

"He's going into cardiac arrest. You don't have much time." Cindy frowned but didn't attempt to resuscitate him as her gaze captured her lover, Ronda, watching the scene unfold.

Toni quickly emptied the remaining fluid into his left hand, then took the other needle and plunged it into the corner of his right eye socket. She prayed she'd hit the right spot to protect his iris enough to fool the computer.

The sound on the alarm changed, and Toni saw the monitor flat line. Cindy's grim expression confirmed what Toni already knew. Alexei had just passed into hell, and she only hoped the new substance would do its job and that she'd picked the correct eye. The clock was now ticking for them to complete the mission.

Ronda uncrossed her arms and strolled over to the bedside. "How long?"

"Two hours, tops," Toni answered.

"What do we need?" Ronda asked.

"His right eye and both hands," Toni answered.

"How come we don't need both eyes?"

"Not enough time."

Ronda nodded and looked Cindy squarely in the eye. "He's dead, you don't need to save him now. Can you retrieve the body parts we need, or…?"

Cindy grimaced.

"Never mind. I'll do it. Now you can attend to someone worthy of your expertise," Ronda said.

"Maggie's stable." Cindy's terse response revealed just how wide a gap there was between the two lovers' core beliefs.

Ronda touched Cindy's arm and her eyes softened. "I know, love. I'm sorry. I didn't mean to suggest anything different."

Cindy turned away and mumbled, "Do what you need to do. You can find surgical instruments for your task in the supply room."

Toni watched Cindy walk away and was sympathetic to her perspective, but she couldn't bring herself to care about the dead man on the gurney.

"How'd you manage to keep Val away?"

"We convinced her that Gina needed her because she was having a hard time with everything that's happened in the last few days," Ronda answered.

"You gonna go get her now?"

Ronda shrugged. "Don't know. I'll let Char make that decision."

"You know the minute you access the files, he's a dead man."

"Yup, and I intend to let Val have those honors. I've never taken a Hippocratic Oath." Ronda grinned. "Can you handle that, or do we need to get Dani to come with us to access those files?"

"I'll come, but I don't need to watch what happens after…."

"Go on, you don't need to see this either. You're a pantywaist, but you do invent cool stuff." Ronda chuckled.

Toni left the infirmary trying not to think about the gruesome removal of Alexei's hands and eyeball. She pulled her phone from her back pocket and dialed Char. She needed to hear her voice because it grounded her, but she also needed to provide her with an update. Maggie had never been out of the picture before, but everyone knew Char was her second-in-command.

†

Val opened the door to her quarters and saw Gina sitting in the teal wing-back chair reading a book.

"Is it over?" Gina asked.

245

"Not yet. They need Alexei alive so they can gain access to their accounts and wipe them out." Val looked away, trying to regain control over her emotions.

"Hey, what's going on?" Gina was out of the chair and moving toward her. "Talk to me."

Val shook her head as tears stung the backs of her eyes. "Those bastards took my youth and innocence, and I want them to look in my eyes when I kill them." Tears rolled down her cheeks.

Gina pulled her close, wrapping her arms around Val's waist. "Let it out, baby," she whispered. "I've got you."

The kiss was soft and full of promise. Val parted her lips in invitation. When Gina accepted, it didn't take long for them to be skin to skin. Val soon became lost in the heady sensations coursing through her body.

Lips gently caressed Val's face, neck, breasts, and abdomen before Gina's fingers began sliding between velvety, wet folds. Val tightened around the digits, drawing them in and moving her hips in time with them. Lips latched on to a turgid nipple, and Val's hand instinctively held Gina's head in place, urging her to take her fully.

Her body was screaming in want and need, and she surrendered completely as wave after wave of pleasure coursed through her. The loneliness and desolation she had known her entire life faded away. In that moment, Val knew with certainly that she was no longer alone.

Later, sated and holding Gina, Val smiled. "Never has anyone ever made me feel so loved."

"Hmm, I know exactly what you mean. Can we stay like this forever?" Gina kissed the shoulder her head was resting on.

"Forever isn't long enough." Val turned so she was facing Gina and caressed her belly. "I didn't hurt the baby, did I?"

Gina smiled. "No. She is safe."

"She?"

"Yes. I'm sure of it."

"This baby will know the love of its parents unlike our upbringing."

"You still want her even knowing who the father is?"

Before Val could answer, there was a loud knock on the door. The unmistakable sound of Char's voice said, "Get dressed. It's time."

†

Char had an important decision to make. She'd just finished talking with Toni and wrestled with whether to knock on Val's door or leave it be and allow Leonid to live. She wasn't necessarily opposed to eliminating the enemy, but she also respected Maggie's leadership and principles.

This time it wasn't about differing views of how to handle the enemy; it was about giving one of her sisters a sliver of peace and closure. She owed it to Val to allow her a much-needed resolution to the nightmares Char knew plagued the damaged young woman. With a certain level of trepidation about her decision, she walked quickly to Val's domicile.

Char rapped lightly on the door and waited patiently for someone to answer. When the door opened, Val was disheveled but had an aura of serenity about her. She recognized that look, because it was the same one she saw in the mirror every time she and Toni connected on such a deep level that she was sure no one else could compete with that bond.

Val raised her eyebrow. "Now what?"

"It's time to finish this. The team is heading to Leonid's estate, and then we're going to be so busy sweeping his mansion for leftover men that we probably won't be able to—"

"Understood." A feral grin blossomed on Val's face.

Chapter Twenty-four

Val strode with purpose to the SUV waiting outside the cottage above the compound that carefully hid the main underground structures. She raised her eyebrow at Ronda, who leaned casually against the vehicle with her arms crossed, when she saw the body slumped against the window. Alexei looked as though he had simply passed out. The movement of the car as it rocked shifted her attention to the front seat.

She approached the smirking woman as Leonid yelled and struggled against his restraints. "What the hell, Ronda? I thought we only needed his eyeball and severed hands?" Val shook her head. "Cindy's making you soft. You couldn't do it, could you?"

Ronda shrugged. "Didn't want to go to the same hell as both of them." She gestured at the SUV with her head. "I'd like to think there's two kinds of hell—the one where they'll end up and a slightly less odious version for us. Maybe they keep all the badass lesbians in one place. Now that's a hell I'll look forward to going to."

"You're dragging the body," Val growled. "And can't you control the animal in the front seat?"

"Didn't want to have to pry both their eyes open," Ronda responded.

"You think you've won, but you haven't, you filthy *pizda*," Leonid yelled from inside the vehicle.

Val stalked around to the passenger side and yanked the door open. "Shut the fuck up or I'll slice you up like your little brother, and I won't have any hesitation about removing your eyeballs and hands while you're still alive."

Leonid strained forward one more time and then spit in Val's face. "You'll finally get what's coming to you. See you in hell, *pizda*, and I'm sure we are all going to the same place."

Val grabbed Leonid by his shirt and slammed his head against the dashboard. "I hate when some asshole tries to be a back or front-seat driver," she said as Leonid's body crumpled against the dash. "Come on, let's go, and then I assume you all will sweep the mansion while I tie up loose ends. I'm driving this time."

Char frowned but crawled into the backseat next to Alexei's dead body. Ronda quickly followed.

Val glanced in the rearview mirror, and the minute both seat belts were fastened, she peeled out of the driveway. "I assume Toni and Sophie are on their way. We don't need Dani, do we? The kid doesn't need to see this part—"

"Jesus, Val, you're the same age as Dani. I'm not exactly happy about Toni being involved, either. How'd you get Gina to stay behind?"

Val didn't quite know why Gina had capitulated so easily. She suspected Gina wanted to preserve her memory of the passionate woman who'd just made love to her and not the monster Val really was. She'd quietly requested for Gina to please remain at the compound because it was the only

250

way she could finish this without totally losing her shit. Gina had simply nodded her assent but followed it with the simple statement that she'd be waiting for Val when she returned.

"I asked politely." Val heard Leonid stirring beside her and elbowed him in the temple before her eyes returned to the road. His head smacked against the glass, and she smiled in satisfaction. "Damn, he's like a Friday the 13th movie. Never knows when to give up."

†

Toni was shaking as she sat in Leonid's office chair waiting for Ronda, Char, and Val to arrive. The buttery-soft leather was far too comfortable for the gravity of the situation. She'd forged ahead and broken through the preliminary layers, and now she had nothing to do but wait. She was steeling herself for what she would have to do. Sure, she'd seen a dead person before and that was traumatic enough, but she wasn't sure she could sit idly by without getting sick as she directed the team to place the body parts in front of the security camera embedded in the computer security protocols.

"Stop fidgeting," Sophie exclaimed.

Before Toni could answer, Ronda, Char, and Val arrived and the scene was like something out of a bad B movie. Ronda was dragging Alexei's body by his arm, and his head was bobbling around smacking the floor as she jostled him into the office. Val held a knife to Leonid's neck as she pushed him forward. With his legs shackled and arms cuffed behind his back, he could only shuffle inside. He had a look of pure hatred on his face.

"I'm not playing here, Leonid. If I have to listen to one more word, I'll slice off your dick and stuff it into your mouth," Val murmured into his ear just loud enough for Toni to hear her icy words.

"Where do you need Alexei?" Ronda asked.

"Um, well, I need Leonid first," Toni responded.

Ronda let go of Alexei's arm and he remained immobile in the center of the office.

When Val brought Leonid over to the monitor, Toni thought he was far more compliant than she thought he would have been under the circumstances. She noted the self-satisfied smile on his face as the computer moved to the second level of security after accepting his retinal access.

Toni moved quickly through the next steps they were fairly confident about, and then braced herself for Alexei's dead body. She was relieved she wasn't dealing with body parts. She and Dani hadn't seen everything they'd need to understand how to bypass all the levels, but they used their deductive reasoning to determine the most likely sequence.

A bead of sweat formed on Toni's brow as she saw the last door open, and her fingers flew over the keyboard. Everything seemed to be progressing smoothly, and then she made the mistake of looking at Leonid. He was smirking at her.

She breathed a sigh of relief when the words *transfer complete* flashed on the screen, and then the screen went black and a neon green clock displaying five minutes began ticking down, *4:59, 4:58, 4:57*...and then she knew why Leonid was smiling.

"See you all in hell, *pizdas*," he yelled.

Toni was eerily calm when she announced, "I'm pretty sure we now have a little over four minutes to escape, and I suspect the place is wired to light up the sky."

Total pandemonium ensued as the women sprang into action.

Val wanted to be the one to personally make Leonid pay, but now there wasn't any time for that. When Toni didn't make a move and continued to type, Val shouted, "What the hell are you doing, Toni? Time to leave—"

"Fuck, we're screwed," Sophie exclaimed from inside Leonid's office.

Val reluctantly left Toni sitting in Leonid's chair and rushed to where Char, Sophie, and Ronda were immobile at the entrance. In less than five seconds, Val processed the scene as she looked at the crisscrossed pattern of thin infrared beams. The transfer Toni just completed had unfortunately also activated Leonid's trap. Everything clicked into place all at once. Leonid's arrogant smile. Toni furiously typing away on the keyboard. The trio's shocked expressions.

Val didn't have to check the other exits to know they were all wired in the same manner. If anyone crossed the laser barrier, the whole place would blow to smithereens. They needed to find Leonid's exit plan, and there wasn't a lot of time.

Val began to operate on instinct. She'd survived an impossible situation before, and now that she had someone to come home to, she wasn't about to give up without a fight.

"That bastard has to have either a way out or maybe a safe room. Toni, clear these lasers, now."

"Got it, I'll work on the other traps. Go, go," Toni yelled.

"Thanks. Okay, Let's start with his bedroom. A small prayer wouldn't hurt right about now." Val ran down the hallway on her way to Leonid's master suite.

"Where's Toni?" Char asked.

Val turned her head as she ran and answered, "I think she's trying to break the code or whatever the hell started the clock."

"We have three and a half minutes left until this place lights up." Ronda appeared beside Val.

"You three find that needle in this about-to-explode haystack. I'll go get Toni," Char announced, breathing heavily.

Val jerked open the door to Leonid's sanctuary and collided with Gina. "Gina, what—"

"No time, come on, follow me, I know the way," Gina said.

"We have to wait for Char and Toni," Val answered.

Gina grabbed her hand and pulled. "It's stuck, I tried to pry it open, but it wouldn't budge. I need your help."

"Shhh." Val halted their progress. "Where-where is it?"

"His walk-in closet. We have to hurry." Gina began to cry.

"Ronda, you wait here for Char and Toni. Sophie and I will get this damn thing open," Val said.

Val and Sophie followed Gina into the bedroom, and when they reached the closet, Val saw the opening to the hidden passageway. In the center of the small space was a brass wheel. She dropped to her knees and grunted as she attempted to move the circle to the left. Nothing. Sophie dropped down on the other side.

"On three. One, two, three," Sophie counted.

As both women worked, the covering began to move a few inches. Droplets of sweat fell against the metal as the threads on the secured entrance to the bomb shelter finally loosened and they managed to unscrew the lid.

"Sixty seconds, Val," Ronda called out.

Val and Sophie finally removed the heavy brass seal, and Val peered down into a dark tunnel. There wasn't time to evaluate whether the shelter would hold six grown women.

Toni and Char rounded the corner and skidded to a stop two feet from the hole.

"Go, go, go," Val barked. "Gina, you're first, please don't argue, we don't have time."

Gina crawled into the dark hole, and the rest of the women quickly followed. Val was the last to find the stairs. She kept her feet anchored to them before grabbing the heavy cover and screwing it tightly. She hoped the seal would hold and protect them.

She'd barely tightened the cover when she heard and felt the vibrations from the blast. Val slumped against the cement and ran her hand through her hair. Today wasn't a good day to die after all. She felt a soft hand on her leg, and the light from a cell phone illuminated the small space as she looked into Gina's loving eyes.

The compulsion to gather Gina in her arms was so overwhelming, Val took Gina's hand, quickly scrambled down the stairs, and pulled her close. She held on for what felt like hours but was probably less than a minute.

Tiny bursts of light from four other cell phones illuminated the small space as the women huddled together in the ten-by-fifteen-foot cement box with reinforced steel. The space was crude, containing a few chairs and minimal supplies for survival. Val suspected it wasn't intended as a place for a person to hole up for more than twenty-four hours.

"I don't think we need to hang out in this little rathole too long, but maybe it would be prudent to stay a few minutes to make sure all the tremors subside and there isn't some residual bomb that acts like a time-release medication to catch the unsuspecting person in Leonid's insidious trap.

I'm glad you had help finding the needle." Char's face had an eerie glow from the flashlight app on her smartphone.

"Anyone have a good ghost story?" Ronda asked.

"That is a really bad joke," Toni answered.

Char turned her penetrating gaze toward Gina. "Not that I'm ungrateful for your help, but what made you come back?"

"Dani found some code thingamajig in that monitor of hers and banged on the door. It scared the crap out of me. I guess she figured if anyone knew of an escape route it would be me, and thankfully I did. Nosing around paid off, I guess."

"So what are your plans now that you're a widower?" Sophie asked. "You sticking around? The compound isn't really a place to raise a kid."

Val glared at Sophie. "Shut up, Sophie."

The women grew silent as the seconds ticked away.

†

The group had agreed to wait ten minutes before venturing into the ruins above. Val unscrewed the cover to the shelter and poked her head up from the hole. She was convinced that nothing could have survived the blast, but she wanted evidence of Leonid's demise.

The place looked like a tornado had blasted through, and Val had a difficult time deciphering where the master bedroom ended and the hallway began. As she picked through the debris, she wondered if she might be able to find solace in Leonid's shattered world as her own fragile pieces began to mend.

The six agents carefully navigated the mansion and found Leonid's body under the vast wreckage. A trickle of blood leaked from the corner of his mouth, and Val didn't need to place her fingers against his neck to know he was dead. His eyes reminded her of one of those dead fish displayed on the ice in an open-air market. His brother lay five feet away in the same position Ronda had unceremoniously left him after they'd pushed his hand against the computer for the last security hurdle required from Alexei. A fine dusting of powder covered everything, including his body.

Val felt Gina brush against her side and take her hand. After she spit on Leonid's body, she murmured, "I hope hell is hot."

"Come on, let's get out of here. We don't want to be anywhere near this mess when the authorities arrive." Char hopped over a large wooden beam.

"You sure you don't need me to do a quick sweep of the place?" Ronda asked.

Char shook her head. "No, he never kept any of the young girls here."

Toni shuddered. "I'll be happy to get back to my lab. We better call and tell them we're okay. I'm sure Dani is freaking out right about now."

"We can call in the car. Char's right, this place is gonna be crawling with cops soon. I'd rather not try to come up with a reason why six women are stomping all over their crime scene." Ronda led the group to their cars.

"She wanted to come, but I told her it would take too much time, um, you know, with her injury. I hope I didn't hurt her feelings or anything," Gina said.

"Nah, Dani is very practical. She would have known that time was important and she can't move very fast. Besides, we didn't need to put another person in danger," Char answered. "Toni and Dani belong in the lab, not out in the field. No offense, hon, but you don't have the constitution for field work."

"None taken." Toni grinned as she pulled open the door to one of the SUVs.

After a brief debate on who was driving with whom, the group peeled out of the driveway and headed back to the compound.

†

When the quiet of the infirmary was disturbed by a tapping sound, Maggie's eyes blinked open. She focused on Dani's grim expression as she hobbled quickly into the room on her metal braces. Maggie was surprised to see Dani using her crutches again and surmised that this time of great stress was the culprit.

"Dani dear, come over here and tell me what has you so worried," Maggie directed.

"I...I...didn't find it right away. It's all my fault."

"Slow down and tell me what you didn't find."

"The code, the fucking code." Dani slumped into the chair next to Maggie's bed and laid the crutches on the right side of the chair.

Maggie took a deep breath. "Tell me about this code."

"I was running through the tape just to make sure Toni had the right sequence, and then I looked at the computer code and saw a strange line, and that's when it hit me. The bastard put some failsafe into the code that triggers something. I'm pretty sure that something isn't pleasant."

"Explosives," Antonio murmured.

Maggie's eyes narrowed at him. "You knew this was a possibility and you didn't think this was important to share." Her tone didn't reveal her controlled anger.

"I didn't know for sure, but it's something we suspected. Paulie told us what he overheard. I apologize for

258

not remembering until now. My worry for your health was distracting," Antonio answered.

Maggie's eyes softened. "Dani, you must have faith in the team. Each one is ingenious in her own right. I believe they'll come through this."

"I sent Gina. She mumbled something about getting there in time and it sounded like she possessed key information to help," Dani added.

"Then we will wait for their arrival." Maggie closed her eyes as the drugs affected her ability to remain awake.

✝

Dani sat on the other side of Maggie with her head bent. She felt helpless. Feeling the vibration of her phone in her pocket, she stood quickly and hobbled off to a corner, hoping she wouldn't disturb Maggie while she rested.

When she saw that the call was from Char's cell phone, her sigh of relief echoed in the quiet room. Antonio looked up at her with a quizzical expression.

"Char! Thank God you called. Please tell me everyone is okay…. Okay…. No, I'm in the infirmary with Antonio and Maggie…. No, no, she's fine. I'll head to the lab now and you can give me a full debrief, but I think we should let Maggie rest…. I'll see you in a few minutes. Thanks for calling, I was so worried."

Antonio stood and walked toward Dani. When he reached her, he asked, "Everything okay?"

Dani nodded. "They're on their way. I'm going to meet them in the lab right now. You can stay with Maggie and we'll debrief you both later on."

Antonio touched Dani's arm. "Thank you. I agree we should let Maggie rest. There will be time to bring her up-to-date."

259

Dani grabbed Antonio and hugged him before leaving the infirmary.

†

Val pushed the door to her quarters closed and heard the familiar click of the automatic lock. She needed a minute to gather her emotions as she processed the aftermath of the mission and the possible ramifications of what may have occurred. The residual adrenaline had finally subsided, and she was left with a myriad of confusing feelings about everything she'd experienced over the last several months.

She knew she and her sister agents owed Gina their lives, but Val was unsure of her future with her. Val wasn't exactly the nurturing type. She knew that everyone respected her, but she wasn't blind or deaf to the whispers behind her back. Maybe she was bat-shit crazy like they said. A robot incapable of emotion.

Pressing her head against the hard door, she was reluctant to turn around and face the object of her confusion. Soft hands wrapped themselves around her waist, and Gina's head pressed against the middle of her back.

"I'm not letting you overthink things. Please don't pull away from me."

Val turned around and accepted Gina's embrace. "Maybe Maggie is right. This isn't really the perfect place to raise a child and I'm not exactly mother material. I can barely remember my mother and, well, my father—"

Gina grabbed her hands. "Tell me your story. How you ended up on the streets. How come you speak fluent Russian. You tell me yours and I'll tell you mine."

Maggie was the only one who knew most of her story. Suddenly, Val felt an overwhelming need to bare her soul and allowed Gina inside. She let Gina lead her to the soft leather, and they sat with their knees barely touching. Gina kept hold of one of Val's hands.

"My mother was a nurse and the person who brought home the paycheck because my father was a drunken bastard. He'd been a big shot in Russia before screwing over the wrong man," Val began. She looked away. "They needed to make an example of my father, and when they finally found us after we escaped to the US and had started a new life, my mother was the exclamation point in their message to him. I came home from school to find her broken body on the front doorstep. She didn't make it. I was the final payment for his debts."

Val felt Gina stroking her hand. "He sold you?"

"After I escaped, I went looking for my father. I wanted to kill him, my own father, but someone had beaten me to it. Not long after I saw you, Maggie caught me trying to fleece someone and brought me back here. I suppose she took the place of my mother, sort of, but what she had to teach was nothing like what my mother taught me. She was a gentle soul." Val turned her focus to Gina and caught her gaze. "How'd you end up on the streets?"

Gina laughed, but it didn't sound happy. "Nothing quite so dramatic. Our parents were a piece of work. We were always dirt-poor and our folks cared more about the next fix than making sure we were fed and clothed. I don't really know what happened to them, probably OD'd." Gina shrugged. "We were better off on the streets. They moved one day and didn't leave us the forwarding address. Paulie and I were on our own after that."

"Maybe you should consider…getting rid of it—"

"No! We can do this. We can break the cycle. Besides, I have a feeling a baby will be a positive influence on the rest of the group. We'll have plenty of babysitters, and if I'm not mistaken, Char is angling for her and Toni to have a baby of their own. Maybe it will keep everyone from jumping on the next dangerous mission." Gina looked at Val with tears in her eyes. "Don't you know by now that I love you and can't imagine raising our little girl without you?"

"Our little girl?" Val's heart beat wildly as she considered the ramifications of her next words, even though she knew the truth of them. "I think I should get myself into therapy, and I love you too."

"You do?"

"I do. I can't believe I'm even considering this crazy plan and therapy." Val put her hand on Gina's stomach. "Our baby."

"Yes, our baby. I'm proud of you."

"Before we spring this on Maggie, I better talk with my fellow badass agents. She can't argue if we're all on the same page. Besides, she'll be so sidetracked with my agreement to seek therapy, that'll likely throw her off her game." Val grinned. "Oh my God, we need to go see Cindy right now. She'll put you on prenatal vitamins, and then we need to shop for clothes, and toys, and...."

"Whoa...she's not even the size of a peanut yet. We have time." Gina brought her lips to Val's.

Val felt an enormous sense of peace in that one brief kiss, and her reservations about raising a child in The Organization melted away.

I can do this. I love Gina, and that's all that matters. The rest is just details.

"We do have time, don't we? Do you think she'll like ice cream?"

Gina's musical laugh floated in the air before their lips met again and deepened in a precursor of the blaze of passion that would last all night.

About the Author

Author

Annette Mori

Annette is an award-winning author and healthcare executive living in the beautiful Pacific Northwest with her wife and their five furry kids. Well, actually, it might be more than five, but they do not count the ones they only feed. Annette believes it is not too late to try something new.

As an avid reader, she is pleased there are thousands of good books to choose from, and hopes that one day hers will be one of the many for readers to consider. She reads at least three to four books a week, so please, keep them coming. She has a habit to feed, after all.

No matter if you loved one of her books or hated it, Annette would love your comments. Feel free to e-mail her at annettemori0859@gmail.com. She believes she will always be a WIP (work in progress—she just learned that), so feedback is a gift.

Follow Annette's blog at:
https://annettemori0859.wordpress.com/
or
her YouTube channel:
https://www.youtube.com/channel/UCIqz8e_k-vNXsRby4M_gXFg

Erin O'Reilly

Erin O'Reilly is an accomplished author with twenty-three published works, including her newest collaboration with JM Dragon *Take Me as I Am* and *Ready for Love*. She was the Sapphic Readers Award winner for her book *Deception*. Her focus as a writer is to develop strong characters that make a dramatic impact on her storylines.

When not writing, she is the Technical Director and CEO of Affinity eBook Press.

Contact Erin at:
erinoreilly@affinityebooks.com

Other Books from Affinity eBook Press

Running From Love by Jen Silver
Sam Wade returns home from a business trip to discover her wife, Beth left her for another woman, Lydia. To take her mind off the break-up Sam accepts an assignment to learn to play golf at the newly opened Temperley Cliffs Golf Resort in Cornwall not knowing that is where Beth and Lydia plan to go too. There is more than one way to run from love; from never having to make a commitment and say those magical three words, "I love you." Find out what happens when they find themselves together—sport, betrayal, jealousy, and love form an unforgettable fusion of emotions.

Specter of Fear by Erin O'Reilly
Anne and Bailey are in love and planning a future together. Only the letters that Anne keeps getting are filling her with fear and doubt. Could the love they share really be a sham? Or is there something more behind the letters? Is the sender of the letters after Anne, Bailey or both women? Find out in this suspenseful tale...or is it a real story?

Back in the Saddle by Ali Spooner
The crew from *Cowgirl Up* are back in the saddle for more

fun. In their new adventure, Coal, Stormy, and Gene get the chance to be part of something they have always dreamed of—a cattle drive. Even without the gang being at the MC2 ranch, there's still plenty of action going on with a new addition, Doc Bo, brings a hint of jealousy and maybe the start of a new romance. Pull on your boots and hats, and hold on tight as you ride along with the crew of the MC2.

Faith in Rayne by Dannie Marsden
Welcome back Rayne and Lisbet from *Rayne Comes to Town* and *Rayne's New Beginnings*. Their life has flourished since meeting. Rayne ventures to Telluride, Colorado, where both adventure and trouble land at her feet. Lisbet heads to Telluride to reunite with Rayne, her head filled with dreams of their future only to have her dreams come crashing down. Can she find the strength to fight for Rayne, allowing her faith to guide them back to their love?

Ruined by Ali Spooner
Kade, a seasoned battlefield soldier has had enough, refusing to fight for greed. Now on a quest to return to her homeland she meets Iza.
Iza, a slave from the army defeated by Kade, begs the warrior to take her on as a servant.
Kade, sympathetic to the slave's request, allows her to travel as a companion and a friendship begins to form.

Refractions Trilogy by Angela Koenig
Follow the adventures of Rhodes Scholar Jeri O'Donnell who becomes embroiled in Ulster's fight for independence from Britain. Later Jeri travels through the Himalayan highlands where she meets Kelly Corcoran, a tourist from the

United States. Kelly is willing to gamble her heart, as Jeri struggles against involving anyone in her perilous and chaotic life. For Jeri, the true battle is confronting her attraction to violence as she struggles against losing herself in the exhilaration of combat.

Fortunes by Alane Hotchkin
Despite the curves life has thrown Remmy Garrick, her life is going along pretty good. Running her father's construction company fills the void left after the death of her lover. State Investigator Kira Kirpatrick is assigned the case, and meeting Remmy, a beautiful and alluring woman is the last thing she wants or needs. Does Kira have the courage to step up and accept the love Remmy is offering, or will she continue to hide behind her secrets and let them control her?

Captivated by Annette Mori
Juliet Lewis has one too many quirks for her own well-being. Snooping was bound to get her in trouble. Sexy police officer Tanner Sullivan gets Juliet's attention and she wants to know more. Will Tanner turn out to be her jailor or savior? Sparks fly when the obsessive-compulsive Juliet and the paranoid Tanner cross paths in this quirky thriller with a new twist around every corner.

Pausing by Renee MacKenzie
Jordy Chapman is the Emergency Service Coordinator at Cypress Haven mental health facility in Naples, FL. Keira Yeager's family owns an upscale furniture store in Naples and orchestrates a generous donation of furniture to Cypress Haven. When the two meet, they hit it off immediately. Will a Yeager family's anguish and misunderstanding threaten

their new relationship?

Breaking the Silence by JM Dragon
Still grieving five years after the death of her father, Dilana Sterling is a shadow of the woman she once was...a successful author with a string of best sellers, and a longer string of women. Rachael Alderman, a teacher at the local orphanage, lives a quiet, yet satisfying life. When Dilana and Rachael meet, they develop a friendship that leads them on personal journeys of self-discovery. Will their memories of the past prevent them from moving towards each other, or will they find a path that leads to each other so they can experience life together?

The Termination by Annette Mori
Codee is having a bad day and it's only going to get worse. Sawyer, a compassionate young woman, is resigned to her fate. Her only question is what fate is that? After slipping on ice, Codee wonders if she is hallucinating and fallen into an Alice type rabbit hole. The only thing she knows is that she needs to save Sawyer. Enjoy this satirical romance, with all of its twists and turns, that just might make you go hmm...

The Next Time by Erin O'Reilly
What if you had the chance to make history stop repeating itself? Would you sacrifice today for a chance at a better tomorrow? There is a moment in everyone's life that defines their future. For Jac and Carol, that time is now. Jump ahead twenty-five years and meet Carol's granddaughter Livvy. She is ready for a challenge and is fleeing the nest and getting on with her life. Read this wonderful love story that spans several lifetimes.

Affinity
Rainbow Publications

E-Books, Print, Free e-books

Visit our website for more publications available online.

www.affinityebooks.com

Published by Affinity E-Book Press NZ LTD
Canterbury, New Zealand

Registered Company 2517228